PRAISE FOR PAUL LEVINE
and
THE DEEP BLUE ALIBI

"A smart, enjoyable page-turner . . . Levine once again supplies plenty of quirky characters and witty banter between Steve and Victoria." —*Publishers Weekly*

"Courtroom drama has never been this much fun. A cross between *Moonlighting* and *Night Court*, *The Deep Blue Alibi* takes off with crisp writing and sharp dialogue that will delight readers. Levine captures the essence of the Key West characters at their quirkiest and gives the added bonus of a solid mystery. I loved it!" —*Fresh Fiction*

"A delicious, fun read . . . Sometimes hilarious, always amusing, *The Deep Blue Alibi* is highly recommended." —*Oakland (MI) Press*

"A smartly plotted and often funny novel . . . Levine again shows his acumen, skewing the law and showcasing Florida scenery while delivering an action-packed plot." —*Fort Lauderdale Sun-Sentinel*

"Wonderfully entertaining (think TV's *Moonlighting*), the blue blood lawyer from Miami and the Coconut Grove beach bum attack each case with vigor and wit. Don't miss this series."
—*Mystery Lovers Bookshop News*

"A must read for those who are familiar with the Florida Keys and enjoy thrilling intrigue, mystery, humor and sexual tension . . . You can't put the book down." —www.floridaboatersguide.com

"A delightful mystery to enjoy."
—www.armchairinterviews.com

"A worthy sequel to the winsome *Solomon* vs. *Lord* . . . The laughs keep coming in this furiously fast paced, rollicking good read."
—www.bookbitch.com

"An entertaining, witty comedy caper . . . Sparkles with promise, humor, and more than a dash of suspense." —www.blogcritics.org

"Always enjoyable . . . A novel fans of legal thrillers and Jimmy Buffet can enjoy together."
—Craig's Book Club

SOLOMON *VS.* LORD

"The legal thriller *Solomon* vs. *Lord* not only delivers a humorous yet solid tale about lawyers, it also proves how much Paul Levine's novels have been missed. . . . Authentic dialogue, rich characterizations, complicated relationships and even pathos bolster *Solomon* vs. *Lord*. Unique plot twists and well-paced humor help, too." —*Fort Lauderdale Sun-Sentinel*

"A delightful mix of legal thriller and romantic comedy . . . Terrific legal entertainment."
—*Connecticut Post*

"A hilarious, touching and entertaining twist on the legal thriller that makes Levine's return a welcome one . . . Levine's book is remarkably fresh and original, with characters you can't help loving, and sparkling dialogue that echoes the Hepburn-Tracy screwball comedies. *Solomon* vs. *Lord* is the first in what we hope will be a long and successful series."
—*Chicago Sun-Times*

THE VERDICT IS IN ON PAUL LEVINE'S LEGAL THRILLERS

"Paul Levine is guilty of master storytelling in the first degree." —Carl Hiaasen

"Irreverent . . . genuinely clever . . . great fun." —*New York Times Book Review*

"Delicious." —*Los Angeles Times*

"Take one part John Grisham, two parts Carl Hiaasen, throw in a dash of John D. MacDonald, and voilà!" —*Tulsa World*

"Cracking-good action-mystery . . . funny, sardonic, and fast paced." —*Detroit Free Press*

"A blend of raucous humor and high adventure . . . wildly entertaining." —*St. Louis Post-Dispatch*

"Mystery writing at its very, very best." —Larry King, *USA Today*

"First-rate . . . The prose is as smooth as a writ for libel." —*Boston Globe*

"Highly readable and fun." —*USA Today*

"Tense, sexy, and sublime." —*Philadelphia Legal Intelligencer*

"A rip-roaring read. Vivid, funny and tense . . . Twice as good as Turow and Grisham and four times the fun." —*Armchair Detective*

Kill All
the Lawyers

A
SOLOMON

Lord
Novel

Paul Levine

BANTAM BOOKS

KILL ALL THE LAWYERS
A Bantam Book / September 2006

Published by
Bantam Dell
A Division of Random House, Inc.
New York, New York

Bantam Books and the rooster colophon are registered trademarks
of Random House, Inc.

ISBN-13: 978-0-440-24275-8
ISBN-10: 0-440-24275-4

Printed in the United States of America
Published simultaneously in Canada

www.bantamdell.com

OPM   10   9   8   7   6   5   4   3   2   1

To the memory of Margaux Renee Grossman
(1986–2001)

www.margauxsmiracle.org

ACKNOWLEDGMENTS

Thanks again to fellow wordsmith and friend Randy Anderson for his criticism and suggestions. Another round of drinks to my Florida crew: Rick Bischoff, Roy Cronacher, and Paul Flanigan for their nautical advice; Ed and Maria Shohat for their criminal law expertise; and Angel Castillo Jr. for brushing up my *español*.

Thanks to Kate Miciak for her editing; Sharon Propson for her publicizing; and Al Zuckerman for his agenting. Much appreciation to everyone at Bantam Books for their support.

Gratitude, too, to Carol Fitzgerald, Sunil Kumar, and Wiley Saichek for masterminding www.paul-levine.com.

FISH OUT OF WATER

Wearing boxers and nothing else, eyes still crusty with sleep, Steve Solomon smacked the front door with his shoulder. Stuck. Another smack, another shove, and the door creaked open. Which was when Steve noticed the three-hundred-pound fish, its razored bill jammed through the peephole. A blue marlin. Dangling there, as if frozen in midleap.

He had seen alligators slithering out of neighborhood canals. He had heard wild parrots squawking in a nearby park. He had stepped on palmetto bugs the size of roller skates. But even in the zoo that was Miami, this qualified as weird.

Steve glanced up and down Kumquat Avenue, a leafy street a mile from the brackish water of Biscayne Bay. *Nada.* Not a creature was stirring, not even a crab.

He checked the front of his bungalow, the stucco faded the color of pool algae. No other animals lodged in windows or eaves. No pranksters hiding in the hibiscus hedge.

A squadron of flies buzzed around the marlin's head. The air, usually scented jasmine in the morning dew, took on a distinctively fishy smell. A trickle of sweat ran down Steve's chest, the day already steaming with moist heat. He grabbed the newspaper, sprinkled with red berries from a pepper tree, like blood spatter at a crime scene. Nothing on the front page about a late-night tidal wave.

He considered other possibilities. Bobby, of course. His twelve-year-old nephew was a jokester, but where would he have come up with a giant fish? And who would have helped the kid hoist it into place?

"Bobby!"

"Yeah?"

"Would you come out here, please?"

"Yeah."

Yeah being the oxygen of adolescent lungs.

Steve heard the boy's bare feet padding across the tile. A moment later, wearing a Miami Dolphins jersey that hung to his knees, Bobby appeared at the fish-sticked front door. "Holy shit!"

"Watch your language, kiddo."

The boy removed his black-framed eyeglasses and cleaned the lenses with the tail of his jersey. "I didn't do it, Uncle Steve."

"Never said you did." Steve slapped at his neck, squashing a mosquito and leaving a bloody smear. "Got any ideas?"

"Could be one of those he-sleeps-with-the-fishes deals."

Steve tried to remember if he had offended anyone lately. Not a soul, if you didn't count judges, cops, and creditors. He scratched himself through his boxers, and his nephew did the same through his Jockeys, two males of the species in deep-thinking mode.

"You know what's really ironic, kiddo?"

"What?"

"My shorts." Steve pointed to his Florida Marlins orange-and-teal boxers, where giant fish leapt from the sea.

"You're confusing irony and coincidence, Uncle Steve," the little wise guy said.

* * *

Twenty minutes later, Victoria Lord showed up, carrying a bag of bagels, a tub of cream cheese, and a quart of orange juice. She kissed Steve on the cheek, tousled Bobby's hair, and said: "I suppose you know there's a marlin hanging on your front door."

"I didn't do it," Bobby repeated.

"So what's up?" Victoria asked.

Steve shrugged and grabbed the bagels. "Probably some neighborhood kids."

He had showered, shaved, and put on jeans and a tropical shirt with pictures of surfers on giant waves, his uniform for days with no court appearances. Before Victoria came into his life, he would have moseyed into the office wearing shorts, flip-flops and a T-shirt reading: *"Lawyers Do It in Their Briefs."* At the time, Steve's cut-rate law firm had the embellished name of Solomon & Associates. In truth, Steve's only associates were the roaches that crawled out of the splintered wainscoting.

Now it was Solomon & Lord. Victoria had brought a touch of class along with furniture polish, fresh lilies, and an insistence that Steve follow at least *some* of the ethical rules.

Today she wore a silk blouse the hue of a ripe peach, stretchy gray slacks, and a short jacket woven with intricate geometrical shapes. Five foot eleven in her velvet-toed Italian pumps. Perfect posture. Blond hair, a sculpted jaw, and bright green eyes. An overall package that projected strength and smarts and sexiness.

"You listen to the radio this morning?" Victoria asked.

Steve poured her a thimbleful of café Cubano, syrupy thick. "Sure. Mad Dog Mandich's sports report."

"Dr. Bill's talk show."

"That quack? Why would I listen to him?"

"He was talking about you, partner."

"Don't believe a word he says."

"Why didn't you tell me you were his lawyer?"

Steve took his time spreading cream cheese on a poppyseed bagel. "It was a long time ago." Evading all questions about Dr. William Kreeger. Pop psychiatrist. Mini-celebrity. And now ex-con. "What'd he say?"

"He called you Steve-the-Shyster Solomon."

"I'll sue him for slander."

"Said you couldn't win a jaywalking case if the light was green."

"Gonna get punitive damages."

"Claimed you barely graduated from a no-name law school."

"The Key West School of Law has a name; it just doesn't have accreditation."

"He said you botched his trial and that he'd sue you for malpractice, except he has no faith in the justice system. Then he ranted about O. J. Simpson and Robert Blake and Michael Jackson."

"I saw O.J. at Dadeland the other day," Bobby said, munching a bagel. "He's really fat."

"So did you screw up Dr. Bill's case?" Victoria asked Steve.

"I did a great job. The jury could have nailed him for murder but came back with manslaughter."

"Then why's he so mad at you?"

"Aw, you know clients."

"I know mine are usually happy. What happened between you and Dr. Bill?"

If he told her, Steve knew, she'd go ballistic. *"You did what? That's unethical! Illegal! Immoral!"*

"Nothing happened. He did time, so he blames me."

"Uh-huh." She sipped at the Cuban coffee. "Bobby, you know how I can tell when your uncle's lying?"

"His lips are moving," the boy answered.

"He speaks very quietly and puts on this really sincere look."

"I'm telling the truth," Steve said. "I don't know why the bastard's mad at me."

Technically, that was true. Steve knew exactly what he did wrong in Kreeger's case. He just didn't know what Kreeger knew. On appeal, the guy never claimed ineffective counsel. He never sued for malpractice or filed disbarment proceedings. Instead, he went off and served six years, worked in the prison mental health facility, and got early release.

Before he was indicted for murder, William Kreeger had a clinical psychiatry practice in Coral Gables and had achieved notoriety with a self-help book, *But Enough About You*. He peddled a simplistic me-first philosophy, and after a puff piece on *Good Morning America*, he landed his own syndicated TV show where he dispensed feel-good one-liners along with relationship advice. Women adored the guy, and his ratings shot into *Oprah* territory. "You ever see Kreeger on TV?" Steve asked.

"Caught his show when I was in college. I loved the advice he'd give those women. 'Drop the jerk! Drop-kick him out of your life right now.' "

"Ever notice his eyes?"

"A killer's eyes?" Bobby sneaked a sip of the café Cubano. It only took a thimbleful to turn him into a whirling dervish. "Like Hannibal Lecter. Or Freddy Krueger. Or Norman Bates. Killers, killers, killers!"

"They're fictional characters, not real killers," Steve corrected him. "And put down the coffee."

The boy stared defiantly at his uncle, hoisted the cup, and took a gulp. "Ted Bundy. Ted Kaczynski. John Wayne Gacy. Real enough, Uncle Steve?"

"Cool it, kiddo."

"David Berkowitz. Dennis Rader. Mr. Callahan . . ."

"Who's Mr. Callahan?" Victoria asked.

"My P.E. teacher," the boy replied. "He's a real dip-stick."

Bobby's rebellious streak had started with the onset of puberty. If it were up to Steve, his nephew would have stayed a little kid forever. Playing catch, riding bikes, camping out in the Glades. But the kid had become a steaming kettle of testosterone. He was already interested in girls, dangerous terrain for even the well-adjusted. For a troubled boy like Bobby, this new frontier would be even more treacherous.

"Last warning, and I mean it." Steve poured some molten steel into his voice. "No more coffee, no more murderers, or you're grounded."

Bobby put down the cup, and drew a finger—*hush, hush*—to his lips.

Steve nodded his thanks and turned to Victoria. "What were you saying about Kreeger's eyes?"

"Hot," Victoria said. "Dark, glowing coals. The camera would come in so close you could almost feel the heat."

"Turned women on," Steve said.

"What about that woman in his hot tub? Did he kill her?"

"Jury said he did, in a manslaughterly kind of way."

"What do you say?"

"I never breach a client's confidence."

Victoria laughed. "Since when?"

"Dr. William Kreeger is out of my life."

"But you're not out of his. What aren't you telling me?"

"Wil-liam Kree-ger," Bobby said, drawing out the syllables, his eyes narrowing.

Steve knew the boy was working up an anagram from Kreeger's name. Bobby's central nervous system deficit had a flip side. Doctors called it "paradoxical functional facilitation." The kid had a savant's capacity to memorize reams of data. Plus the ability to work out anagrams in his head.

"William Kreeger," the boy repeated. "I EMERGE, KILL RAW."

"Nicely done," Steve complimented him.

"So you do think he's a murderer?" Victoria cross-examined.

"The jury's spoken. So has the judge and the appellate court. I respect all of them."

"Hah."

"Don't you have to get to court, Vic?"

"I've got lots of time."

"But I don't. Bobby, let's go to school."

"I'd rather watch you two fight," the boy said.

"We're not fighting," Steve said.

"Yet." Victoria studied him, her eyes piercing green laser beams. "This morning, Dr. Bill challenged you to come on the air and defend yourself."

"Forget it."

"I thought you'd leap at free publicity."

"Not on some third-rate radio program."

"Aren't you the guy who bought ads on the back of ambulances?"

"Ancient history, Vic," Steve said. "I've decided to become more like you. Principled and dignified."

"Uncle Steve's speaking softly again," Bobby said, "and trying to look sincere."

* * *

Thirty minutes later, Steve was headed across the MacArthur Causeway toward Miami Beach. He had kissed Victoria good-bye and dropped off Bobby at Ponce de Leon Middle School. Now, as his old Mustang rolled past the cruise ships lined up at the port, Steve tried to process the morning's information. What was this feeling of dread creeping over him? The last time he'd seen Kreeger was at the sentencing. It had been a messy case with just enough tabloid elements—drugs, sex, celebrity—to attract media attention.

A woman named Nancy Lamm had drowned in three feet of water. Unfortunately for Kreeger, the water was in the hot tub on his pool deck. That wouldn't have been so bad, except for the gash on Nancy Lamm's skull. Then there was the tox scan revealing a potent mixture of barbiturates and booze. The pills had come from Kreeger, which was a big no-no. He was a court-appointed expert in Nancy's child custody case, so he shouldn't have been playing footsie with her in a Jacuzzi. In an unseemly breach of medical ethics, Kreeger and Nancy had become lovers. The state claimed they'd had a spat, and she was going to blow the whistle on him with the state medical board. Armed with proof of motive, the state charged Kreeger with murder.

Steve could still remember his closing argument. He used the trial lawyer's trick of the loaded rhetorical question.

"Is Dr. William Kreeger a stupid man? No, he has a near-genius IQ. Is he a careless man? No, quite the contrary. He's precise and meticulous. So, ask yourselves, if Dr. Kreeger were inclined to kill someone, would he do it at his own home? Would he be present at the time of death? Would he admit to police that he had provided a controlled substance to the victim? I think you know the answers. This was an unfortunate accident, not an act of murder."

The jury returned a compromise verdict: guilty of involuntary manslaughter. Not a bad result, Steve thought—but then, he didn't have to serve the time. Now he dredged up everything he could remember about the moment the jury came back with the verdict. Kreeger didn't even wince. Not one of those clients whose knees buckle and eyes brim with tears.

Kreeger didn't blame Steve. Thanked him, in fact, for doing his best. Kreeger hired another lawyer for the appeal, but nothing unusual there. Appellate work was brief writing. Steve was never much for book work, and footnotes gave him a headache.

He never heard from Kreeger again. Not a call or postcard from prison. And nothing when he got out.

So what's with all the insults now? Why is he calling me a shyster and challenging me to debate him on the air?

Steve didn't like the answer. Only one thing could have changed.

He found out. Somehow, he found out exactly what I did.

Meaning Kreeger also figured out that he would have been acquitted if any other lawyer on the planet had defended the case. And that marlin on the door? It had to be a message from Kreeger, something they both would understand.

A marlin.

Not a grouper or a shark or a moray eel.

A marlin had significance for both of them.

So what's Kreeger want?

Steve tried the loose-thread approach, something his father taught him. *"Whenever you're stumped and feeling dumb as a suck-egg mule,"* Herbert T. Solomon used to drawl, *"grab a loose thread and pull the cotton-picking thing till you find where it leads."* Now Steve pulled at the idea of Kreeger suddenly attacking him on the radio and jamming a rotting fish into his front door. Where did that thread lead?

Probably not to a lawsuit or disbarment proceedings. No challenge for Kreeger's towering ego to seek redress through official channels. No chance to show his obvious superiority. Steve pulled at the thread some more. It kept leading back to a dead woman in a hot tub.

"The bitch betrayed me."

That's what Kreeger had told Steve, even while denying that he'd killed Nancy Lamm. Kreeger's hot eyes notwithstanding, there was an icy coldness to the man that could make you shiver. And now the answer Steve was seeking emerged with chilling clarity.

The bastard doesn't want to sue me. He wants to kill me.

Two

THE FACE IN THE WINDOW

Walking down the noisy corridor at school, dodging bigger kids with Mack truck shoulders, Bobby tried to remember the dream.

It was a dream, right?

The face in his bedroom window. He tried to picture the face, but it was lost in the fog of sleep. Dammit, his brain was letting him down. All that stuff in his head, but where was the face?

When I close my eyes, why does all this useless 411 pop up?

In one corner of his brain, floating letters, constantly rearranging themselves into new words. In another corner, the periodic table of elements, 118 of them, from hydrogen to ununoctium. *So where did the face go?*

He hadn't told Uncle Steve about the face in the window because it was just a dream.

Or was it?

Bobby decided to put his brain in reverse and logically consider the events of the past twelve hours. The same night someone stuck a giant fish on the front door, he dreamed of a face in the window.

Okay, think! What else do you remember?

A noise! There'd been a noise in the backyard. A palm frond falling, maybe? No, different than that.

Someone bumping into the old windsurfer propped against the house? Maybe. And a second sound. Metallic. The mast clanking against the boom? Could be.

Noise. Face. Fish.

The words flashed in his brain. Just like the warning sign in front of the school.

Slow Children. Slow Children. Slow Children.

Which could be rearranged to spell SIN HELL CROWD.

A raging river of words cascaded through his brain. He could shatter the words with a hammer, the letters scattering then re-forming, an endless scrawl of graffiti. Sometimes Bobby thought he could hear the synapses in his brain, crackling like a power line he once saw in the street after a storm, throwing off sparks, dancing like a thick black snake. Sometimes, listening to the sounds grow louder, watching the letters multiply, he would walk into walls or get lost heading home from the bus stop. When that happened, Uncle Steve would teach him the concentration game. That's how his uncle stole all those bases when he played baseball at U.M. Focusing on the pitcher, studying every twitch, knowing whether he would go to the plate, or try to pick him off first base.

"You're gonna be even better than me at the concentration game, kiddo, because your brain's a Ferrari and mine's an old pickup truck."

But it didn't feel that way. Sometimes Bobby thought there was too much floating around in his head, like

Grandpop's stews where he tossed in snapper heads and mackerel tails and called it bouillabaisse.

Bouillabaisse. USE A SLOB ALIBI.

The letters ricocheted inside his skull.

Noise. Face. Fish.

He tried to clear out all the other images and draw a picture of the face in the window. For several moments, nothing. Then . . .

A woman!

What else? Bobby played cop, like on the TV shows. What color hair? How old? Any identifying marks?

She looked familiar.

She looked like Mom!

Only cleaner. Bobby remembered the way his mother had looked on the farm. She was carrying cold soup into the shed where he was locked up. Her face streaked with soot from the fireplace, her eyes watery and far away. Totally zonked on stuff she smoked or inhaled or injected. That night, Uncle Steve broke into the shed to take him away. Lots of images there.

The bearded man with the walking stick.

The man smelled like wet straw and tobacco. Sometimes he slept in Mom's bed, and sometimes, after they yelled and hit each other, he would spend the night on the floor of the shed, farting and cursing. Bobby had watched the man carve the stick from a solid piece of wood. It was as long as a cane, but thicker, with a curved top like a shepherd's staff. The man had polished it and painted it with a shiny varnish.

Whoosh! Ker-thomp!

The sounds from that night. The man had tried to hit Uncle Steve with the staff. But Uncle Steve was very quick and strong, too, stronger than he looked. He wrestled the staff away and swung it like a baseball bat. *Whoosh.* Then, *ker-thomp,* the stick struck the man's head, sounding like a bat hitting a ball. Home run.

Bobby remembered Uncle Steve carrying him through the woods, slipping on wet stones, but never falling. Bobby could feel his uncle's heart beating as he ran. Instead of slowing down, he ran faster, Bobby wondering how anyone could go so fast while carrying another person, even someone as skinny as him.

Ever since that night, Bobby had lived with Uncle Steve. They were best buds. But Bobby couldn't tell him about Mom in the window. Uncle Steve hated Mom, even though she was his sister.

"My worthless sister Janice."

That's what he called her when he didn't think Bobby was listening.

There was another reason to keep quiet, too. It might only have been a dream.

* * *

Bobby spotted Maria kneeling at her locker, her shirt riding up the back of her low-rise jeans, revealing the dainty knobs of her spinal column, like the peaks of a mountain range. He caught a glimpse of her smooth skin, disappearing into the top of her black panties.

Black panties. PACK A SIN BELT.

Maria was the hottest hottie in the sixth grade. Caramel skin, hair as black as her panties. Eyes as dark as the obsidian rock Bobby handed her in earth science class, their hands touching.

Maria Munoz-Goldberg.

Bobby crouched down at his own locker. He wanted to say something, but what?

Maria had taped photos of Hillary Duff and Chad Michael Murray to the inside of her locker. Bobby had seen them in that dipshit movie, *A Cinderella Story,* but maybe slamming Maria's favorite actors wasn't the way to go.

What could he do? Maria lived only a block away on Loquat, 573 steps from his front door. Should he tell her that?

No, she'll think I'm a stalker.

"Hey, Bobby," she said.

"Hey." He turned too quickly and bashed his elbow into his locker door. *Owww!* His funny bone, the pain so intense it momentarily blinded him.

"You read the history junk?" she asked.

He mumbled a "yeah" through the pain.

"The Civil War has too many battles," she complained. "I can't remember them all."

Bobby thought about saying he'd memorized the battles alphabetically from Antietam to Zollicoffer. But that would sound so dorky. "For the quiz, just know Gettysburg and both Bull Runs," he said.

"There's so much to read." A faint whine, but coming from her parted lips, it sounded musical.

Antietam, Bachelor's Creek. Chickamauga, Devil's Backbone, Ezra Church . . .

He couldn't help it. His brain was reciting Civil War battles from A to Z.

"Do you think you could help me?" she asked.

"You mean . . . study together?"

"I could come over to your house after school."

He tossed his shoulders, as if that would be okay, but no big deal. "Sure. Cool. You know where I live?"

She smiled, perfect teeth, the orthodonture having been removed at the beginning of the school year. "I know it's gotta be close. I've seen you outside my house."

Busted!

"I, uh . . . walk . . . sometimes. The neighborhood. Kumquat. Loquat. Avocado . . ."

Shut up already! You sound like a total wingnut.

"My hood, too." She stood up, and so did Bobby, miraculously managing not to drop his books or bang his shins into the locker.

"Give me your address," she said. "I'll come over around four."

Bobby wrote the address on a slip of paper. He knew that some people couldn't remember things the way he could.

"I'll bring some DVDs," Maria said. "If we get done early, maybe we can just hang and watch a movie."

"Great. Have you ever seen *A Cinderella Story*? It's pretty cool."

"Are you kidding! I *love* that movie. I've seen it like a zillion times."

Another smile, and she spun on her heel and headed off, breathing a "See ya later" over her perfect shoulder.

Holy shit.

Maria Munoz-Goldberg was coming to his house with her history book, her DVDs, and her black panties. He watched her walk toward home room, the symphony of her voice still echoing in his brain, along with . . .

*Fredericksburg, Gettysburg, Harper's Ferry, Irish
Bend, Jenkins' Ferry, Kennesaw Mountain . . .*

The names wouldn't stop. But they were so soft, he
could still hear Maria's voice and could still see her
parted lips, warm and sugary in his brain.

Three

GAFF FROM THE PAST

Steve parked the car and admired the twenty-foot-high likeness of himself. It was a part of the day he always enjoyed.

The two-story mural was painted on the chipped stucco wall of Les Mannequins, the modeling agency where Solomon & Lord maintained its offices. There was Steve, sitting on the edge of a desk, wearing a charcoal gray suit, reading a law book. Something he never wore, something he never did. Standing next to him was Victoria, in a ruby red knit suit with a two-button, ruffled-trim jacket, her breasts fuller, her hips rounder than in real life.

Artistic license.

Then the caption, in fancy script:

Solomon & Lord, Attorneys-at-Law
The Wisdom of Solomon, the Strength of the Lord
Call (555) UBE-FREE

Victoria had been appalled, of course. "Cheesy" and "blasphemous" were two of her kinder adjectives. The mural was the handiwork of Henri Touissant, a sixteen-year-old Steve had represented in Juvenile Court. One of the best graffiti artists in Little Haiti, Henri was busted while tagging an overpass with a drawing of President Bush having intimate relations with a goat. "Profound political satire," Steve argued in the lad's defense. The judge gave Henri probation, and Steve hired him to paint the mural, in lieu of attorney's fees.

Now, heading into the building, Steve was plagued by a question that had been bothering him all morning.

Just how much should I tell Victoria?

It was one of the recurring issues of their relationship, both professional and personal. He'd been more open with Victoria than with any other woman he'd ever known. Of course, he'd never cared for any other woman with the depth of feelings he had for her.

But she can be so damn judgmental.

Steve remembered the fireworks in Bobby's guardianship case. Faced with the possibility that the state would take his nephew away, Steve had secretly paid Janice, his drug-addled sister, to change her testimony. When Victoria found out, she exploded.

"You can't bribe a witness."

"I'm paying her to tell the truth. If I don't, she'll lie and we'll lose."

"It's still illegal."

"When are you gonna grow up? When the law doesn't work, you've got to work the law."

Smack. Vic slapped him. Hard. Sparring partners instead of law partners.

So just how would Victoria react if he told her the truth?

"Oh, by the way, Vic. State versus Kreeger. Forgot to tell you. I tanked the case."

She'd clobber him with his Barry Bonds rock-hard maple baseball bat. Or his Mark McGwire, Jose Canseco, or Rafael Palmeiro models. Steve favored bats by baseball's most notoriously juiced players.

Or maybe not. Would she even believe him?

"You took a dive? You, the guy who cheats to win?"

As he walked through the front door, Steve decided to tell Victoria everything about the Kreeger case. What he did and why he did it.

Women appreciate honesty. He'd read that in one of Victoria's magazines, a relationship column tucked away in the ads for overpriced Italian footwear. Expose your doubts, express your fears, confess your weaknesses, and she'll be understanding and forgiving.

Okay, he'd bare his soul. He'd do it today. He made that promise to himself. He wished he had a Bible to swear on, wondering what happened to the one he lifted from a hotel room in Orlando.

* * *

"Ste-vie! Ste-vie!" A high-pitched whine.

"Wait up!" A second voice. Louder and more insistent.

The shouts came from somewhere between the photo studio and the wardrobe room.

Damn. If I don't hustle, they'll cut me off at the stairs.

"Stevie, wait!"

Steve heard the *clackety-clack* of leather hoofbeats, and in a second there they were. Lexy and Rexy. Pale blond twins. Models, six feet tall. As litigious as they were leggy.

One wore florescent orange spandex shorts and a white halter top. The other was in Daisy Duke cutoffs with a leopard-print halter. Both wore strappy sandals with stiletto heels that could take out an eye.

"You gotta help me," Lexy demanded. Or maybe it was Rexy. Who could tell?

"Got to," her sister agreed.

"What now, Lexy?" Taking a shot at the name. "I'm really busy."

"I'm Rexy! My belly button is an inny."

"And mine's an outy," Lexy confirmed.

"Everybody on South Beach knows that." Rexy shook a long index finger at him, the lacquered nail festooned with gold stars. "Margaux says you have to represent me. It's in your lease."

Margaux being the owner of Les Mannequins. Solomon & Lord got free office space under the litigate-for-rent clause he'd thought was such a great idea. Now he was spending half his time handling *mishegoss* for the models.

"Haven't I done enough for you two?" he asked.

"Hah." Rexy again.

He'd already gotten them handicapped parking stickers, successfully arguing that bulimia was as much a disability as paraplegia. He'd skated Lexy out of a RWI case—Rollerblading while intoxicated—even though she'd plowed into a group of tourists on Ocean Drive, knocking them over like bowling pins. And he'd beaten back a lawsuit against Rexy by an angry suitor who had spent two thousand bucks on dinner, drinks, a limo, and a Ricky Martin concert, only to have her go home with a member of the band.

"A man who dates a South Beach model takes the risk she'll be a rude, inconsiderate airhead," Steve had argued to the judge. Rexy thought he'd been brilliant.

Now the sisters blocked his path to the stairs, bony elbows akimbo, like wooden gates at a railroad crossing.

"Look at this!" Rexy waved an eight-by-ten flyer at him. An advertisement for a South Beach plastic surgeon with before-and-after shots of a woman's breasts. She pointed at the photo. "Can you believe *this*?"

"Boobs. What about them?"

"Don't you recognize them?" She yanked down her halter, exposing two coconut-size, gravity-defying breasts with pointy nipples.

"Ah," he said. "The afters." Suddenly, Steve was happy Victoria was across the causeway in the courthouse. Not that he kept his past a secret from her. Still, sleeping with a room-temperature IQ model wasn't something he'd post on his résumé. "They're your boobs, right?"

"You gotta sue that quack for my mental anguish." Rexy kept the top pulled down and stood, hipshot in model pose, as if Richard Avedon might record the moment for a coffee-table book. "A million dollars, at least."

Steve was about to say: *"A million bucks of mental anguish seems excessive for a twenty-dollar mind,"* then realized he'd told her that every time she wanted to sue someone.

"They're handing these out in the clubs," Rexy wailed, shaking the flyer in his face.

"I don't know, Rexy. Your face isn't even in the photo. What are your damages if you're the only one who knows it's you?"

"Are you nuts? You know how many guys already called me, saying they saw my tits on the way to the men's room?" She pulled her top back up, and Steve took the opportunity to brush past her and hightail it up the stairs.

"I'll go to the library, research the law," he called out, with as much sincerity as he could muster.

"Like you know where the library is," Rexy shot back.

At the top of the stairs, Steve was just about to open his reception room door when he heard a *thump,* followed by a woman's scream. Another *thump,* as if someone had bounced off a wall, then a woman's angry voice: *"No me toques, idiota!"*

Cece's voice!

Steve threw open the door and saw a jumble of images. His secretary, Cece Santiago, in red panties and bra. A man hoisting her into the air, swinging her left and right, her feet sailing off the floor.

"Hey, put her down!" Steve thundered.

"Fuck you!" The man was bare-chested and big, with a watermelon gut. Mid-forties, face lathered in sweat. He wore suit pants with suspenders and was barefoot.

Steve crossed the room in two steps. The man let go in midswing, and Cece flew across her desk, knocking files to the floor.

Steve grabbed the man by the suspenders.

"Hey! I don't do guys," the man protested.

"Steve, *no te metas*!" Cece shouted, just as he uncorked a straight right hand. It caught the man flush on the chin, and he fell to the floor like a sack of mangoes.

"Jesus! You knocked him out," Cece wailed. "I'll never get paid."

"What are you talking about? This guy was trying to rape you."

Cece stepped into a pair of spandex workout shorts. "Rape me? That limp-dick pays me two hundred dollars to *wrestle*."

"But you screamed. I thought—"

"I let him think he's gonna win, then I pin him."

"Here? In my office? You're running a sex service *here*?"

"Not sex, *jefe*. Fantasy wrestling. Some guys get off on it."

She tugged a sleeveless T-shirt over her head, her deltoids flexing, and the tattoo of a cobra coiling on her carved right bicep. Cece spent more time lifting than typing, and it showed, both in her ripped physique and in Steve's typo-laden legal briefs.

The guy moaned and tried to get to his feet.

"You all right, Arnie?" Cece asked.

"Gonna sue," the man mumbled, rubbing his jaw.

"Sorry I hit you, Arnie," Steve told him. "I didn't know."

"Yeah. Well, I know all about you, Solomon. I heard on the radio. You're that shyster who couldn't win a jaywalking case if the light was green."

"Aw, jeez."

"Gonna file criminal charges." Arnie grabbed his shirt from a corner of Cece's desk, picked up his socks and shoes from the floor, and hurried out the door.

"Are you gonna get in trouble, *jefe*?" Cece asked Steve.

"Me? What about you? This violates your probation."

"Doubt it. Arnie's my probation officer."

"No way."

"*Verdad, jefe*. On his reports, he says I enjoy competitive sports as a hobby."

Cece Santiago had been Steve's client before she became an employee. A little matter of beating the stuffing out of a cheating boyfriend, then driving his car off the boat ramp at Matheson Hammock.

Steve walked to his desk. "Do you think we can do a little work this morning, assuming it doesn't interfere with your hobby?"

"What work? Nobody called. Mail's not here yet. But you did get a personal delivery." She nodded toward the corner of the reception room.

Propped against the wall was a graphite pole, maybe eight feet long with a stainless-steel hook at the end.

"Fishing gaff," Steve said. "Who sent it?"

"*No sé*. It was outside when I opened up the store."

Steve picked up the gaff, hefted it, ran his hand over the sharp, lethal hook. "For landing big fish. Like marlin."

Kreeger on the radio. The marlin in the door. And now the gaff. It was all coming together, Steve thought, and he didn't like where it was heading.

Kreeger's telling me he's killed before, and he can kill again.

Steve felt a chill run up his spine. He sensed a presence behind him, whirled around, but no one was there.

The bastard's getting to me.

Which had to be part of Kreeger's plant, too. It would give him pleasure to inflict fear as well as pain.

"Deep-sea fishing?" Cece said. "Didn't you get seasick when you took Bobby on a paddle boat at Water World?"

"The gaff's not for me to use. It's to remind me of something."

"Of what, *jefe*?"

"Of the time a client of mine went fishing with someone else and only one of them came home."

SOLOMON'S LAWS

1. I'd rather lie to a judge than to the woman I love.

Four

LOGICAL LOVE

I hate lying.
  Strike that. I hate lying to someone I love.
  Some lies were worse than others, Steve thought. In court, lies come in all shapes and sizes. Outright false-hoods, cautious evasions, clever prevarications. Lies are as plentiful as the silk-suited lawyers mouthing them. Not to mention clients, cops, witnesses, and the guy peddling stale empanadas on the courthouse steps. Judges and juries do not expect to be told the truth, the whole truth, and nothing but the truth. And their ex-pectations are always fulfilled.

But you should not lie to the woman you love. This morning, Victoria had asked what happened with Kreeger, and Steve had skated around the thin ice of the truth. Now, headed to meet Victoria at a condo open house, he tried to work up the courage to tell her everything. Just as he passed Parrot Jungle on the MacArthur Causeway, his cell phone rang.

"If you been tuned to the AM dial, you ain't got no cheery smile."

Steve recognized the mellifluous voice. "Good morning, Sugar Ray."

Seven years earlier, when he prosecuted Kreeger, Ray Pincher was just another deputy in the major crimes unit. Now the ex–amateur boxer, ex–seminary student, ex–rap musician was the duly elected State Attorney of Miami-Dade County. "Too bad the dude got out the clink. That crook, that bum, that shady shrink."

"I didn't listen to the show," Steve said. Figuring he was the only one in town who hadn't heard Dr. Bill torch him.

"Said you were more crooked than a corkscrew. Lower than a rattlesnake's belly. As rotten as week-old snapper. And those were the compliments."

"So what? The man's a convicted felon. He's got zero credibility."

"You figure he knows what came down?"

Steve felt a chill. Why the hell bring that up? And on the phone yet? "You taping this call, Sugar Ray?"

"Now, that gives me pause."

"And probable cause?" Steve completed his rhyme.

Pincher laughed. "Golly, Solly. You must have a guilty conscience."

On Biscayne Boulevard now, Steve passed Freedom Tower, the Mediterranean Revival building some called Miami's Ellis Island. Hundreds of thousands of Cuban refugees were processed there in the 1960s. Now a developer planned to envelop it with a sky-scraper.

"As I recall, Sugar Ray, your hands aren't exactly clean."

Pincher exhaled a breath that whistled through Steve's earpiece. "My job was to prosecute the dude. Yours was to defend him. I did *my* job, Solomon."

The conversation had taken a nasty turn. Was Pincher threatening him? "Why you calling me, Sugar Ray?"

"To say I can't protect you. If I'm subpoenaed, I'm gonna tell the truth. Only way I can get screwed is by covering for you. Malfeasance. Obstruction. Perjury."

"Hell, you do that before breakfast."

"Ain't gonna be funny, dude after your money."

"I don't have any, and Kreeger'd know that."

"Then he'll get excited to see you indicted."

Steve stayed silent. The conversation was sailing in rough waters. Approaching the Brickell Avenue Bridge, he beeped the horn at a lane-changer, a PT Cruiser with rental plates. *Damn tourists. Why don't they all stay at Disney World and let us clog our own streets?*

Running late, he could picture Victoria impatiently tapping the toe of her hand-stitched pump on the marble floor of the high-rise condo. Steve's mood had dipped. His desire to buy overpriced real estate was waning by the minute.

"I never asked you to do anything wrong," Pincher continued. "You remember that, don't you, Solomon?"

Sure, he's recording this. Making exculpatory statements and trying to get my corroboration.

"Only thing I remember," Steve said, "when your wife was out of town, you asked me to fix you up with the Les Mannequins girls."

"You prick, Solomon."

"And now that I think about it, I seem to recall you asking where you could score some crystal meth."

Play that for the grand jury, Sugar Ray.

"You're just like your old man, you know that, Solomon?"

"Leave him out of this."

Pincher laughed, the sound of a horse whinnying. "Both of you hold yourselves above the law. And you're both gonna end up the same way. Wouldn't that be something, father and son, both disbarred?"

"Dad wasn't disbarred. He quit the Bar. That's one difference between him and me, Pincher. I don't quit anything."

But the State Attorney had already hung up.

* * *

Victoria stood on the balcony of the high-rise condo, forty-one stories up, staring at the bay, where a dozen sailboats were rounding buoys in a triangular race. To her right was Rickenbacker Causeway, the sky bridge to Key Biscayne. The MacArthur Causeway was to the left, connecting the mainland with Watson, Palm, and Star islands on the way to Miami Beach. In the distance beyond, the greenish-blue waters of the Atlantic.

Not bad. She pictured herself waking up each morning at sunrise, carrying a glass of orange juice onto the balcony. Peaceful. Relaxing. Quiet. Until Steve put on *Sports Center* to get the late scores from the West Coast.

A breeze from the southeast kicked up, wafting perfumed scents. A gorgeous apartment, a spectacular view, a Chamber of Commerce day.

So why am I so irritated?

Because of Steve, of course. He was late, as usual. But that wasn't what was bothering her. When you love a man, you accept his annoying idiosyncrasies.

Hogging the remote.

Drinking milk straight from the carton.

And Irritating Habit Number 97, sending me to the

courthouse to take the heat in a crummy case he brought in the door but didn't want to handle.

All of that came with the territory, the territory being the sometimes enchanting, often exasperating land of relationships. A far more important issue was on her mind today. They were shopping for a place to live—together—and that raised scary questions of its own.

Is this the man I want to spend my life with? Can two people so different somehow make it work?

She tried to answer logically, but could matters of the heart ever be determined by reason? Once she had thought so. Marriage was a partnership, right? She'd aced Mergers and Acquisitions as an undergrad, then gotten the book award for Partnerships and Corporations in law school. Business arrangements were based on cooperation between like-minded individuals with a common goal. So why shouldn't love be similarly logical? Why shouldn't marriage be a synergistic partnership of two people with similar interests and tastes? That calculated reasoning had led her into the arms of Bruce Bigby, real estate developer, avocado grower, Kiwanis Man of the Year. An All-American, all-around good guy. She believed their mutual interests—opera, Impressionist art, and summers on Cape Cod—represented a balanced life relatively free of stress. But once engaged to Bruce, she discovered that life was devoid of excitement and fun and . . .

Electricity.

Which is what she found with Steve. Perhaps too much electricity. Is that possible? She supposed it was. Electrocution, for example.

What was it about Steve, anyway? He had dark hair a little too long and a little too messy. He tanned easily and looked great in shorts with his strong runner's legs. Then there were his eyes, a liquid brown, and his half smile, flashing with mischief.

"You're what my mother would call Mediterranean sexy," she once told him.

"You mean a handsome Hebe?"

"There's just something about your whole look. Those full lips. That aquiline nose. Like a Roman emperor."

"You sure you don't mean a kosher butcher?"

Now, waiting for him, she wondered if moving in together was a good idea. And *she* was the one who had suggested it.

She had taken a roundabout route, starting with Bobby, worried about his reaction. They had a great relationship. Still, being the girlfriend who slept over was different than being the full-time surrogate mom. A few weeks ago, she asked Bobby whether he was okay with her moving in. Bobby thought for a second, then grinned and high-fived her.

"All of us racking together? Cool."

Steve signed on, too, without any apparent reluctance. But she could tell he hadn't given it much thought. Maybe she should have waited for *Sports Center* to be over before bringing it up.

"Good idea," he had said, during the NFL highlights. *"We'll save money, cut down on driving time."*

Mr. Romance.

Then came the housing dilemma. Steve's bungalow on Kumquat Avenue was too small. Ditto, her condo. So today, Victoria had rushed from the downtown courthouse to the high-rise canyon of Brickell Avenue to check out this three-bedroom, three-bath beauty.

She liked it and hoped Steve would, too. Problem

was, he wanted a house with a yard; she wanted an apartment with a balcony.

He says po-tay-to, and I say po-tah-to.

She'd been irritated with Steve at breakfast when he sidestepped her questions about Kreeger. On the drive to her hearing, she listened carefully to Dr. Bill's tirade, trying to determine if it was just a shtick or part of something deeper and more menacing. Kreeger, after all, had been charged with murder and convicted of manslaughter.

Underneath the wisecracks, Kreeger sounded deadly serious. Aggrieved and angry. Just what was Steve hiding from her?

So typical of him. It was, she decided, Irritating Habit Number 98. Always thinking he could shield her from unpleasantness. Protecting the little woman, as if that were his job. Not understanding that she could handle anything he could.

I'm a trial lawyer. I can stare murderers in the eye and never blink.

"So where's the bad boy, Tori?" Jacqueline Tuttle walked onto the apartment balcony, the curtains trailing behind her in the breeze. "If he's not here soon, you won't have time to try out the bed."

"Or the inclination," Victoria said.

Jackie Tuttle, real estate broker, was Victoria's best girlfriend. A tall, buxom bachelorette with a curly mane of dyed red hair and a penchant for Spicy Nude lipstick, she drove a Mercedes convertible and worked the king-of-the-jungle market, high-rise condos where she hoped to find a wealthy, single man just dying to marry a tennis-playing, water-skiing party gal. Unlike Victoria, Jackie was uninhibited, with a loud laugh and a bawdy sense of humor.

There didn't seem to be a filtering device between Jackie's brain and her mouth. No subject was off-limits. Orgasms: number and intensity. Penises: shapes, sizes, and proficiency. Credit ratings: guys lacking a seven-figure net worth should not bother calling. She cataloged potential mates on a sliding scale she called "Minimum Husband Standards." Two extra points for the man who puts the toilet seat down. Two-point penalty for the guy who keeps his Rogaine next to the skim milk in the re-frigerator.

Sometimes she would recite the names and attri-butes of her former beaus by creating a song to the tune of "Do-Re-Mi."

"Jack, a jerk, a cheapskate jerk. Dick, a drop of worthless scum . . ."

When she could no longer remember the names of all the men she'd slept with by counting on her fingers, Jackie peeled off her Jimmy Choos and computed on her toes. When she'd run out of toes, she created a spreadsheet on her computer.

"Do you think Steve will like the place?" Jackie asked, fingering a button on her silk and cashmere cardigan, which was purposely one size too small.

"Doubt it. He hates elevators."

"So why are we here?"

"It's a partnership." Victoria looked to the north where the drawbridge began to open on the Venetian Causeway, a sailboat with a tall mast waiting to pass through. "He doesn't get to choose where we live."

"Ooh. Assertiveness raises its well-coifed head."

"I mean, why should Steve call all the shots?"

"You go, girl."

"If we're going to move in together, shouldn't I have equal say?"

"*If?*"

"What?"

"Vic-a-licious. You just said 'if' you move in together. I think you have cold feet and sweaty palms."

"What are you talking about?"

"You're a commitment phobe."

"That's absurd. I'm committed to Steve."

"How many men have you lived with?"

"You know the answer. None."

Jackie belted out a laugh that made her breasts jiggle underneath the Calvin Klein cardigan. "I've lived with three in one year."

"You call that commitment?"

"I call it courage. Tori, you're a scaredy-cat."

"Am not."

"Are too. You love Steve. You have from the day you met him."

"I hated him the day I met him."

"Same difference."

"Sometimes, Jackie, you're as exasperating as Steve is."

"Really? Well, if you ever dump that bad boy into the recycling bin, have him page me."

Jackie laughed again, Victoria joining in. A moment later, Steve came through the open door and onto the balcony. "What's so funny?"

"Men," the women said simultaneously.

Jackie looped an arm around Steve's elbow. "Have you seen the master bath? The Jacuzzi? The marble floors?"

"All I've seen are the damn elevators. You have to take one from the parking garage and another from the lobby."

"But did you check out the pool?" Victoria chimed

in. "Bobby will love it. You know how swimming soothes him."

"Swimming with dolphins soothes him. I didn't see any in the shallow end."

"C'mon, handsome," Jackie said. "Keep an open mind."

"There's no land. No grass." Steve gestured toward the ground, forty-one floors below. "It's all concrete down there. Where am I going to play catch with Bobby? And what's with that sign on the seawall? *No Fishing?*"

"You hate fishing," Victoria said.

"I hate rules. I love fishing. I come from a long line of anglers."

"You come from a long line of liars."

"Shows what you know. My *zayde* Abe Solomon caught a record herring off Savannah."

"There are no herring off Savannah."

"Grandpop Abe must have caught them all."

"Don't be difficult," Jackie intervened. She put both hands on her hips in a motion that pushed her breasts higher. "Steve, you have a few things going for you in the husband sweepstakes. You're single, straight, and self-supporting. But frankly, I've pulled your credit report, and you're not exactly Donald Trump."

"I'll dye my hair orange if that'll help."

"You drive a ratty old car, you dress like a Jimmy Buffet roadie, and except for what I've been told are your talents in the bedroom—"

"Jackie!" Victoria blushed.

"You're not all that great a prize," Jackie continued, "and my best bud deserves the best. So why not just chill and let Tori choose a place to live?"

"Hey, I get a vote here, Jack-o," Steve said.

She dismissed the notion with a wave of her finger-nails, painted the pinkish color called "Italian Love Affair." "I've seen your house, Steve. You obviously have *no* sense of design or style."

"You mean I have no pretensions like those trust-fund boys you run around with."

"Stop it, you two," Victoria ordered. "Steve, don't be mean to Jackie."

"Me? She's the one who wishes you'd married Bigby."

"True," Jackie admitted. "But I told her to keep you on the side." She gestured toward the interior of the apartment. "Now, why don't we look at the master suite?"

"I hate this place," Steve said.

Sounding like a child, Victoria thought. A petulant child.

"I'm wasting my time here," Jackie said. "Toodles." She waved and headed back through the balcony door.

Victoria gave Steve one of her piercing looks.

"What? What'd I do, besides tell the truth?" he asked.

"You walked in throwing hand grenades. Why didn't you just call and say there's no way you'd live here?"

"I wasn't sure until the concierge spoke French to me."

"I'm serious, Steve. It's unfair to Jackie. She's doing us a favor."

"Not unless she kicks back half her commission." Steve took a deep breath. "Look, Vic. We need to talk."

"I know. You want a house with a yard and crab-grass."

"It's not that." He cast a long look toward the sailboats, as if he wanted to be on one. "I need to tell you about Kreeger."

"You do?" She didn't even try to hide her surprise.

"This morning, I wasn't entirely truthful with you. Now I want to tell you everything."

"You do?" Sounding as skeptical as she felt.

"I've been too closed off. I'm going to share more of myself."

She studied him a moment. "Are you gaming me?"

"Jeez, when did you get so cynical?"

"When you taught me that everybody lies under oath."

"Look, I'm not saying I'm gonna become Mr. Sensitive. I'm as scared as the next guy to show weakness, but what I did this morning wasn't fair. I answered your questions about Kreeger like I was before the Grand Jury. So I'm gonna tell you what happened with him and maybe use that to open up on other stuff, too."

She threw both arms around his neck and drew him close. "You're a wonderful man, Steve Solomon, you know that?"

"Before you make that final, you might want to hear me out."

SOLOMON'S LAWS

2. **Thou shalt not screw thy own client . . .
   unless thou hast a damn good reason.**

Five

SURVIVAL OF THE HOMICIDAL

A pelican sat on a coral boulder, scratching its feathery belly with its beak. Steve and Victoria walked along Bayfront Drive, a wall of condos on one side, the flat, green water of Biscayne Bay on the other. Her sunglasses were perched on top her head and her long stride tugged her Sunny Choi pencil skirt tight at the hips. Steve didn't know Sunny Choi from chicken chow mein, but he'd started picking up slivers of fashion information by listening to Victoria's end of phone conversations with Jackie.

They headed in and out of shadows cast by the high-rises, the sun slanting toward the Everglades. In the light, Victoria's hair glowed with butterscotch highlights. In the shadows, her green eyes gave off their own light. She seemed happy, already forgiving Steve for being late, for being obstreperous, for being . . . Steve.

"I did something in Kreeger's case I'd never done before and haven't since," he said. "And I'm not proud of it."

"Tell me. Tell me everything, Steve."

Her nurturing tone. That was it. Women were born

nuturers. Cling to their warm bosoms, and everything will be all right. This would be easy. Victoria was, by nature, supportive and caring. And forgiving.

"The case against Kreeger was purely circumstantial," he said. "I thought I could win."

"You always think you can win."

"Yeah, but this was different. I thought Kreeger was innocent."

He didn't have to say, *"as opposed to not guilty."* Victoria knew the difference. In criminal cases, you seldom defend a person who is truly I-didn't-do-the-crime innocent. But you'll often defend someone who almost certainly did the crime; the state just can't prove it. That's the difference between *innocent* and *not guilty.*

As everyone knows who watches blabbermouth lawyers on TV dissecting the latest trial of the century, the state must prove guilt beyond every reasonable doubt. The prosecutor is the sturdy workman at the center of a storm, carrying sandbags to the dike, staving off the flood that will swamp the state's case. The defense lawyer is the vandal, poking holes in the sandbags, pissing in the river, and praying for even more rain. Steve believed he was second to none in the hole-poking and river-pissing departments. He took seriously the lawyer's duty to zealously defend his client. And he always had. Except once.

"Kreeger had no criminal record," Steve continued. "He was wealthy, well known, respected. He was the court-appointed expert in a nasty child custody fight. At the same time, he was having an affair with the mother."

"Not nice."

"A woman named Nancy Lamm. Not only does

Kreeger seduce her, he gives her bushel baskets of pills, overprescribing antidepressants and sedatives. They have a falling-out, and she threatens to file a complaint with DPR, go after his license."

"Sounds like the state had its motive. Kill her. Shut her up."

"That's what Pincher argued to the jury, but think about it, Vic. If Kreeger planned to kill her, would he do it at his house, in his hot tub, with his drugs in her system?"

"If criminals were smart, we'd be out of business."

"Kreeger has a genius IQ. If he wanted to kill Nancy Lamm, it would have been a lot cleaner."

"Unless he snapped."

"He's not given to rages. He's a smart, calculating man who just happens to have a woman drown in his hot tub after mixing booze and barbiturates."

"Any signs of trauma?"

"Excellent question, Counselor. Laceration on the skull. Pincher's theory was that Kreeger bashed her with something, then tossed her into the hot tub. Kreeger told me he was in the house mixing a pitcher of daiquiris. When he came out, he found her in the tub. My theory was that she was zonked out of her mind, slipped on the wet pool deck, hit her head on the rounded edge of the tub, and tumbled in."

"Sounds pretty far-fetched to me."

"I had a human-factors expert who backed me up. Said it was within the realm of reasonable probability. We also put together a video animation that looked pretty convincing."

"So you made the slip-and-fall argument without blushing?"

"I never blush."

"Right. Not even when you claimed your client shouldn't have to return the engagement ring she accepted when she was . . . what was the term you used?"

" 'Temporarily unavailable for matrimony.' "

"Right. Solomon-speak for 'already married.' "

They walked past the Sheraton Hotel and neared the bridge to Brickell Key, once an undeveloped island, now a concrete jungle of high-rises, with barely a tree or shrub that wasn't potted on a condo balcony. A heavyset shirtless jogger plugged into an iPod lumbered past them.

"What did the coroner say about the laceration?" Victoria asked.

"Inconclusive. Could have come from impact with the tub or something else with a rounded edge."

"Such as?"

"The skimmer pole used to clean the pool."

"Did they test it, match up the marks?"

"Couldn't. The pole was missing. Never found."

"Oh, isn't that convenient?"

"Yeah, Pincher ranted and railed about that. Suggested to the jury that Kreeger smacked the woman with the pole, then got rid of it before he called nine-one-one."

They approached the small park at the point where the Miami River pours into Biscayne Bay. Off to one side was Miami Circle, the archeological site that dates back two thousand years. Long before Brickell Avenue was populated with lawyers and investment bankers and CPAs, a hardwood hammock stretched along the bay, a prairie ran inland, and Native Americans camped on the banks of the river, cooking their wild game over open flames and making carvings in the limestone.

"You already know what the jury did," Steve said. "Acquitted on murder and convicted on manslaughter."

"The curse of the lesser included offense."

"Exactly. A no-guts compromise verdict. They should have either convicted Kreeger of murder or acquitted him. But forget that for a second, Vic. You be a jury of one. What's *your* verdict?"

"I hope you don't think I'm being critical," she began. Her feminine way of softening whatever might follow, couching her criticism in terms as comfy as bedroom slippers. "I'm surprised the jury didn't acquit. Without a murder weapon, with a reasonable alternative scenario for the head wound, your guy should have walked."

"I thought you'd say that. But it wasn't a fair question. I left something out."

"Something incriminating?"

"You tell me. Let's go back almost twenty years. Kreeger's just finishing med school at Shands. To celebrate, he takes a weekend trip down to Islamorada with a couple classmates. One's his best friend, a guy named Jim Beshears. The other is Beshear's girlfriend."

Victoria seemed puzzled. "What's a trip to the Keys have to do with the dead lady in the hot tub twenty years later?"

"Like I always say to the jury, please wait until my entire case is presented before reaching any conclusions."

Victoria shrugged and he continued. "The three of them—Kreeger, Beshears, and the girlfriend—charter a boat to go after marlin. Now, they've been drinking all weekend, and everything they know about fish they learned at Red Lobster, but somehow Beshears' girlfriend manages to hook a marlin and fight the thing till it's alongside the boat. Not a huge one as marlins go, but still a couple hundred pounds or so. The captain's on the fly bridge, and Kreeger and Beshears are like Abbott and Costello trying to land the fish. Kreeger's waving a gaff and Beshears is leaning over the gun-wale, and somehow the fish lands in the cockpit and Beshears lands in the drink."

"Okay, so he went overboard. They haul him aboard, right?"

"The girlfriend throws him a life ring but he can't reach it. Beshears is swallowing water and panicking. Kreeger leans over the side, holding the gaff for Beshears to grab on to. But the boat's rocking and Beshears is riding up and down on the waves, and somehow in the confusion, Kreeger brains him with the gaff. The captain's trying to maneuver the boat and they lose sight of Beshears until he's dragged into the props and chopped into sushi."

"Oh, God. You're not saying Kreeger intended to kill him? I mean, there's no proof of that, right?"

"No more than with Nancy Lamm in the hot tub."

"Meaning what?"

"All weekend long, Beshears had been busting Kreeger's balls about some paper he wrote, claiming Kreeger'd phonied up research to justify his conclusions about evolutionary psychology. Kreeger believed that murder is a natural consequence of our being human, that evolution favored those who kill their rivals."

"Survival of the homicidal."

"Exactly. Kreeger wrote that killing is programmed into our DNA, rather than being aberrational conduct. He did some studies with undergrads, measuring their propensity for violence. Beshears needled him the way guys do, calling him a fraud. Kreeger warned him to shut up, and it just kept getting uglier."

The sun had angled lower in the sky and was shooting daggers into their eyes. Victoria slipped her sunglasses down from the top of her head. "Pattern conduct," she said softly, as if thinking aloud. "Beshears and Lamm. Two people who pose threats to Kreeger. Each one gets clobbered on the head and knocked into the water. Both end up dead. Each time it looks like an accident. Similar facts under the Williams Rule."

"Which is how Pincher got the Beshears story into evidence, crippling my defense."

"Pincher's usually so lazy, I'm surprised he discovered the earlier case."

"He didn't."

"So how'd he find out about the fishing trip and the guy dying?"

"I told him," Steve said.

"No. You didn't."

"I did, Vic. I gave Pincher all the evidence he needed to convict my client."

Victoria's lower lip seemed to tremble. Then she shook her head, as if trying to cast out the memory of what she just heard. "You violated your oath?"

"I had a good reason."

"There's never a good reason," Victoria said, turning away.

Six

THE LOVE CHILD OF
AYN RAND AND TED BUNDY

Victoria tried to process what she had just heard. Just yards away, students at the dig site worked on hands and knees with trowels and whisk brooms, searching for archeological treasures.

She could hardly believe what he'd told her. Steve never rolled over and played dead for anyone. In court, he always fought hard and sometimes dirty. More than once, he had spent the night behind bars for contempt.

"A lawyer who's afraid of jail is like a surgeon who's afraid of blood."

He'd told her that the day they met. At that moment, they were ensconced in adjacent holding cells. He had provoked her in the courtroom. She'd lost her cool and they'd been held in mutual contempt. Which is the way they felt about each other. In the lockup, he had ridiculed her propriety; she'd railed about his ethics, or lack thereof.

"You make a mockery of the law."

"I make up my own. Solomon's Laws."

She knew that Steve cut corners to win. But breaking the law to *lose*? That was a new one. And perhaps even more frightening because it cut to the heart of the lawyer's oath. A lawyer was supposed to zealously defend—not double-cross—his or her client.

"Come on, Steve. You didn't give incriminating evidence to the state."

"Yes, I did."

"Why?"

"Kreeger lied to me, and I caught him at it."

"Then you should have withdrawn from the case."

"Then he would have lied to his next lawyer, and he would have gotten off. Like you said, without evidence of the earlier death, the state had a weak case."

"That's the system. The net has holes in it. Sometimes the guilty fall through so the innocent won't be snared. You, of all people, must know that."

Here she was, a former prosecutor, telling Steve-the-Shyster that it's okay for murderers to walk. She couldn't believe the role reversal at play.

"Somebody had to stop him," Steve said. "Kreeger killed Jim Beshears and Nancy Lamm."

"Dammit, Steve! You don't know that."

"I felt it in my bones. I was dead-solid certain."

"Even if you're right, a defense lawyer can't be a secret agent for the state."

She glared at the man she loved, the man she planned to live with, might even someday marry. But this was just astonishing. Something her mother once said came back to her.

"Men's deceptions are always the tip of the ice cube."

"You mean iceberg, Mother?"

"Not if they're drinking Scotch on the rocks. My point, Princess, if you catch them in one lie, others will surely follow."

In her chosen career as a glamorous widow, Irene Lord, The Queen, had developed a healthy cynicism about men. Victoria had picked up some of that. But it never seemed to apply to Steve. Most men put on a front and hide their aggravating traits. Like the archeology students at the dig site, you have to scrape with shovel and trowel to find their true nature. Not so with Steve. He hid his softer, caring side—his love for Bobby, his pro bono work, his passionate commitment to justice—under an exterior that could be both overbearing and unbearable.

She forced herself to speak to him in even, measured tones. "I understand your motive, but you stepped so far over the line, I have to question whether you're fit to be a lawyer."

"Jeez, why are you taking this so personally?" Sounding hurt.

"How am I supposed to take it? I'm your partner. And your lover."

"You weren't either one when this went down."

She clenched her teeth so hard, she felt her jaw muscles ache. "Would you like to restore the status quo ante?"

"Aw, c'mon, Vic. I didn't mean it that way. More like, you weren't around to influence me, so I did some things I wouldn't do now."

"Nice recovery, Slick. But what you did was still unethical and illegal."

"Okay, already. I've gotten over it. You should, too."

"Just like that! Could you give me a few minutes first?"

One of the students at the dig site, a young woman in khaki shorts, stood and yelled. She held something in her hand and waved to the others. From this distance it was impossible to make out the item. A shard of pottery, an arrowhead, some artifact of the Tequesta Indians? Scratching away to learn secrets of the past.

Victoria went into her lawyer mode. Speaking softly, as if thinking out loud, she said: "Kreeger probably can't sue you because the statute of limitations has run. But there's no limitations period on ethical violations. He could have you disbarred."

"Or hit me with a marlin gaff."

He told her then about the gaff delivered to the office. "The marlin on the door. The gaff. Kreeger's way of saying he knows I torpedoed his case."

"But why tell you?"

"To let me know he can do the same thing to me he did to Beshears and Lamm."

"So selling out your client wasn't just blatantly illegal," she said, shaking her head in disbelief. "It was also unbelievably stupid."

* * *

Her anger surprised him. What happened to that warm and comfy nurturing he'd expected?

What happened to clinging to her warm bosom?

Steve thought back to the day he'd discovered Kreeger's secret. He'd been looking for helpful witnesses, not damning ones. Kreeger had become a bit of a celebrity. The psychiatrist had done work with the FBI's Behavioral Science Unit and gained some credibility as an expert on serial killers. Turn on CNN or Court TV, and he'd pop up every time some freak was loose. Then he moved into personal relationships, which Steve figured wasn't all that different than homicide. Relaxed in front of the camera, Kreeger got his daytime TV show, dispensing wisdom to women fed up with their men, an inexhaustible and ever-growing audience.

Steve traveled to the med school in Gainesville, trying to find character witnesses. He spoke to a professor who remembered Kreeger and told a murky story about a fishing trip gone bad. A few more calls turned up the former girlfriend of the late Jim Beshears. The girlfriend told Steve that Kreeger had been enraged by Beshears' charges of academic fraud. The two men had argued, and from her vantage point in the cockpit of the boat, she thought Kreeger might have pushed Beshears overboard, then intentionally hit him with the gaff. But everything had happened so fast and she'd been so shaken, she couldn't be sure. Officially, the death was declared an accident without a full criminal investigation.

Then Steve read Kreeger's bestselling book: *Looking Out for Numero Uno*. The man's views of human nature were downright macabre. In chapter one, "Screw Thy Neighbor," Kreeger posited that greed, hedonism, and selfishness are good. Altruism, charity, and sacrifice are stupid. Self-interest is the only interest. Be the screwer, not the screwee. The more he read, the more concerned Steve became.

He went back to Gainesville and puttered around in the Shands Hospital library. He found Kreeger's monograph, *Murder Through the Eons: Homicide as an Essential Element of Evolutionary Biology*. While a hospital resident on the psychiatry staff, Kreeger had argued that human beings were bred to be murderers. Homicidal instincts, he wrote, are survival tactics dating from prehistoric times. By historical practice, it is rational and sane to kill anyone who threatens your cave, your mate, or your dinner. Our DNA carries those instincts today.

"Murder should not be considered a perversion of human values. Murder is the essential human value."

Then Kreeger went even further. To kill rationally, he declared, does not require one to be engaged in self-defense. Setting aside man-made notions of right and wrong, it would be logical to kill a rival for a promotion at work or for the love of a woman or even for the last seat on a bus.

Suddenly, preparing for the man's trial, it had all become clear to Steve.

William Kreeger, MD, was the love child of Ayn Rand and Ted Bundy.

A man so possessed of narcissism and self-interest and so devoid of feelings for others that he would eliminate anyone he believed was a threat.

His classmate. His lady friend. Or his lawyer.

Sure, Victoria was right. Not only was it illegal to turn over incriminating evidence to the state, with Kreeger as a client, it was also dangerous. So what now? Kreeger wouldn't be satisfied with pranks involving dead fish, marlin gaffs, and trash talk on the radio. Those were just preludes.

Kreeger could be planning his attack right now.

Which meant Steve needed a counterattack. Or better yet, an offensive. A way to bring down Kreeger *before* he took his shot. But how?

Storm into the radio station, jack Kreeger up against the wall, and rattle his fillings.

Nah.

Steve was a lawyer. A schmoozer. He could bob and weave in front of a jury and play rope-a-dope with opposing counsel. But violence? Not his style. Sure, he'd taken one swing with a stick that cracked a man's skull, but that had been necessary to rescue Bobby. What else?

Punching that probation officer in dubious defense of Cece's virtue? Not very impressive. Starting a brawl years ago by spiking the Florida State shortstop while breaking up a double play? Nah, nobody even got bruised.

But Kreeger? The man had a track record of deadly violence. So Steve needed a plan. But a problem there, too. How do you outsmart a man who is both brilliant and a killer, when you are neither?

SOLOMON'S LAWS

3. When you don't know what to do, seek advice from your father . . . even if he's two candles short of a menorah.

Seven

KING SOLOMON AND THE
QUEEN OF SHEBA

Steve needed advice. He needed to talk to the man who had once peered down at assorted miscreants, pronouncing them guilty, dispatching them to places where the only harm they could inflict was on one another. The Honorable Herbert T. Solomon had a feel for this sort of thing.

What do I do, Dad, when some nutcase is after me?

Steve walked out the kitchen door into his backyard. His father and nephew sat cross-legged on the ground, in the shade of a bottlebrush tree. Pieces of plywood and two-by-fours were strewn on the grass, along with a hammer, a saw, and an open toolbox.

"*Shalom*, son," his father called out. Chin stubbled with white whiskers, long silvery hair swept straight back, flipping up at his neck. With a bottle of sour mash whiskey within arm's reach, Herbert T. Solomon looked like Wild Bill Hickock in a yarmulke.

Or maybe a biblical prophet. He held a weathered copy of the Old Testament in one hand and a drink in the other. "The Queen of Sheba," Herbert intoned in his Southern drawl, "having heard of Solomon's fame, came to test him with tricky questions."

"Get to the sexy part," Bobby said. "Where Solomon slips it to Sheba and all the concubines."

Herbert took a sip of the whiskey. "In due time, boychik."

"What's going on, Dad?"

"Ah'm teaching Robert the good book." Herbert flipped a page. " *'The Queen of Sheba gave Solomon gold and spices, and—'* "

" 'Spice' is Bible talk for nookie," Bobby interrupted, grinning at Steve. "Grandpop taught me that."

"Grandpop's a regular Talmudic scholar."

Bobby went on, excitedly: "In the first book of Kings, it says that Solomon gave Sheba *'everything she desired and asked for.'* You get it, Uncle Steve?"

"I think I can figure it out."

"Did you know King Solomon had seven hundred wives and three hundred concubines?"

"No wonder he wanted to get out of the house and conquer Mesopotamia." Steve turned to his father, who was pouring whiskey over ice. "Dad, why are you filling Bobby with this nonsense?"

"Our roots are not nonsense." Herbert took a noisy pull on his drink and turned to his grandson. "Robert, our ancestors were warriors in the court of King Solomon. We're direct descendants from His Honor's own wise self."

"Oh, for God's sake," Steve groaned.

"Don't you blaspheme in mah presence."

"And what's with the yarmulke? You covering a bald spot?"

"Ah pray for you, Stephen. You've become a Philistine."

"And you've flipped out. Going orthodox at your age is just plain weird."

Herbert shook his head. "Cain't believe mah son's a heathen and mah daughter's a whore."

"Hey, Dad. Cool it in front of Bobby with that stuff, okay?"

"*Nu?* What's the big deal? You think the boy doesn't know his mother's a junkie and a tramp?"

"Dad, that's enough." Not that it wasn't true, Steve thought, but you don't smack a kid in the face with that kind of talk.

"It's okay, Uncle Steve." Bobby fiddled with a two-by-four, showing no apparent concern. But Steve knew that look. A blank, neutral mask. It was how the boy hid the pain. What the hell was wrong with his father, anyway? Didn't he realize how sensitive Bobby was? Probably not. When Steve was a kid, his father treated him just as callously. Hadn't he called him a "wuss" when four *Marieltos* at Nautilus Middle School beat him up for his lunch money?

Without looking up, Bobby said: "The other day in the cafeteria, one of the kids asked about my parents."

Steve held his breath. Kids can be so cruel. Little predators preying on the one who's different.

"I told them I didn't know my father, and my mom was in prison," Bobby continued.

"You take some heat over that, kiddo?"

Bobby shook his head. "Everybody thought that was way cool. Manuel said he wished he didn't know his old man. Jason asked if I ever visited Mom in prison."

The boy let it hang there. His way of asking Steve why they never drove down to Homestead Correctional. So hard to understand the boy's longing. Janice had neglected and abused him. Locked him in a dog shed, starved him while she got stoned. And

Bobby, what . . . *missed* her? Steve decided to let it go. What could he say, anyway?

"If you visit your Mom, those nightmares will come back, kiddo."

No, he would rather stay clear of the subject of Janice Solomon, junkie, tramp, and utterly worthless mother.

"If mah son won't go to *Shabbos* services with me," Herbert declared, "maybe mah grandson will."

"I have to study," Bobby said.

"On a Friday night? You oughta be praying, then chasing tail. Maybe praying you catch some."

"Dad, what the hell's going on? You haven't been to synagogue in thirty years."

"The hell you say. When ah was a practicing lawyer, ah went to High Holy Days every year."

"Right. You handed out your business card on Yom Kippur. What's up now?"

"Mah grandfather was a cantor, you know that?"

Steve had heard the stories since he was a child. Herbert claimed to have traced the family tree back nearly three centuries. Ezekiel Solomon was among the first English colonists to settle Savannah in the 1730s. The Solomons grew and prospered, and over the generations the family sprawled to Atlanta and Birmingham and Charleston. According to Herbert, who specialized in the tradition of exaggeration employed by lawyers, peddlers, and Southerners, the tree that sprouted from old Ezekiel produced farmers and weavers, stone masons and mill owners. Even an occasional rabbi and cantor. Not to mention a stock swindler and a bookie who went to prison for fixing college football games in the 1940s.

But what was this crap about the court of King

Solomon? It was one thing to trace your ancestors back to James Oglethorpe. But quite another to lay claim to a royal name three thousand years old.

Until recently, Herbert hadn't cared much about spirituality. So, why now? He was getting older, of course. Probably sensing his own mortality.

Then there's his fall from grace.

Nearly fifteen years ago, snared in a bribery and extortion scandal, Herbert had protested his innocence but nonetheless quit the bench and resigned from the Bar in disgrace. That had to be it, Steve thought.

Lost and found. My old man found religion to make up for what he's lost.

Career and status, gone. Wife—Steve's mother, Eleanor—dead of a vicious cancer. Daughter Janice in and out of jail and drug rehab. A touchy relationship with Steve.

Herbert picked up a hammer and a handful of nails and grabbed a two-by-four. "Gotta get to work, son."

"On what?"

"Gonna make a scale model of the Temple of Solomon," Herbert said.

"You got a building permit for that?"

"Got the blueprints. How long's a cubit, anyway?"

Steve doubted his father could drive a nail straight. When Steve was Bobby's age, Herbert couldn't glue the wings of a balsa airplane to the fuselage.

"Robert, the temple is where King Solomon kept the Ark of the Covenant," Herbert said, "the very tablets the Lord gave to Moses."

"I know, Gramps. I saw *Raiders of the Lost Ark*."

Enough was enough. "Bobby, I need to talk to your grandfather for a few minutes," Steve said.

"So?"

"There are fresh mangoes on the counter. Go make yourself a smoothie."

"You can't order me around. I'm descended from King Solomon." Bobby squeezed his eyes shut. "King Solomon. SOLO GIN MONK."

"Fine, kiddo. Now, give us a few minutes."

"Okay, okay." The boy got to his feet and slouched toward the kitchen door.

"I've got a problem, Dad. I need advice."

"Then you damn well came to the right place," Herbert Solomon said.

* * *

Just as he had done with Victoria, Steve told his father everything. How he learned Kreeger's philosophy by reading his monograph on rational murder. How he uncovered Beshears' death, then sold Kreeger out in the murder trial by tipping off Pincher. How he found the marlin on his door and the gaff in his office, symbols of Kreeger's homicidal fishing trip. And how upset Victoria became when he confessed his lawyerly sins.

When he was finished, Herbert exhaled a long, low whistle. "Jesus and Magdalene, David and Bathsheba."

"I don't think those two couples are equivalent," Steve said.

"Then you didn't read *The Da Vinci Code*. Son, when you stroll through the cow pasture, you best not be wearing your wingtips."

"What the hell's that mean?"

"You stepped in deep shit. So what is it you want? Girlfriend advice or Florida Bar advice? 'Cause if it's girlfriend advice, ah'd say it's high time that shiksa converts. A dip in the *Mikvah,* the gateway to purity. Miriam's well in the desert."

"Jeez, Dad. Can you focus? I'm telling you this guy's coming after me."

"You mean to do you harm?"

"No, to wish me happy Chanukah. Don't you get it? Kreeger killed two people. I was supposed to defend him, and I double-crossed him. He's out of prison and he's pissed. It's a *Cape Fear* deal."

"Cape Fear, cape schmere. Ah heard him on the radio today. Talking about what a shitty lawyer you were. Some of it was damn funny."

"Glad you enjoyed it."

"He was riding you hard, sure. But it didn't sound mean. More like joshing."

"So what's the message he's sending?"

"The way Ah figure, he's saying he knows what you did. Confirming you were right about him being a killer. Boasting about it. Thinking maybe you would appreciate the artistry of it."

"Why would I appreciate him killing two people?"

"From what you say, he admires men who break the rules. That's you, son."

"But not by killing. Not like him."

"Dr. Bill probably considers you just a step or two up that slippery slope from where he stands."

"And what do you think he wants from me?"

"Take the man at his word. He said he wanted you to come on his show. Maybe he thinks he's Johnny Carson and you're his Ed McMahon. His sidekick. Ah don't believe Kreeger wants to kill you, Stephen. Ah believe he wants to be your pal."

"That's crazy."

"Just listen to the man flap his gums. He's a talker.

But who's he gonna talk to about killing those people? You, son. In his head, you're the only one who understands."

"I don't want to talk to him. I want him off my back."

"Okay, go tell him that. But what if he won't let up?"

"Then I'll bring him down. I don't know how, but I will."

"You best be careful about that."

"You saying I should do nothing, let him smear me?"

"Ah'm saying, you call me if you plan to take him on. That sumbitch ain't a one-mule load."

*　*　*

Bobby sliced the mangoes, taking care to cut around the pit so it would pop out, the way Uncle Steve had taught him. He could hear the two men talking in the yard. On the farm, when Bobby had been locked in the shed in the dark, his sense of hearing had sharpened. At night, he'd listened to the coyotes until he could tell one from another as they sang their songs. He could hear the horses shuffling in the barn, their rumps smacking the wall. Could almost feel the hot breath of their snorts and whinnies. During the days, he'd heard the trucks, their doors slamming, men cursing. When he was let out to work in the fields, he would listen to the birds chirping and the bees buzzing.

He'd liked it outside, even if the men would sometimes hit him for not working hard enough. The men smelled funny, and their beards were tangled and yucky. The women worked in the vegetable garden, bent over, greasy hair falling in their eyes.

Mom said they were organic farmers, but Bobby

saw drums of insecticide and bags of artificial fertilizer. And he knew the leafy green plants were marijuana. On moonless nights, he heard the trucks pull in, heard the men grunting as they hoisted bales, heard them yelling at the moon, whooping after their women, guns blasting empty liquor bottles to smithereens.

Now Bobby listened as Uncle Steve told Grandpop about the psychiatrist named Kreeger. Uncle Steve sounded worried, which was weird. He was always getting into trouble but it never seemed to bother him. But this was different. Was Uncle Steve scared?

Bobby tossed the mango slices into the blender with a sliced banana, a handful of ice, and two scoops of protein powder. He wanted to gain weight so he didn't look like such a weenie, but it wasn't working. Despite the smoothies and ham paninis and all the pistachio ice cream he could eat, his body still was all wires and bones. With the blender whirring, he could no longer hear the men. Were they talking about his mother?

Uncle Steve doesn't understand. He thinks just because Mom messed me up, I don't want to see her. But she's still my mom.

There was something he needed to tell Uncle Steve, but didn't know how. His mother had called him yesterday. She cried on the phone, and he did, too. Said she loved him and was sorry about everything and she had completely changed.

"*I'm a new woman, Bobby. I'm clean and sober.*"

"*That's great, Mom.*"

"*I'm never going back to those old ways. I have a new purpose. A guiding light.*"

"*What's that, Mom?*"

"*I found Jesus. I let Jesus Christ into my heart.*"

Wait till Grandpop hears, Bobby thought.

But that wasn't what Bobby needed to tell Uncle Steve. What he needed to tell him was the last thing Mom had said.

"I'm coming to get you, Bobby, honey. I'm coming back to be your mother again."

Eight

WAXING NOSTALGIC

Without really intending to, Victoria Lord was staring straight into The Queen's crotch. "Maybe this should wait, Mother."

"Nonsense. It's your duty to relieve my insufferable boredom." Naked from the waist down, Irene Lord lay on her back, her hands under her butt, her legs raised and spread. "Benedita, you will be quick about it, won't you, darling?"

"I will be *queek* so your lover can be slow," Benedita vowed in a thick Brazilian accent. A young woman with cinnamon skin and flaming red lipstick, Benedita wore pink nylon shorts, a crimson sequined wrestler's singlet, and knee-high suede boots.

They were in a private booth at the Salon Rio in Bal Harbour for The Queen's monthly bikini wax. Already, Victoria regretted coming here, but she was desperate for personal advice.

Should I move in with Steve? Why is the thought of All-Steve, All-the-Time, so terrifying?

Victoria hadn't expressed her fears to him. How could she? Moving in together had been her idea. Of course, if Steve were more attuned to the subtleties of her moods, he would have picked up the vibes. Instead, she had asked: *"Are you absolutely sure you're ready for this?"*

He quickly said yes, not realizing she had been expressing her own doubts. Typical tone-deaf male.

Now she was in full-blown crisis mode. Could she really work with him all day, then come home to the same house? Was 24/7 simply too much?

Something else, too. After that bombshell today, Steve nuking the ethical rules by turning on his own client, could she even work with him?

Then she wondered if she was overreacting. Or even worse . . .

Am I subconsciously using what Steve did years ago as a reason not to advance our relationship?

She wanted to ask her mother all these questions. After all, The Queen's experiences with men crossed several continents over several decades and were exponentially greater than her own. But her mother, as usual, was engrossed in her own affairs.

"You really must meet Carl," Irene said, peering over her pubic region. "He's a dreamboat and a dead ringer for George Clooney. They could be twins."

"Which would make him how much younger than you, Mother?"

"Actually, I haven't told him my age, but I implied I was too young to remember Neil Armstrong landing on the moon."

"Which means you gave birth to me when you were, what—ten?"

"It's been known to happen, dear."

"Stop moving," Benedita ordered as she dusted Irene's private parts with perfumed puffs of baby powder. Snow falling on pubies.

"Princess, you really should get waxed," Irene said.

"No thank you, Mother."

"I've seen that bush of yours. You could use a weed whacker."

"Mother!"

Benedita hoisted one of Irene's legs over a shoulder.

"I'm just trying to help, dear. Men love those bare, smooth loins. Probably the Lolita fantasy."

"I'm not having this discussion."

"Just trying to help, dear." The Queen studied her daughter a moment, pursing her lips. "And what have you done to your hair? Your *other* hair."

"Nothing."

"You've tinted it. I can tell."

"I haven't done anything except wash it."

"I liked it better the other way."

"What other way! Dammit, Mother, you're impossible."

"Don't raise your voice. Men can't stand a woman who's shrill."

Victoria sighed. "God, why did I come here?"

"Why, to keep me company, of course."

Victoria blurted it out: "I'm not sure about moving in with Steve."

"Well, I am. It's a terrible idea. Why you ever suggested it is beyond me. A man won't buy the cow if he's getting the crème fraiche for free."

"I thought you didn't want me to marry Steve."

"Oooh," The Queen sighed as Benedita slathered the warm beeswax concoction over her crotch. "I don't, Princess. The man is totally unsuitable for you."

"Why? Because he's not Episcopalian or because he's not rich?"

"Ouch!" A tearing sound and The Queen yelped. "Jesus, Benedita . . ."

Benedita smiled as she examined the glob of hardened wax she'd just yanked from The Queen.

"I'm not a bigot and I'm not *that* materialistic," Irene said. "But I can't help wondering, dear. If you're going to be with a Jewish man, why couldn't it be one with some wherewithal? Goodness knows, there are enough of them."

"I knew this would be useless."

Another rip. Another *"Ouch!"*

"I'm just worried that we're too different, Mother."

"Of course you are, dear."

As if it's a given. As if there's no need to discuss it.

"Keep the landing strip narrow, Benedita," Irene instructed as the Brazilian woman plucked stray hairs with tiny tweezers. "It makes the man look bigger."

More concerned about the aesthetics of her private parts than about her only child's happiness.

Victoria decided to try once more. One more stab at drawing her mother away from her own sybaritic pleasures. "Steve did something incomprehensible, and I just can't come to grips with it."

"He cheated on you?"

"Of course not! It involves a case."

"You know how legal talk bores me, dear."

But still, Victoria told her the story of Steve handing over evidence that helped convict his client. By the time Victoria finished, The Queen was left with a landing strip the width of a popsicle stick. The surrounding skin was flaming pink.

"I don't know, dear. What Stephen did doesn't sound that terrible to me. His client's a murderer who was going to get away with it. At least Stephen took him off the streets for a few years."

"But that's not his job. You don't understand, Mother. It cuts to the essence of the profession. A lawyer who'll do that . . . who knows what else he might do? If Steve represents a corporation, will he give away trade secrets if he decides the company's behaving badly? In a divorce, if his client tells him she's been cheating on her husband, will he tell the judge? Once you break the rules, where does it stop?"

"Did I mention that Carl is a fantastic golfer?"

"What?"

"He wants to take me to Scotland, play all the great courses."

What a breathtaking leap, Victoria thought, her mother vaulting to her own love life without breaking stride.

Of course, she already devoted nearly five minutes to my problems. How much more could I expect?

Victoria decided to surrender. What else could she do? "That's fascinating, Mother."

"Carl's family came over on the *Mayflower*. Personally, I never cared for cruises, though the S.S. *France* had foie gras to die for. Which reminds me. Are we going to the club for my birthday?"

"It's up to Steve, Mother. He's picking up the check."

"If he mentions that chili dog place on the causeway, tell him to forget it."

"Will you be bringing the fantastic golfer?"

"Of course. It will be the perfect time for our announcement."

"What!"

"Don't furrow your brow, dear. Little lines today,

deep ditches tomorrow. And don't worry. Carl and I are not getting married." She smiled mischievously. "Yet."

"I had no idea the two of you were so serious."

"Because you don't listen to your mother. All wrapped up in your own problems. My life drifts along, unnoticed and unadorned."

"Hardly, Mother. Don't project your personality onto me."

"Nonsense. You're my only child, Victoria. My entire *life*."

There was no way to win the argument, Victoria knew.

"As for Carl," Irene continued, "I haven't been drawn to any man this way since your father died. We fit together so perfectly. He has such a—*je ne sais quoi*—I find almost indescribable."

Something felt out of kilter, Victoria thought. The Queen made men swoon, not the other way around. "So what exactly is the big announcement?"

"Sur-prise," Irene sang out. "You'll have to wait. But I'll say this. I haven't been this happy in years. Just look at me. Am I glowing?"

"Your crotch certainly is, Mother."

* * *

Well, that was useful, Victoria thought ruefully as she crossed the Broad Causeway on her way back to the mainland. Indian Creek Country Club was to her left across a narrow channel. She had played tennis there as a child, had consumed gallons of root beer floats in the clubhouse restaurant, had learned to sail in the calm waters of the bay. She hadn't envisioned an adulthood filled with complications, both professional and personal. When her father was still alive, when her mother seemed to care for more than just herself, the future promised rewards that thus far eluded her.

I have to make decisions. About Steve. About me. About life.

Ten minutes later, she was on Biscayne Boulevard, stopped at a police barricade. A parade passed by. A steel band from one of the islands. Marchers carrying signs that either celebrated some holiday or protested conditions in their native land. From five cars back in line, she couldn't tell which.

She decided to go with her gut. Wasn't that what Steve always taught her?

"Throw away the books, Vic. Go with your gut."

Okay, so he'd been talking about jury selection, but didn't the advice apply to mate selection, too?

Her gut told her she loved Steve. But did that mean they should live together? Then there was Bobby to think about. Bobby kept talking about "family," and she was included. The boy'd had so many disappointments. She didn't want to add to them.

So, as the parade passed and the police barricade gave way, Victoria hit the gas. She decided to plunge ahead. Her gut was telling her to move in with Steve, to give the relationship every chance, to see if they would have a *je ne sais quoi* that would be almost indescribable.

SOLOMON'S LAWS

4. If you're going to all the trouble to make a
   fool of yourself, be sure to have plenty of witnesses.

Nine

THE SHRINK AND THE SHYSTER

"You gotta look out for *numero uno*. You gotta do what gives you pleasure, not what others want you to do. Hedonism is good. Selfishness is good. Greed is good. No, I take that back. Greed is great!"

The voice was deep, rhythmic, and spellbinding. Wearing a headset and a beige silk guayabera, Dr. Bill Kreeger crooned into a ceiling-mounted microphone. Steve stood in the control room, looking over the shoulder of the board operator, watching through the window. So far, Kreeger, his mouth close enough to the microphone to kiss the cold metal, hadn't seen him. Steve had come here to deliver the message that would get Kreeger off his back.

"Self-interest is the highest morality," Kreeger prattled on, "and selflessness is the deepest immorality. You can't make another person happy, so don't even try. Give a hundred bucks to a charity at Thanksgiving, they'll hit you for two hundred at Christmas. Bake a tuna casserole for the neighborhood shut-in, next week she'll expect filet mignon. The people you sacrifice for won't appreciate it, so forget them. Wait, you say. That's cruel, Dr. Bill. Wrong!

Don't be a sucker. The moral life is one of self-interest. If everyone pursued his or her own happiness, there wouldn't be a bunch of losers who always need help. And what a beau-ti-ful world it would be."

Putting a tune to it. Then laughing, a deep rumble. Kreeger had gone a little gray around the temples since Steve had seen him last. But he looked remarkably healthy and fit. Wavy hair combed straight back revealed a widow's peak. A firm jawline that never even sagged when he looked down at his notes. No more than five-nine, he had a square, blocky build and seemed to have put meat on his chest and shoulders. Prison weight lifting, maybe.

"After a short break," Kreeger said into the microphone, "my seven tips for living the life of self-fulfillment. Tip number one. The word 'invincible' starts with 'I.' And *I'll* be right back."

Kreeger hoisted his coffee cup and turned toward the window. He spotted Steve on the other side of the glass and smiled broadly. For an instant, the smile seemed genuine, a look of pleasant surprise at seeing an old friend. Then the corners of his mouth dropped a bit, as if Kreeger just remembered the old friend owed him money. A second after that, the smile turned chilly, a frozen mask.

* * *

"To what do I owe this honor?" Kreeger asked, waving Steve into the seat next to him.

"I came here to tell you just one thing: I'm not scared of you."

"Why would you be?"

"If you come after me, I'll land on you like a ton of concrete."

"That's two things, actually. You're not scared and you're a ton of concrete."

"I'm not some stoned woman in a hot tub."

"Not sure I know where you're going with that, Counselor. Are you saying you'd *like* to be a stoned woman in a hot tub? Some gender confusion issues?"

"What I'm saying, Kreeger, is I can handle myself."

"Interesting choice of words. 'Handle myself.' Did you masturbate excessively as a child? Or do you now?"

"Fuck you, Kreeger."

A mechanical *beep* came from the speaker mounted on the wall.

"Whoa, Nellie," Kreeger laughed. "Good thing we're on a seven-second delay."

Confused, Steve looked toward the control room. A red light illuminated the words: "On Air."

Oh, shit. Is this going out on the airwaves?

Kreeger leaned close to the microphone. "You're listening to Dr. Bill on WPYG, broadcasting live from South Miami, with our special guest, Steve-the-Shyster Solomon. Phone lines are open from Palm Beach to the Keys, from Marco Island to Bimini."

Steve was halfway out of his seat when Kreeger punched a flashing button on his telephone. "Jerry in Pinecrest, you're on the air."

"Gotta question for the lawyer."

"Shoot, Jerry," Kreeger said. "But don't make it too tough. It took Solomon four times to pass the bar exam."

"Three," Steve corrected him.

"What's the difference between a lawyer and a catfish?" Jerry asked.

"Aw, c'mon," Steve said.

"One is a scum-sucking bottom feeder," Jerry answered. "The other is a fish."

Kreeger bellowed as if Jerry in Pinecrest were the new Robin Williams.

"I said what I had to say." Steve headed for the door.

Kreeger hit the cough button, silencing the mike. "Stick around, Solomon. At the break, I got something good to tell you."

Steve stood in place a second. Kreeger looked at a monitor and punched another button on the phone. "Lou in Miramar, you're on with Dr. Bill."

"I'm a big Hurricane baseball fan and I remember when Solomon played."

"Hear that, Solomon?" Kreeger asked, motioning Steve back into his seat. "You got a fan here. Obviously, he's never been a client."

"What I remember best," Lou in Miramar said, "was Solomon getting picked off third base in the College World Series."

Steve groaned.

Why did I come here, anyway? To show some toughness. To warn Kreeger off. And what do I get? Ridicule on talk radio, the cesspool of broadcasting.

"I was safe," Steve protested, moving toward the microphone. "Ump blew the call."

"No surprise, Lou. When Solomon loses a case, he always blames the judge." Kreeger punched another button. "Lexy, on South Beach, you're on the line."

Lexy? No. It can't be.

"Why don't you get off Stevie's case, anyway?" A young woman's whiny voice. Yep, Lexy.

Whatever you do, Lex, don't try to help.

"He's a terrific lawyer and he's cute, too."

Kreeger flashed Steve a smile. It was the same smile a barracuda shows to a porkfish. "So Solomon has represented you, has he?"

"He got me out of like a zillion dollars in parking tickets."

"Traffic court. Now, that's Solomon's speed."

"You don't understand, Doc. The tickets were all for parking in a handicapped zone. But Stevie found a chiropractor who said I had bulimia, so I got off."

"Fabulous," Kreeger enthused. "With Solomon, the guilty go free and the innocent do six years in prison." The psychiatrist lowered his voice, as if letting his listeners in on a secret. "Now, friends, you won't believe this, but Steve-the-Shyster Solomon once sued a surfer for stealing another surfer's wave. And who says we don't need tort reform?"

"Surfers consider waves their property," Steve said. But music was already coming up, and the board operator was pointing an index finger at Kreeger from the other side of the window.

"We'll be right back after this news update," Kreeger said. The *On Air* sign went dark, and he slipped off his headset. "That was great. We should take this on the road. *The Shrink and the Shyster.* Maybe get a syndication deal. Satellite radio within a year."

Maybe his father was right, Steve thought. Maybe Kreeger just wanted a sidekick.

"I'm vox populi," Kreeger continued. "The voice of an aggrieved populace that hates lawyers. You keep playing the dunce."

"I wasn't playing."

A newsman's baritone voice came over a speaker. The stock market was up. The water table was down.

City fathers were shocked, *shocked* to discover that prostitution was rampant along Biscayne Boulevard. Kreeger turned a dial and lowered the volume a notch. "You know, I really admire you, Solomon. What you did to me took balls."

Steve stayed quiet.

"You're not curious how I found out?" Kreeger asked.

Steve took a long breath, said nothing. On the speakers, the news anchor was giving the fishing report. Mackerel were running. Snapper, on the other hand, were merely swimming.

"Right in the middle of my trial," Kreeger continued, "the State Attorney files a notice about a so-called similar incident. What's it called?"

"Williams Rule material," Steve said. "The state can introduce similar incidents from a defendant's past to show a pattern of conduct."

"Yeah. Poor Jim Beshears drowns down in the Keys. And years later, wretched Nancy Lamm drowns in my hot tub. Kind of a stretch tying those two together, don't you think, Counselor?"

"Not when each person got hit on the head with a pole you happened to be holding. The judge thought the first incident was similar enough to be admissible."

"My quibble's not with the judge, Solomon."

In the background, Steve could hear a commercial for a local dating service for overworked and horny executives.

"One day, when the appeal was pending," Kreeger went on, "I looked through every piece of paper in the file. You know what I found? Two copies of the police report of the boat accident. One attached to the State Attorney's brief and one in your file."

"So what? Pincher was required to give me a copy when he filed his Williams Rule notice."

"Right. Except your copy had an earlier time stamp. *You* had the police report first and you gave Pincher a photocopy. You dropped the dime on your own client."

Steve didn't say a word. There could be a tape recorder rolling. They were, after all, in a recording studio.

The damn time stamps. He'd been sloppy, Steve realized. Well, what could you expect? He'd never sold out a client before.

"At first," Kreeger said, "I was mad enough to kill you. And you, of all people, know I'm capable, right? Then I realized you do whatever it takes. You live by your own code. You violated your attorney's oath in order to put your own client away." Kreeger rumbled a laugh. It sounded like coal pouring down a chute. "I get goose bumps just thinking about it. You put my theories into practice, Solomon. We're like long-lost brothers, you and I."

"I don't kill people."

"Not yet." Another laugh. Then, with what seemed like dead-earnest sincerity, Kreeger said, "We're gonna be great friends. We're gonna spend some quality time together."

"The hell we are."

"C'mon, Solomon. You owe me that much. In fact, you owe me six years. There I was, eating all that starchy food, living in a cell with a metal toilet, and you were out here enjoying the good life. You've got yourself a lady. What's her name? Victoria, right? I look forward to meeting her. And you have your nephew with you. Robert. Has some medical problems, doesn't he?

And you had a bit of a dustup with the state over custody. Well, you'd better keep your record clean. Wouldn't want to upset those hard-asses at Family Services. And how's your father, by the way? Judge Solomon drinking too much these days?"

There are lots of ways to threaten someone, Steve thought. At one end of the spectrum, your lawyer can send a letter, advising that you intend to use all lawful means to enforce your legal rights. At the other end, you can jam the barrel of a gun into someone's mouth, breaking off teeth and yelling you're going to blow their brains all over the wall. Or you can take a middle ground. You can mention everyone in the world the person loves and just leave it at that. Steve felt his face heat up, and his stomach clenched itself into a fist.

"Stay away from them, Kreeger. Stay the hell away or I'll cut you into little pieces and feed you to the sharks."

"Doubt it. Like you said, Steve, you're not a killer."

"And like you said: Not yet."

"Pardon me for not peeing on my socks, but I've just spent six years in a rattlesnake nest and never got bit."

"Maybe your next stay, you won't be so lucky."

"Now, why would I go back to prison?"

"It's just a matter of time before you feel wronged by someone. You'll use that bullshit philosophy of yours to justify your actions, and before you can say, 'Man overboard,' there's another body floating facedown. So maybe I will stick close to you, Kreeger, because I want to be there the day the cops come knocking on your door."

No one knocked, but the cushioned door to the control room popped open and two City of Miami

Beach cops walked in. Weird, Steve thought. But life is like that sometimes. You think of a woman you haven't seen in three or four years, and that day she comes knocking on your door, with a little boy at her side who looks alarmingly like you. Not that it had ever happened to him, but he'd heard stories.

So what were the Beach cops doing out of their jurisdiction? Had Kreeger slashed some tourist's throat while waiting in line at Joe's Stone Crab?

"Are you Stephen Solomon?" The cop wore sergeant's stripes and had a mustache. He was in his forties, with a tired look.

"Guilty," Steve said. "What's this about?"

He was vaguely aware that Kreeger was leaning close to the microphone, his voice a portentous whisper. "Exclusive report. Breaking news here at WPYG. You're live with Dr. Bill. . . ."

"You're under arrest, Mr. Solomon," the sergeant said wearily.

"For what! What'd I do, curse on the air?"

"Steve-the-Shyster Solomon *arrested*, right here in Studio A," Kreeger rhapsodized.

"Assault and battery."

"I haven't hit the bastard yet." Steve nodded toward Kreeger.

"Not him. A guy named Freskin."

"Who the hell is that?"

The younger cop took a pair of handcuffs from his belt. "Please place your hands behind your back, sir."

Damn polite, just like they teach them in cop school.

"I don't know any Freskin."

"I have to pat you down, sir," the younger cop persisted.

"The excitement builds," Kreeger announced, sounding like Joe Buck doing a World Series game. "They're putting the cuffs on Solomon."

"Goddammit. Who's Freskin?" Steve felt a mixture of anger and humiliation.

"State probation officer," the sergeant answered. "Arnold Freskin. You assaulted him in your law office."

Oh, him!

"That freak? He was getting off wrestling with my secretary."

Even as he spoke, Steve knew he was violating the advice he gave to every client he'd ever had.

"Never talk to the cops. You'll only dig yourself a deeper hole."

"You have the right to remain silent," the sergeant reminded him. "You have the right to an attorney. If you cannot afford an attorney—"

"I know. I know."

"They're taking him downtown," Kreeger sang out cheerfully. "Is Steve Solomon not only a shyster, but a violent thug, too? Stay tuned."

Ten

EVEN MURDERERS NEED PALS

Steve stood at the kitchen sink, scrubbing the ink off his fingertips. He'd been booked and processed, finger-printed and photographed, and generally ridiculed by cops and corrections officers who knew him from court. He had spent two hours in a holding cell where the walls were covered with yellowish-brown graffiti. Generations of inmates had used mustard from their state-issued bologna sandwiches to leave their mis-spelled profanities to posterity. Perhaps not as im-pressive as Paleolithic cave drawings, the graffiti nonetheless provided a sociological snapshot of our un-derclass, as well as an indictment of our public schools.

Judge Alvin Elias Schwartz released Steve without bail on the grounds that His Honor used to play pinochle with the defendant's father. Steve would be required to show up in a week to be arraigned on charges of assault and battery and obstructing a state official, to wit: Mr. Arnold G. Freskin, in the perfor-mance of his duties. According to the criminal com-plaint, Freskin's duties included an "on-site interview with a probationer," which Steve figured sounded better than an "erotic wrestling match with an undressed secretary."

Steve had taken a sweaty taxi ride home, the Jamaican driver explaining the A/C was on the blink, but Steve figured the guy was just saving gas. Steve's pants and shirt stuck to the vinyl seats, though the heat didn't seem to bother the driver, who was sitting on one of those beaded back supports.

"You sounded like a horse's ass on the radio today." Herbert Solomon sat at the kitchen table, sipping kosher red wine and eviscerating his son. "A real *putz*."

"Thanks for the support, Dad." Steve was not up for his father's abuse. It had been a shitty day, and it wasn't over yet. In an hour, he would have to put on a smiley face and brush-kiss Irene Lord. The Queen. Victoria's mother. A woman so cold and imperious she made Martha Stewart seem warm and cuddly.

"Ah bailed you out, didn't ah?"

"I was released on my own recognizance. All you did was call the judge."

"That's a helluva lot."

"You could have driven downtown and picked me up from the jail."

"Not after sundown, boychik."

"Why, you got night blindness?"

"*Shabbos*, you *shmoe*!"

"What is it, open-bar night at temple?"

"Wouldn't hurt you to come along. Say a *Sh'ma* or two."

So that explained his father's outfit. A double-breasted blue blazer, rep tie with khaki walking shorts and sneakers. Ever since the old man went ortho, he began adhering to the rule of not driving between sundown Friday and sundown Saturday. Now, looking like a demented Englishman in the midday sun, he was ready for the three-mile trek to Temple Judea.

"It's Irene's birthday," Steve said. "Otherwise, I'd be right there with you in the front row."

"Hah. You don't even know where the shul is."

"On Granada, right across Dixie Highway from the ball field." The *ball field* being Mark Light Stadium at the University of Miami, where Steve couldn't hit a lick but semi-starred as a pinch runner and base stealer. He also occasionally attended class, majoring in theater and minoring in the swimming pool. Herbert had wanted Steve to study political science or pre-law, something that might lead to the legal profession. But the word in the dorm was that the hottest girls were in theater. Enough said. Steve brushed up his Shakespeare and headed for the Ring Theater, which was conveniently located next to the campus Rathskellar.

Only later did Steve realize that the acting skills he accidentally learned would be useful in court. As an undergrad, he played the cynical reporter E. K. Hornbeck in *Inherit the Wind,* a role that came easily. Then he was Teach in *American Buffalo,* a part he enjoyed mainly because he got to say a lot of fuck you's. His senior year, Steve played the older brother, Biff, in *Death of a Salesman.* A jock with early promise, Biff's life crumbled when he discovered that his father was a fraud.

"Pop's going to kill himself! Don't you know that?"

At virtually the same time Steve cried out that line, his own father—Herbert Solomon, not Willy Loman—was being hauled before the Grand Jury. Looking back, Steve knew his onstage tears were real.

For much the same reason he studied theater—hot coeds—Steve joined the campus chapter of the ACLU. The prevailing wisdom then was that liberal chicks were easier to bag than, say, the Young Republican Women for Chastity. The ACLU meetings gave him a feel for the underdog. All considered, the acting lessons and liberal politics provided solid, if unintentional, training for the life of a solo practitioner in the mystical art of the Law.

"So what's your plan?" Herbert asked.

"For Irene's birthday? We're going to Joe's for stone crabs."

"For Kreeger!"

"I'm working on it, Dad. He claims he wants to hang out with me."

"What'd Ah tell you? Murderers need pals, too."

"Except it sounded more like a threat. Be my pal—or else."

"So what's your plan?" Herbert pressed him.

Steve didn't know how much to tell his father. His father's parenting had swung between benign neglect and caustic criticism. And now, that old fear resurfaced. Ridicule and rejection. Not measuring up.

"I need to get down to the Keys. Find a witness."

"What for?"

Steve decided to go for it. His ego had pretty much survived all the welts and bruises his father could dish out. "That fishing trip I told you about. Kreeger and his classmate Jim Beshears."

"Old news. You think Kreeger pushed the guy overboard and clobbered him with a gaff."

"It's all I've got. I can't nail Kreeger for killing Nancy Lamm."

"Double jeopardy. They already convicted him of manslaughter."

"Exactly. But Kreeger was never charged with murdering Beshears. I need someone who was there. A witness. Beshears' girlfriend is too vague about what happened. But there was one more person on the boat."

"The charter captain."

"Oscar De la Fuente. He was on the fly bridge, holding the boat steady, yelling instructions. He had the angle to see everything. But I never found him."

"Shouldn't be hard. The state would have his charter license."

"The computer records only go back ten years. The incident was nineteen years ago. If De la Fuente had a license then, he doesn't anymore."

"County property records?"

"Doesn't own anything in Miami-Dade, Monroe, or Collier. No business license. No fictitious-name license. No phone, listed or unlisted."

"At least you've done your homework."

The compliment sounded grudging, but Steve took it just the same. "Now I'm gonna pound the pavement. Or maybe the sand."

"What? Wear some lawyer's suit down in the Keys, poke around asking questions?"

Actually, he'd been planning on wearing cutoffs and a T-shirt that read: "*Practice Safe Sex. Go Screw Yourself.*" But his father was on a roll, so Steve let him go.

"The Conchs will think you're DEA," Herbert warned him. "No one will talk to you. And if anyone knows this De la Fuente character, they'll warn him to stay away from you. Problem is, you don't know the territory, son."

There it was, Steve thought, his old man hauling out the knives to carve him up. "What choice do I have?"

"You got me, you *shmoe*! Who knows the bars and marinas better than me?"

True. When Herbert wasn't crashing on a sofa in Steve's spare bedroom, he was fishing off his leaky houseboat on Sugarloaf Key. "You'd do that for me?"

"I'm your father. You gotta ask?" Pleased with himself, Herbert grabbed a white straw hat he would wear over his yarmulke for the walk to the synagogue. The hat had a small, upturned brim. Steve thought it was called a porkpie, but maybe not. That didn't sound kosher.

"Thanks, Dad. I really appreciate it."

"Don't mention it. By the way, how much are P.I.'s charging these days?"

"Good *Shabbos,* Dad."

Herbert started for the door. "Bobby's dinner is in the fridge."

"Where is the Bobster?"

"In his room with that gypsy girl."

"What? Who?"

"That harlot-in-training with the jewelry in her belly button. The Juban girl from a block over."

"Not polite, Dad. We don't describe people by their religion or ethnicity."

"That so, matzoh boy?"

"Very old-school, Dad."

"Well, kiss my kosher *tuches.* Ain't my fault the girl's both a Yid and a Cubana. Tell her to change her name if she's so ashamed of it. Like some of our chickenshit *landsmen.* Cohen becomes Kane, Levine becomes Landers. *Schmendricks.*" Herbert gave a snort of disapproval.

"Her name's Maria Munoz-Goldberg, and I doubt she's ashamed of it," Steve said.

"Fine by me, but if I were you, I'd go peek in Robert's bedroom. Or next thing you know, there'll be a little tyke named Munoz-Solomon running around the house."

Eleven

THAT JUBAN GIRL

Steve finished off the glass of kosher wine his father had left on the table. It tasted like liquified grape jelly. Bobby was in the bedroom with Maria, and Steve needed to fortify himself before moseying down the hall. He planned to knock on the door before entering. If it was locked, he'd batter it down like a SWAT team at a meth lab.

Just what were the rules with pubescent kids these days, anyway? Only recently had it occurred to him that Bobby, on the hazardous precipice of puberty, might need a fatherly lecture on the birds and bees. When he talked to his nephew about it, the boy said he knew all about STDs and condoms and even told Steve about a girl at Ponce de León Middle School who got pregnant.

"After that, none of the girls would, you know, do it, but there were a lot more rainbow parties, not that I've ever been invited."

"Rainbow parties?"

"C'mon, Uncle Steve. Where the chicks all put on a different color lipstick and the guys drop their pants, and the idea is to get as many different colors on your—"

"Jesus!"

Now Steve paused outside Bobby's door, sniffing the air like a bloodhound. No tobacco, no pot. But something odd. A citrus scent. Oranges or tangerines.

Steve knocked once and headed inside.

Both kids had textbooks open. Wearing baggy shorts and a Hurricanes football jersey, Bobby was slouched in his beanbag chair. Maria was sprawled across Bobby's bed. She wore low-riding jeans with enough holes and shreds to give the impression she'd stepped on a land mine. A sleeveless mesh T-shirt revealed a lacy bra underneath. Her complexion was a rich caramel, and her bright red lipstick was as slick as fresh paint. A shiny rhinestone peeked out of her twelve-year-old navel.

Bobby waved at Steve but kept talking to Maria, sounding like a little professor. "The Battle of Gettysburg was a big-time accident. Lee and Meade never said, 'C'mon, let's meet in this little town in Pennsylvania and have a big battle.' That's just where the Union decided to stop the Confederate advance. I mean, if they hadn't, Lee's army could have taken Philadelphia, and then maybe Washington, and the South would have won the war."

"That'd suck," Maria said. "Hey, Mr. Solomon."

"Hi, Maria. So what are you guys studying?"

"Duh. Like calculus," Bobby said. Showing some spunk for his little hottie.

"American history, Mr. Solomon. Bobby knows everything that ever happened."

"It's no big deal," Bobby said.

"It is to me." Maria smiled at Bobby. An inviting

come-hither smile. The citrus aroma was stronger here.

"What's that smell?" Steve asked.

"Oh, probably my perfume, Mr. Solomon."

Perfume! Bobby doesn't have a chance.

"Boucheron," Maria continued. "My mom's."

First they take their mothers' perfume. Then their birth control pills.

Steve knew Maria's parents from a Neighborhood Watch committee. Eva Munoz-Goldberg, the proud daughter of an anti-Castro militant, frequently roamed the neighborhood, passing out flyers that called for bombing Venezuela and assassinating Hugo Chávez. As a child, Eva spent weekends with her father and a pack of cousins, trekking through the Everglades, shooting Uzis at cardboard cutouts of Fidel Castro. Later, they would all head home to grill burgers, drink Cuba Libres, and watch the Dolphins on TV. Recently, Steve had seen Eva piloting her black Hummer through Coconut Grove, an NRA bumper sticker pasted on the rear bumper.

Maria's father, Myron Goldberg, was a periodontist with an office on Miracle Mile in Coral Gables. Myron's hybrid Prius sported bumper stickers for Greenpeace and Save the Manatees, and the most dangerous weapon he owned was a titanium root-canal shaft. The Munoz-Goldbergs were Exhibit A in South Florida's paella-filled melting pot of cross-cultural multiethnicity.

Looking at the two kids lounging in the bedroom, Steve was certain he should lecture his nephew about exercising self-control in a time of raging hormones. Another thought, too. A contrary one. Could this little vixen be just using Bobby to pass her courses? As much as Steve adored his nephew, he had to admit the kid was not exactly a candidate for the Abercrombie & Fitch catalog. Basically, Bobby was a skinny, loveable loner in thick glasses who didn't fit into any of the cliques.

"What's this about the high-water mark?" Maria asked, thumbing through the textbook. "It sounds like something that'll be on the test."

"The High-Water Mark of the Confederacy," Bobby said, confidently. "It's where the tide turned the Union's way at Gettysburg."

"Ooh, right." She scribbled a note.

"Pickett's Charge," Bobby continued. "Fifteen thousand Confederate soldiers. Some made it to the Union line, but they were cut to ribbons. A frontal assault moving uphill never works. When the enemy's holding the high ground, you gotta outflank him. Fake an attack on one flank." Bobby threw an imaginary left hook. "But really attack the other flank." With a *whoosh*, he tossed a roundhouse right. "When your enemy zigs, you zag."

"You're so smart." Maria rewarded the boy with another twinkling smile, then turned toward Steve. "We heard you on the radio today, Mr. Solomon."

"Yeah," Bobby added. "Never thought that shrink could school you like that."

"Are you going to jail?" Maria asked Steve.

"Uncle Steve's been to jail lots of times," Bobby declared, a touch of pride in his voice. "Judges make him stay overnight because he gets rowdy."

"Everything's gonna be okay," Steve said. "What I did was only technically illegal."

Bobby snorted. "Yeah, you *technically* beat the shit out of some guy."

"Watch the lingo, kiddo."

"Are you gonna let that shrink keep cracking on you?"

"Nope. I've got a plan to shut him up."

"Ph-a-a-t! How you gonna do it?"

Steve shook his head. What could he say? *"Your uncle and grandfather are trying to nail a killer, but don't worry about it."* No. He wouldn't spook the boy.

"Highly confidential," Steve said.

"Just so you're not doing what that woman in the hot tub did. Because if Dr. Bill killed her . . ."

Bobby let the words hang there, then turned back to his book.

*   *   *

Half an hour later, Bobby scooted deeper into the beanbag chair. Maria was still sprawled on his bed, leafing through the pages of the history book. Moments earlier, Bobby did a trick with his brain, purposely dividing his conscious thoughts in two. Going split screen, he called it, something that let him think two unrelated thoughts at once.

I want to kiss Maria. And . . .

Why does Uncle Steve treat me like a baby?

It was really Bobby's only complaint.

Most of the time Uncle Steve was really cool. Always spending time with him. Tossing the ball, teaching him to dig in at home plate and not bail out even when the pitch was inside. Taking him to court and even to a couple of autopsies, which was way cool, except for the smell.

But he hides stuff from me, afraid I can't handle it.

Uncle Steve was planning to go after Dr. Bill. Which was scary.

But why can't he tell me?

Above him, on the bed, Maria draped a leg over his shoulder. She wiggled her toes, the nails painted some color that looked like flames.

The brain waves carrying thoughts of Dr. Bill suddenly flatlined. Bobby felt a pleasant buzz in his undershorts. But this was awkward. His butt was sunk into the beanbag chair, his back was toward the bed, and he couldn't even see her. To kiss her, he'd have to scoot around, get to his knees, and crawl onto the bed, and then what? It would take several seconds and would seem premeditated and dorky, instead of casual and cool.

Another problem: *to tongue or not to tongue?*

He heard more pages rustling. She couldn't be reading that fast. Could she be getting bored? Was she waiting for him to make a move? He wished he could ask Uncle Steve for advice right now.

Or Mom. Yesterday, she told me she first had sex at twelve. My age!

Now his brain opened another screen. There was Maria on the bed, her flame-toed foot dangling in his face. And there was Mom, talking about sex.

Bobby could never tell Uncle Steve what Mom said. Or even that he'd seen her. Uncle Steve thought Mom was still in prison.

She had shown up at the park, picked him up, just like a regular mother, not an ex-con. They'd gone to Whip 'N Dip for pistachio ice cream. She started talking about her life, the stuff just spilling out, and a lot was pretty icky. The guys—sometimes, she didn't even know their names. The drugs—they'd messed her up bad, and that's why she stole and got in trouble, but now she'd kicked the habit. She thanked Jesus for his help, the Son of God being the true messiah and all, and maybe it was time for Bobby to be baptized.

Sure, Mom. Right after my bar mitzvah.

Bobby had told her about Maria and how much he liked her. She seemed interested, especially in Maria's family, the mother being Catholic and the father Jewish.

"*She sounds like a good candidate for Jews for Jesus,*" his mother had said.

Now Maria draped a second leg over his other shoulder. She pressed her thighs together, squeezing his ears, knocking his glasses sideways. He could smell her perfume, orange and vanilla, like a Creamsicle. He wanted to lick her face.

"I'm tired of studying," she whispered.

All right!

Time for action. But how?

If he could turn around and somehow stand up, his crotch would be at her eye level. Ordinarily, no big deal, but right now, he had a world-class boner. What if she didn't want to kiss him? Would she tell everyone at school he was a horn-dog perv?

A third screen opened in his brain, and Uncle Steve was saying: "*Always show respect for girls. Sometimes you even have to show more respect for them than they have for themselves.*"

And Mom was saying: "*Like Jesus said, if you look at a girl with lust, you've committed a sin. But the cool thing about the Savior, Bobby, is that he's very forgiving. So my motto is to do what feels right at the time. You can always repent later.*"

Twelve

REPORT AND RAPPORT

Why is Steve so quiet?

Victoria pondered the question as they drove across the causeway on their way to The Queen's birthday dinner. Of course, Steve wasn't exactly crazy about her mother, who treated him as she did so many people: like hired help.

The thought of Steve marrying into the family really curdled the cream in The Queen's demitasse.

"Steve has many qualities, dear, but is he really the one for you?"

Translation: *"I hate him, and you can do better."*

It probably didn't help his cause that Steve would sometimes wear a T-shirt with the logo: *"If It's Not One Thing, It's Your Mother."*

Irene Lord considered Steve déclassé. Steve considered Irene Lord a gold digger. Victoria loved them both but, like the lion tamer at the circus, had to occasionally crack the whip to keep them apart.

Taking The Queen and her new beau, Carl, to dinner—and getting stuck with the check—probably wasn't high on Steve's list of favorite things. But still, Victoria wondered, why did he seem so distant? Okay,

so getting humiliated on the radio and arrested for assault might throw a guy off his game. But Steve was
used to verbal combat and was no stranger to jail, so
what was really bothering him?

Thinking back over recent events, it seemed as if
Steve had been out of sorts for a while. When they'd
looked at the condo, he'd been almost hostile to the
idea of moving in together. They were supposed to see
other properties with Jackie, but did Steve really want
to do it? In his typical male fashion, he wasn't talking,
so she had no choice but to ask.

"So what's your plan?" she said as they passed
Fisher Island.

The question seemed to startle him. "Wow, that's
something." With one hand on the steering wheel, he
playfully shook a finger at her. "You're reading my
mind."

"Good. Tell me about it."

"I'm not sure I can."

"Who would you tell if not me?"

"It's dangerous," he said, "and I don't want you to
worry."

She was lost. "Moving in together is dangerous?"

"What? Who's talking about moving in together?"

"We are. Or at least I am. I'm trying to figure out
what you're planning. House or condo? Move in together now or maybe wait a bit?"

"Oh."

"So what are you talking about?"

"Kreeger. How I'm gonna nail him."

Wasn't that just like Steve? Or any man, she decided. Your guy is sitting there, quietly stewing, and
you think he's worried about the relationship. Turns
out he's wondering if the Dolphins can cover the

spread against the Jets. And when men do talk, it's like dispensing the news on CNN. Hurricane in Gulf. Dow Jones up twenty. I-95 gridlocked. Just the facts, ma'am.

She had studied psychology and linguistics at Princeton, and she knew that men and women communicate differently. It sounded clichéd, but it was true. Women talk about feelings, what academics called "rapport talk." Men dispense information, what's called "report talk." When they talk at all.

"Both Dad and Bobby asked me about my plan for Kreeger," Steve told her, "so when you asked 'What's your plan?' I just naturally thought—"

"It's okay, Steve. But maybe you should just let Kreeger go. It didn't work out that great on the radio."

Her feminine mode of communication. She could have said: *You really got your ass handed to you today, partner.* But with a lover, it was best to cloak your criticism in lamb's wool, not lash it with barbed wire.

"I was just getting warmed up when the cops came in."

"It seemed like he enjoyed tormenting you. And if he's as dangerous as you say . . ."

"Exactly. That's why my plan will work."

Steve swung the car off the causeway and onto Alton Road. They'd be at Joe's in three minutes. There'd be a line of tourists snaking through the bar and into the courtyard. But between Dennis the mâitre d' and Bones the captain, Steve would manage to have his party seated within ninety seconds.

"I'm almost afraid to ask," Victoria said.

"Kreeger killed two people, right?"

"Two you know about."

"Right. Each one posed a threat. Jim Beshears was gonna blow the whistle on his phony research. Nancy Lamm was gonna report Kreeger's ethical violations. Suppose someone else poses a threat to him now?"

"What kind of threat?"

Victoria listened as Steve told her about Herbert trying to track down the charter boat captain who would have seen Kreeger brain Jim Beshears with the gaff.

As he went over the details, she began analyzing the plan in her logical way. Then she said, "Even if you found the captain, even if he says, 'Yeah, I think Kreeger shoved the guy overboard, then purposely hit him,' a defense lawyer would slice him up. Why'd it take you all these years to come forward? Why doesn't the other witness, the girlfriend, corroborate your story? And all this assumes you can get an indictment, and the chances of that are—"

"Slim to none."

"Right. So why do it?"

"If I tell you, take a deep breath and think it over before unloading on me."

"So it's got to be illegal."

"I told Dad to make sure he handed out my card everywhere he went, from Key Largo to Key West. Tell every drinker and fisherman and old salt that Stephen Solomon, Esquire, of Miami Beach, will pay a reward for finding Oscar De la Fuente, missing charter captain. Then I took an ad in the *Key West Citizen* and posted some notices on websites, saying the same thing."

It only took her a second. "You don't care if you find the guy! You just want Kreeger to know you're looking for him."

"You're getting warmer. Keep going."

"You're going to tell Kreeger you found De la Fuente, whether you do or not. You're going to say you have solid eyewitness evidence against him. You might even come up with a phony affidavit, De la Fuente swearing he heard Kreeger threaten Beshears, then saw Kreeger push him overboard before clobbering him."

"Hadn't thought of the affidavit. Nice touch."

"So this is your brilliant plan? To use yourself as bait. To get that psycho to try to kill you."

He had a grin on his face that managed to be both childish and clueless. Like a boy who catches a viper and shows it to a girl in the misguided belief she will immediately want to start necking. "I can't get him for either of the two murders he's committed, Vic. But I can get him for attempting a third."

"Has it occurred to you that Kreeger might be better at committing murder than you are at preventing it?"

"I'll have an advantage Beshears and Lamm didn't have. I'll be sober, and I'll know what's coming."

This time, she didn't try to cushion her words. "You are utterly irresponsible. Even worse, you don't care about the people who love you."

"Don't see how you can say that."

"What about Bobby? What about your father? What about me? If you get hurt or killed, what about us?"

"Vic, I'm not scared of Kreeger. The guy's a coward who murdered a stoned woman in a hot tub and a drunk on a boat."

They were the fifth car in line as they pulled up to valet parking in front of the restaurant. Patrons spilled out the doors and clogged the patio. On the outdoor speakers, they heard Dennis the maître d' announce: "Grossman party. Stuart Grossman. Party of eight."

"Now, as for that other thing," Steve said.

"What other thing?"

"The living-together thing. House versus condo."

Wait a second, she thought. *We're not through discussing your asinine plan. You can't move on to the next subject just because you've done your über-male report-talk.*

"I have this great compromise." Steve sounded proud of himself. "You like condos. Low maintenance. Lock and leave. And I respect that. But I like houses. Privacy. Mango tree in the backyard. So how about a townhouse?"

This isn't communication. This is the male of the species setting a brush fire, scorching the earth, and moving on.

"Steve, the townhouse can wait. We're not done here."

Now they were second in line for the valet. She didn't have much time. "You didn't even ask my opinion about your crazy plan, which, by the way, I think is suicidal. And now, what? Subject closed? Now we're supposed to talk about a townhouse and a hibiscus hedge?"

"I was thinking bougainvillea—"

"I'm serious. I'm really unhappy about this, and you'd better deal with it."

Steve's eyes widened. Getting hit with a two-by-four will do that. He chewed at his lower lip a moment. Over the loudspeaker, "Berkowitz party, Jeff Berkowitz. Party of six."

"Okay, Vic. Here it is. There are three people in the world I dearly care about. Three people I love with all my heart. You and Bobby and my crazy father. You're the ones I'd take a bullet for."

His words startled her. "Is that *literally* true?"

He seemed to consider it a moment. "Well, I'd take a bullet for you and Bobby. For my old man, I'd take a punch."

He seemed sincere, she thought. No man had ever said anything like that to her, that her life was more important to him than his own.

"There are some concepts I care a helluva lot about, too," he continued. "That vague, shadowy thing we call justice. Seven years ago, I really screwed up. Everything you said the other day was right. I tried to convict my own client, and I was wrong. Now it's come back to haunt me. But I was right about one thing. Bill Kreeger is a killer. When I was at the radio station today, he mentioned Bobby and Dad by name. And he mentioned you, too, Vic."

She felt a shiver go through her. "Why?"

"Because he wanted me to know he could get to the three of you."

"Did he make any threats?"

"He says I owe him for the six years he spent in prison. He's come back to collect the debt. Six years isn't something I can repay in cash, so I figure he wants to hurt me by going after someone I love. I can't sit back and do nothing. To keep him from coming after one of you, Vic, I need him to come after me."

What could she say? Sure, he was being reckless, but it was a recklessness born of love and care and obligation. That was another aspect of the male of the species. Man, the protector.

"I still hate the idea of you doing this," she said. "Will you at least promise to be careful?"

"Hell, yes. I'll promise that and anything else you want."

"Deal." She gave Steve a soft smile just as the attendant opened the door. "Promise to be nice to my mother tonight."

Thirteen

THE QUEEN AND THE PIRATE

"You're looking lovely, Irene," Steve said, on his best behavior.

"Thank you, Stephen," Irene Lord replied with a smile as brittle as an icicle.

"And your dress." Steve let out a whistle. "What can I say?"

"I'm not sure, Stephen. What *can* you say?"

"Why don't we order?" Victoria interjected. Steve was on his third tequila, and she had no desire to watch him spout ribald limericks, one of his irksome habits when tipsy.

"Bright, Irene," Steve decided, after a moment. "Your dress is very bright."

It was an ankle-length number in flowing turquoise silk and chiffon. A trifle dressy for Joe's, Victoria thought.

"I thought we were going to the club," Irene said, with a tone of disappointment. "Hence, the gown."

"Hence, the frown," Steve added, draining his Chinaco Blanco.

"One would never know from your own wardrobe

that you paid such close attention to fashion," Irene said. Her smile was permafrosted in place.

Victoria tried again. "Mr. Drake, are you ready to order?"

"Call me Carl," the distinguished-looking man said. He was the much-ballyhooed new beau. Forty-five, tops, with shiny dark hair going gray at the temples. Face a little too tan, smile a little too bright. He wore a navy blazer with gold buttons, a blue striped shirt, and a rep tie. His fingernails were manicured and polished to a fine sheen. He had a trim mustache a bit darker than his hair. Victoria thought it might have been dyed, and was trying not to stare at it. He spoke with the faintest of British accents, as Americans sometimes do if they spend time in the U.K. All in all, Drake conveyed the impression of a successful investment banker and a gentleman, an extremely presentable accoutrement for an evening at the opera or country club.

"Might I propose a toast?" Drake inquired.

"By all means, Carl," Irene said. "Perhaps after another drink, I won't hear all the racket." She motioned in the direction of the hungry hordes.

"Loosen up, Irene. We're at Joe's. Center of the culinary universe." Steve leapt to the defense of his favorite restaurant.

"A fish house," she sniffed. "Filled with sweaty tourists." Again, she waved a dismissive arm toward a table of ten. Sunburned faces, aloha shirts still creased from the packaging. "What's going on there, an orthodontists' convention?"

"Is that an ethnic remark, Irene?" Steve fired back.

"What?"

"Orthodontist equals Jew? That it, Irene? Does that table of Israelites offend you?"

"Oh, for God's sake."

Not this again, Victoria thought. For a nonpracticing Jew, Steve could be extremely prickly about ethnic cracks, real and imagined.

The Queen leveled her gaze at Steve. "I have no idea if those loud men with the mustard sauce on their faces are Jewish. I have no idea if most orthodontists are Jewish." She flashed an exaggerated, toothy smile. "I have never required the services of an orthodontist, thank you very much."

True, Victoria thought. But much later, there had been staggeringly expensive periodontal work, and her mother's flawless smile now reflected two rows of glimmering white veneers.

"A toast?" Drake tried again. He hoisted his gin and tonic, forcing the rest of them to join in. "To the lovely Irene, a shimmering diamond in a world of rhinestones, a shooting star in a galaxy of burned-out asteroids, a woman of poise and purpose—"

"My nephew Bobby swims with a porpoise," Steve said.

"I beg your pardon?" Drake appeared puzzled.

"You said Irene had a porpoise."

"*Purpose.* I said she's a woman of poise and *purpose.*"

"Stephen, I'm beginning to wish they hadn't let you out of jail so quickly," Irene said.

"Jail?" Drake echoed. He had the startled look of a man who unexpectedly wakens to find himself in the monkey cage at the zoo.

"Stephen spends more time behind bars than his clients. Don't you, dear?"

"To a lawyer, that's a compliment," Steve said. "Thank you, Irene."

Drake shot looks around the table. "Perhaps I should finish my toast . . ."

Twirling a diamond earing between thumb and forefinger, Irene cocked her head coquettishly. "Please do, Carl. I love a man who's good with words. Which reminds me. Stephen, I heard you on the radio today. So surprising that a trial lawyer of your experience would become so flustered."

"Mother, can we just call a truce?" Victoria decided to intervene before the party of the first part attacked the party of the second part with a jagged crab claw. Steve had already violated his promise to be nice, and her mother wasn't doing much better. "On your birthday, can't we all just get along?"

"Yes, darling. Let's enjoy ourselves at Stephen's favorite, noisy restaurant." She glanced toward the diners who might have been Jewish orthodontists or Protestant stockbrokers, but who were undeniably loud. An overweight man in canary yellow Bermuda shorts was tossing stone-crab claws across the table, where they *clang*ed into a metal bowl. His friends applauded each score.

"If it were up to me," The Queen continued, "we would have gone to the club."

"If it were up to you," Steve counterpunched, "your club wouldn't accept my tribe as members."

"Oh, that's rubbish," Irene said. "My accountant is Jewish. My furrier is Jewish. *All* my doctors are Jewish."

"Yeah. Yeah. Yeah."

"It's true. Do you think I'd go to some *medico clinica* in Little Havana?"

Desperately, Drake *clink*ed his water glass with a spoon and cleared his throat. "A toast to Irene. May this birthday be better than all the ones that came before."

"*All* of them?" Steve prodded. "How will she even remember?"

"To Irene!" Drake repeated, then took a hard pull on his gin and tonic.

"Happy birthday, Mother." Victoria sipped at her margarita and glared at Steve, conveying a simple message: *Behave!*

"*L'chaim.*" Steve drained his tequila, then recited: "There once was a girl named Irene—"

"Steve!" Victoria warned.

"Who lived on distilled kerosene. But she started absorbin' a new hydrocarbon. And since then has never benzene."

Steve chortled at his own joke, a cappella, as nobody joined in. "Bobby made that up for you, Irene."

"How sweet of the child," The Queen replied, her smile now cemented into place.

Steve signaled the waiter for a refill on the drinks, and Victoria felt the beginning of panic. She had hoped to keep the evening civil, at least until the Key lime pie. "Steve, are you sure you want another drink before we eat?"

"C'mon, Vic. You know me. I'm half Irish and half Jewish. I drink to excess, then feel guilty about it."

"Two lies in one sentence," she replied. "You're not half Irish and you never feel guilty about anything."

* * *

Victoria felt like a referee.

In one corner, six feet tall and 180 pounds, the base

stealer from the University of Miami and the unaccredited Key West School of Law, the Mouth of the South (Beach, that is), Steve Sue-the-Bastards Solomon.

In the other corner, five feet ten in her Prada heels, 130 pounds (net, after liposuction subtractions and silicone additions), the woman known both for haute couture and her own hauteur, Irene The Queen.

Here was Steve, spouting his dogma for the underdog, railing against the Establishment, materialism, and Republicans. And there was her mother, who once remarked: *"Diamonds aren't a girl's best friend, darling. A diversified portfolio, including both growth and value stocks, is much friendlier."*

Her mother's economic fortunes hadn't been as bright as the remark indicated. After the suicide of Victoria's father, Irene had been left to fend for herself. She fended fine for a while, attaching herself—like a remora to a shark—to a number of exceedingly wealthy men. There were rides on private jets, tips on stocks, and quite a few diamonds, too. But The Queen never attained the status she both desired and believed herself entitled to. These days, Victoria knew, her mother felt the sand was running out of the glass. Wealthy men cast their nets for younger, perkier fish. Maybe that was why Carl Drake seemed so important to her.

The platters of shelled claws had been removed from the table. The mountains of cole slaw topped with tomato slices had disappeared, the bowls of creamed spinach were empty, and the spears of sweet potato fries had been consumed. Waiting for dessert, The Queen daintily dabbed her lips with a napkin, then turned her crystalline blue eyes on Drake.

"Carl, darling, why don't you tell Victoria our little secret?"

"While you're at it, tell me, too," Steve instructed.

Victoria stiffened. She'd already had enough surprises for today.

The waiter delivered three slices of Key lime pie— mother and daughter would split theirs—and Drake straightened in his chair. "Well, Victoria, it seems your mother and I are related. Distant cousins, you might say."

"Not quite kissing cousins," Irene chirped. "See, dear, my grandmother's maiden name was Drake and if you go back far enough, our Drakes were related to Carl's family."

"Fascinating." Steve was using his fork to spread the whipped cream over the pie filling.

"I haven't gotten to the best part," Irene prattled. "If you go back four hundred years to England, both Carl and I are descended from Sir Francis Drake."

"The pirate?" Steve asked. "That explains a lot, Irene."

"Privateer," Carl Drake corrected. "Queen Elizabeth issued official papers that allowed Drake to plunder Spanish ships."

"Like the Bush administration and Halliburton," Steve said, agreeably.

"Isn't it exciting, Victoria?" Irene said. "We're descended from a famous sea captain."

"My old man thinks we're descended from King Solomon," Steve said. "Of course, he's off his rocker."

"Captain Drake enjoyed an especially close relationship with Her Majesty," Carl said. "So close that the name Virgin Queen might have been a misnomer."

Irene chuckled and Steve burped at the risqué little joke.

"Drake amassed millions in gold and jewels. When he died in 1596, the Crown confiscated his fortune. Now, you might think all that loot went to the royal family. But it didn't. Elizabeth still carried the torch for that handsome rascal. She created the Drake Trust, later administered by the Royal Bank. Well, the money was never spent and never disbursed. It was invested and just kept growing and growing for four centuries. It's now worth north of thirty billion dollars."

"You're quite the expert on the subject," Victoria observed.

"It started as a hobby," Carl confessed. "Once I learned I was related to Captain Drake, I started constructing the family tree. It's quite a task, mind you. All those generations. I didn't even know about the money until the trustees contacted me and offered quite a tidy sum for my research."

"A tidy sum," Steve repeated. "I always wondered what an untidy sum might be."

"My work could save them years of going through musty documents in libraries and museums."

"Why do they want the family tree?" Victoria asked.

"To locate the heirs," Irene answered. "Isn't that right, Carl?"

"Precisely. By a secret ballot, the trustees recently voted to disburse the monies to all known blood relatives of Captain Drake. They want to close the estate."

"I know probate takes a long time, but four hundred years?" Steve questioned.

"It's quite unprecedented; but then, there's never been a case like this," Drake said. "I've located two thousand nine hundred and twelve descendants. The trustees estimate there are another six hundred or so. Thirty billion dollars going to thirty-five hundred heirs. As the kids say, do the math."

"I don't know, Drake. You tell me." Steve's eyes were closed as he savored a huge bite of the tart pie.

"About eight and a half million for each heir," Drake said.

Steve's eyes popped open. "You're saying Irene is going to get *eight million bucks*?"

"Give or take, once she's a certified descendant."

"Irene, have I told you how exceptionally lovely you look tonight?" Steve said.

The Queen rolled her eyes.

"And how much I've always admired you for your . . ." He seemed stumped. "Poise and porpoise," he finished triumphantly.

"Stop being so silly, Stephen," Irene said. "What do you think of my good fortune?"

Steve turned back to Drake. "What's it gonna cost her?"

"Cost?" Drake seemed bewildered. "What do you mean?"

"All these heirs. They've gotta fill out forms, right? Affidavits. Birth certificates. Lots of clerical work before you get your slice of the pie."

"Of course there's paperwork."

"So what are you charging these lucky souls? Ten thousand? Twenty thousand apiece? That's the scam, isn't it? People will gladly pay that if they think they're getting millions. Because I gotta tell you, Carl, this is what my old man would call a *bubbe meise,* a grandmother's story. And it's what I would call a load of crap."

"Ste-phen!" The Queen hissed his name.

"Steve, that's very insulting," Victoria said. "Apologize this instant."

Drake smiled and waved off their protests. "No problem. A savvy attorney should be skeptical. There are no fees, Steve. No charges. I'll help Irene fill out the forms, and if it is her desire, I hope to be by her side the day the trustees disburse the money to all of us."

Three sets of eyes bored into Steve, who was licking the last of the graham cracker crust from his fork. "Perhaps I misspoke."

"That's not much of an apology, Stephen," Irene said.

He gave his lopsided grin, and Victoria tensed; Steve was preparing to misspeak again.

"So, if it's not a big con," he said, "there must be public records in England that'll back up your story."

Drake shook his head as he stirred his coffee. "It's a private trust and is quite confidential. You see, there is no lawful requirement that the trustees disburse these monies to the descendants. They could have just as easily escheated the money to the government or conveyed it to charity. And to prevent phony claimants from climbing out of the woodwork, there's to be no public announcement at all. It's to be all extremely hush-hush."

"If I were you, Irene," Steve advised, "I wouldn't spend that money yet."

"Oh, don't be such a spoilsport," The Queen snapped.

* * *

They were waiting for the check when a voice sounded: "What a surprise. Hello, Solomon!"

Steve didn't have to turn around. He recognized the resonant tones at once. Now, what the hell was *he* doing here?

Dr. Bill Kreeger sidled up to the table. He wore a dark, tailored suit with a yellow silk shirt, open at the neck. A handkerchief the same color as the shirt blossomed from his jacket pocket like a daffodil. Standing a half step behind him was a young woman wearing a stretchy pink top with holes cut out to reveal the contours of her breasts. The top stopped a foot above her hip-hugging slacks, giving a view of a nice set of washboard abs. Strawberry blond hair, wavy and shoulder length. She couldn't have been more than twenty.

"Solomon, this is my niece, Amanda."

Niece?

Steve refrained from laughing. Sure, the girl was Kreeger's niece. And Irene was the heir of Sir Francis Drake. And Steve was a direct descendant of King Solomon.

Hellos were exchanged and Kreeger flashed his smile toward Victoria. "You must be the lovely Ms. Lord." He swept his gaze toward The Queen. "And I'll bet you're her sister."

Irene beamed. "People are always saying that."

"Where?" Steve asked. "At the Lighthouse for the Blind?"

More introductions, a shaking of hands, The Queen saying she listened to Dr. Bill every day and found herself agreeing with him, especially about Steve. The young woman—niece Amanda—stood shyly in place, her eyes darting across the restaurant.

Bored, maybe. Or ill at ease. Steve couldn't tell which. Just who was she, anyway?

"Whoops, that's mine," Steve said, reaching into a pocket for his cell phone.

"That's so rude," Irene said.

"I didn't hear anything," Victoria said.

"It's on vibrate." Steve flipped the phone open and punched a button. "Hey, Bobby. No, Maria may not spend the night. Why not? Because her mother owns automatic weapons."

Steve noticed Victoria staring at him. Was there just a hint of suspicion in those green eyes? Man, he couldn't get anything past her.

"See you later, kiddo." Steve flipped the phone closed.

Bobby had not called. No one had. But Steve had clicked three photos of Amanda, from her strawberry blond hair to her six-pack abs.

SOLOMON'S LAWS

5. When a woman is quiet and reflective, rather than combative and quarrelsome, watch out. She's likely picturing the bathroom without your boxers hanging on the showerhead.

Fourteen

THE SERPENTINE PATH

One week after the birthday bash, a cold front was pushing down from Canada. The orange groves upstate braced for freezing temperatures. The TV reporters wore their colorful parkas and warned people to bring their dogs and cats and ferrets indoors. And an even deeper chill settled over the offices of Solomon & Lord.

Driving to the office, Steve reviewed the events of the past week. The deep freeze started on the way home from dinner with The Queen. They had just passed the port where the cruise ships were lined up in a neat row like the fleet at Pearl Harbor. Then, out of the blue, a sneak attack. "You were absolutely horrid to my mother," Victoria said.

"Not once I learned she's gonna be rich."

"You promised to be nice. Then you went out of your way to be horrid."

"Horrid" being the word of the day, Steve figured. A word doubtless passed down from The Queen to The Princess like an heirloom necklace.

"And you were monstrous to Carl Drake," she continued.

" 'Monstrous' is a little strong, Vic."

"All right. Ill-mannered and boorish."

"Often boorish. Seldom a bore. That's me. As for Drake, I don't trust a guy with polished nails and a phony accent."

She glared at Steve long enough for him to stage a strategic retreat.

"Okay. Okay. If I offended anyone, I'm sorry."

Even a semi-apology didn't placate Victoria, so now, a week later, he waited for both cold fronts—the Canadian and the Episcopalian—to pass.

Driving the old Mustang solo across the causeway with the top down despite the chill, listening to Jimmy Buffet ask "Jamaica Mistaica," Steve took further inventory of the past seven days. He and Victoria had spent the time running back and forth to court, going through the motions of looking for a new abode . . . and not making love. Victoria hadn't slept over once, a world record *schnide*. Steve had dropped a few casual mentions about having a quiet dinner, and got shot down three nights in a row. Victoria had other things to do—dinner with Jackie Tuttle, shopping with her mother, even legal research, of all the lousy excuses.

He had called his father for company, but the old man was in the Keys on his fruitless search for the missing boat captain, Oscar De la Fuente. Steve just hoped Herbert was making a fuss everywhere he went so word would get back to Kreeger.

Feeling lonely, Steve wanted to spend time with Bobby. Maybe they'd rent a pitching machine at the park, hit some balls. But the kid was hanging out with Maria. Girls will do that, split up guys and keep them from taking their practice swings. At least Bobby had helped download the photos of Amanda-the-Niece from Steve's cell phone.

"A hottie," Bobby had proclaimed as he printed out the pictures.

"How old, you think?"

"Old. Twenty, maybe."

Just yesterday, Steve had tried to engage Victoria in a discussion about Kreeger and Amanda. "So what do you think? Niece or girlfriend or something else?"

"What difference does it make?"

"I need to gather everything I can on Kreeger. Knowledge is power."

"Uh-huh."

"C'mon, Vic. I'm asking for help here. You're really good at sizing up people. The way you pick juries, it's amazing."

"Oh, please. You're so transparent."

"See what I mean? You knew I was gaming you. But it's still true. You're better in voir dire than I am. So tell me, when you looked at Amanda, what did you see?"

She sighed and seemed to give it some thought. "The top she was wearing. It's right off the rack at The Gap or Victoria's Secret. But the jeans were True Religion. Expensive. And did you notice her shoulder bag?"

"Should I have?"

"I don't know how you could miss it. Kiwi green. Alligator skin. Probably a Nancy Gonzalez. At least fifteen hundred dollars."

"I know a poacher who'll get you the whole gator for a hundred bucks."

"And those sandals with the hundred-millimeter heels . . . ?"

"You measured them?"

"I can tell. They're Blahniks. You don't want to know the price."

"This is good, Vic. Very good."

"Why?"

"Because all those dollars add up to a girlfriend of a guy with money."

"What an unbelievably sexist statement. Maybe Amanda earned the money. She could be a model. Or a personal shopper at Saks, where she gets a discount. Or she could work for her uncle Bill."

"Bill Kreeger has one sister with two sons. And he's never been married. He doesn't have a niece."

"So if you already knew . . ."

"I needed to know what you picked up. I've been looking for a way to get inside Kreeger's head."

"And you think his girlfriend will help you?" Sounding skeptical.

"What if I proved to her that he was a killer?"

"She'll never believe you."

"Maybe I can get close to her, establish my credibility."

"How?

He gave her his best lounge lizard smile. "Using all my charm."

"That and a baseball bat ought to do it."

"Have a better idea?"

"All I'm saying, Steve, even assuming you can find Amanda, and you start trying to hang out with her, the first thing she'd do would be tell Kreeger."

"Maybe that's not such a bad thing. Especially if it puts more heat on him."

Victoria gave Steve one of those looks that would wilt petunias. "So, now you're going to hit on Kreeger's girlfriend, hoping he finds out. At the same time you want him to believe you're building a murder case against him. Why not burn down his house while you're at it?"

"I've got to do something. From the day he stuck that fish on my door, I've been on the defensive. All that trash talk on the radio. Those veiled threats about you and Bobby and my father. Even his showing up at Joe's. He's worming his way into our lives and I want him out. I need to knock him off his stride, force him to make a move he hasn't planned."

"When Kreeger makes a move," Victoria reminded him, with an air of exasperation, "people tend to die."

* * *

Tourists clogged the causeway as Steve neared the Fisher Island Ferry terminal. He wove in and out of lanes, trying to find the quickest route across the bay. His mind drifted back to the dinner at Joe's, the source of the skirmish with Victoria. Okay, he hadn't been on his best behavior, but The Queen was partly to blame. Her very presence brought out his sarcastic side.

The Queen and The Princess.

Guys always say to study a girl's mother to see just what your girlfriend will look like in thirty years or so. Well, no problem there. Even without her artificial enhancements, The Queen was still a dish, to use another one of her expressions.

But what about personality traits? Does a daughter pick up those, too? Victoria seemed to have rejected her mother's values. She had ditched filthy rich Bruce Bigby and she had rejected the advances of lethally handsome and equally rich Junior Griffin. Her devotion and selflessness toward Bobby nearly matched Steve's.

But something troubling had come up in the search for a place to live. Why was Victoria steering him toward seven-figure penthouse condos and mini mansions? If they bought something beyond their means, Solomon & Lord would have to start wooing banks and insurance companies and other well-heeled clients.

Is this her secret plan? Maybe in cahoots with The Queen?

Was there some mysterious genetic factor at work here? An invisible time bomb, a materialism gene embedded in her family's DNA. Maybe it went all the way back to Sir Francis Drake, plundering Spanish ships for their gold doubloons.

A minivan with Michigan plates swerved into his lane, cutting him off. Steve banged his horn, then sped around the doofus. In five minutes, he'd be at the office, sidestepping anorexic models and dashing for the stairs. He wondered if Victoria was already there. Usually, she arrived before him, and there'd be coffee brewing and fresh lilies in a vase by the time he arrived.

But the past week, she'd been the tardy one. Not only that, she'd been unusually quiet. She hadn't been giving him grief, another bad sign. The other day, he'd worn an old T-shirt, with the logo *"Please Forgive Me; I Was Raised by Wolves."* No reaction from The Princess. The next day, he wore one reading, *"Oh, No! Not Another Learning Experience."* Still nothing. This morning, he'd actually put on a suit and tie. The suit was friendly brown, not powerhouse navy or gray. The duds were not for Victoria; he was due in Criminal Court later. The arraignment in the case of *State v. Solomon.*

But now, all his thoughts were stuck on Victoria. Should he be alarmed at her silence? Where were the sparks? Where was the heat? Sound and fury, he could deal with. Stillness and indifference, he could not. In Steve's experience, when a woman was enmeshed in quiet reflection, best be prepared for oceanic change, a reversal of tidal flows. What was going on? Just what the hell was she thinking?

* * *

Driving her Mini Cooper across the causeway, Victoria spotted Steve just ahead in his Mustang convertible, hair blowing in the wind. Why was the top down on such a chilly day? Why did he have to be such a contrarian? She heard a horn blare, knew it was his, watched as he cut hard to the left and passed a minivan with Michigan plates.

Here they were, Solomon and Lord, headed the same direction but traveling in different lanes. At different speeds. About to take different routes.

Is this some sort of metaphor for our lives?

She would stay on Fifth Street all the way to the beach and swing right on Ocean Drive. One simple turn and the Les Mannequins building would be two blocks away. Steve would sail south on Alton, hang a left on Fourth Street, a right on Meridian, and a left on Third.

Why does he always choose the serpentine path?

Presumably, their destination was the same . . . but was it really? She loved Steve, but sometimes she truly wondered why. He could be so aggravating. Ordinarily, his churlishness with her mother wouldn't have bothered her. God knew, Irene brought a lot of it on herself.

And The Queen enjoyed needling Steve as much as he enjoyed returning the favor.

But it was her birthday!

And what about the way he'd treated Carl Drake? Her mother really cared for the guy, and Steve practically called him a crook. As for the booty of Sir Francis Drake, sure, it all sounded a little fanciful. But Drake said he had some confidential paperwork he was going to give The Queen that should resolve any questions. And she wasn't laying out any money. So what was the harm? And maybe it was all real. Some people go to a garage sale and buy a Jackson Pollock for ten bucks.

Just ahead of her, she saw Steve's Mustang swing onto Alton, just as the light turned from yellow to red. Yep, taking his circuitous shortcut. She decided not to go to the office. Instead, she would drive to Lummus Park, walk along the ocean, think for a bit.

Did Steve even understand the problem? Or was he totally unaware of just how precarious their relationship was?

Fifteen

THE CASE OF THE
OVERBOOKED RABBI

"Let me get this straight," Steve said. "The rabbi was late for your wedding."

"Causing us emotional distress," piped up Sheila Minkin.

"And costing us like a thousand bucks in extra liquor charges," added Max Minkin, newly minted groom. "We had to start the reception before the wedding. Do you know how much the Ritz-Carlton charges per bottle?"

Steve didn't know and didn't care. He just wanted to get the basic facts of this *farshlugginer* case, then head to court for his own arraignment. It wouldn't hurt if his lawyer—Victoria Lord, Esq.—showed up so she could go along, too.

Where the hell is she?

In the past two minutes, Steve had learned that Max was a stockbroker downtown, Sheila a personal shopper for Neiman Marcus in Bal Harbour. Bride and groom were in their early thirties and well dressed. Steve figured the case was worth fifteen minutes of his time, twenty if he liked the couple. So far, he didn't.

They were sitting in the interior office of Solomon

& Lord on this chilly day. A northwest wind had definitely replaced the soft Caribbean breezes, and the windows rattled in their panes. Across the alley, on the balcony of an apartment occupied by a Trinidad steel band, wind chimes banged against one another, loud as cymbals. Still, that was preferable to half a dozen bare-chested men with dreadlocks beating sticks against metal pans. In the reception room, Cece Santiago did her bench presses, her grunts interspersed with the clang of the bar dropping into its brackets.

"Three hours late," Sheila Minkin was saying. "Rabbi Finsterman showed up three hours late, and he smelled of liquor."

"He got our names wrong during the ceremony," Max Minkin tossed in. "That's got to be worth something, right?"

Steve tried to pay attention. It was a shit case, no doubt about it. But sometimes you can write a demand letter. . . .

"My clients have suffered grievously as a result of your negligence."

And the guy coughs up five grand to make you go away. One-third of which was $1666.67. Not a bad day's pay, even if he had to listen to the newly wedded Minkins piss and moan, kvetch and noodge.

"First the rabbi said traffic was blocked getting over the Rickenbacker because of the tennis tournament. Then he said a Purim festival in Aventura ran late. But I did a little sleuthing."

Sheila Minkin paused, as if waiting for applause. "The big *k'nocker* triple-booked. He had another wedding at the Diplomat in Hallandale and a third at the Church of the Little Flower in the Gables."

"A Catholic church?"

"A mixed marriage," Sheila explained. "Finsterman's reform."

"A thousand bucks in extra booze," Max Minkin repeated. "My uncle Sol got so *shikker* he pinched Aunt Sadie instead of a bridesmaid."

"I have to tell you," Steve said, "this isn't a big-money case. Not much in hard damages."

Working his clients. Preparing them for pin money. And hoping to get them out of his office as quickly as possible.

Just where the hell is Victoria, anyway?

"What about my emotional distress?" Sheila insisted. "I broke out in hives when the band played 'Hava Nagila.'"

"A lot of brides experience tension and stress." Steve played devil's advocate, the devil being the opposing lawyer.

"There's more. Tell him, Max."

Her husband reddened but didn't say a word.

"Okay, I'll tell him. Max couldn't get it up that night. A six-hundred-dollar suite at the Ritz-Carlton, and he couldn't get it up. A groom, on his wedding night! There's a name for that in the law, right?"

Buyer's remorse, Steve thought, but what he said was: "Lost consortium."

"Right. We didn't consort for two days. That's hard damages, right?"

Or soft damages, as the case may be.

"It's a cognizable claim," Steve said, trying to sound like a lawyer. "I just don't want you to think we're talking big money here."

The door opened, and Victoria walked in. Cheeks pink. Her fair complexion showing the effects of the wind. Meaning she hadn't just gotten out of her car.

She'd been walking. Alone. As she did when troubled. Not a good sign. He needed Victoria on so many different levels, and here she was, going all introspective on him.

"Sorry to interrupt," Victoria said softly. "Steve, don't you have to go to court?"

"*We* do."

"Do you need me? It's all worked out, right?"

True, the hearing would take all of five minutes. The state had agreed to lower the charges to a misdemeanor; Steve would plead nolo contendere and take an anger management course. Adjudication would be withheld, and when Steve got his certificate saying he was gentle as a pussy cat, all records would be expunged. In a strict legal sense, he didn't really *need* Victoria to stand alongside him in court, but he *wanted* her there. Saying that was something else. He wasn't going to beg.

"Nah. You don't have to go, Vic. Why don't you finish up here?"

He introduced her to Max and Sheila Minkin and described the facts, which he termed "a shocking case of rabbinical malpractice."

"Shocking," Victoria agreed, with just a smidgen of sarcasm. She turned to the lovebirds and said, "I'm sure we'll be able to achieve a fair and just result for you."

"Fuck that," Sheila Minkin said. "I want you to put that rabbi's nuts in a vise and make him squeal."

Sixteen

DISORDER IN THE COURT

Harry Carraway, a young Miami Beach cop, was riding his Segway down Ocean Drive, looking like a complete dork in his safari shorts and shades.

"Morning, Steve," he called out, above the hum of the machine.

"Dirty Harry," Steve called back. "Catch any jaywalkers?"

"No, sir. You walk any felons today?"

"Day ain't over yet."

The cop waved, gave the Segway some juice, and buzzed down the street.

The bicycles were bad enough, Steve thought, the Beach cops pedaling up and down Lincoln Road in their tight shirts and canvas shorts, flirting with sunburned coeds. But the sissified Segways were just too much. Cops should be straddling Harleys or driving big ugly Crown Vics.

Steve hopped into the Mustang and headed to the Criminal Justice Building.

Alone.

Victoria had jumped ship. Not that he couldn't handle this himself. But he never would have left her alone if the situation were reversed. Of course, it never would be reversed. Victoria would never have to step into a courtroom to enter a plea to a crime. *But that aside,* he wondered, *what's going on here?* Approaching the civic center, listening to "Incommunicado," Jimmy Buffet singing about driving solo on a road with a hole in it, Steve asked himself yet again: *Just what the hell is going on?*

* * *

"What's cooking, Cadillac?" Steve said as he crossed the courthouse patio.

"Baby backs, oxtail soup, ham croquettes," answered Cadillac Johnson, an elderly black man with a thick chest and a salt-and-pepper Afro.

Steve stopped at the counter of the Sweet Potato Pie, a trailer permanently parked on the patio. Cadillac, former blues musician, former client, current owner emeritus of the Pie—he was officially retired—slid a cup of chicory coffee across the counter to Steve. "You want me to save you a slab of ribs, Counselor?"

"Nah. I've become a vegan."

"Sure. And I've become a Republican." Cadillac poured a cup of coffee for himself. "You hear Dr. Bill on the radio this morning?"

Steve shrugged. "I listen to Mad Dog Mandich talk football and Jimmy B sing about tequila."

"The doc was talking about you."

"I know all about it. Solomon the Shyster. Steve the Snake."

"Not anymore. Today he said you had psychological issues you needed to deal with, but underneath, you were a good person."

"You're kidding."

"If I'm lying, I'm dying."

Five minutes later, Steve walked along the fourth-floor corridor, sidestepping cops and probation officers, court clerks and bail bondsmen, girlfriends and mothers of the presumably innocent hordes who were being led in shackles from the jail tunnel to the holding cells.

"Hey, *boychik*! Hold your horses!"

Marvin the Maven Mendelsohn toddled up. A small, tidy man around eighty, Marvin had a neatly trimmed mustache and a gleaming bald head. His black eyeglasses were too large for his narrow face, and his powder blue polyester leisure suit must have been all the rage in the 1970s. "What's your hurry, Stevie? They can't start your arraignment without you."

"You still reading the dockets, Marvin?"

The little man shrugged. "State versus Solomon. Assault and battery. In front of that *alter kocker* Schwartz."

At eight A.M. each day, Marvin the Maven could be found thumbing through the printouts attached to the clipboard outside each courtroom. As unofficial leader of the Courthouse Gang, a group of retirees who preferred trials to television, Marvin chose which cases to observe.

"So where's Ms. Lord?" Marvin asked.

"Don't need her," Steve said.

"What *mishegoss*! Of course you need her."

"I've got a plea all worked out."

"You gotta know, a man who represents himself has a *shmendrick* for a client."

"And a *shlemiel* for a lawyer?"

"Exactly."

As they neared the door to Judge Schwartz's courtroom, Marvin said: "So did you hear Dr. Bill today?"

"Apparently, I'm the only one in town who doesn't listen to the guy."

"He was saying nice things about you. That you have a lovely girlfriend. And in his experience, a man must have some good qualities if a fine, upstanding woman sees something in him."

"He's talking about himself, Marvin."

"I don't get it."

"He's sending a message that the two of us are alike somehow."

Steve headed into the courtroom, Marvin in tow. Inside, it was "shoot-around time," Steve's term for the chaos of a motion calendar. Lawyers and cops, clerks and clients drifting all over the courtroom, defendants filling the jury box, everyone talking at once. A basketball team's shooting practice, a dozen balls launched toward the rim at the same time. Presiding over the disorder was the Honorable Alvin Elias Schwartz, the only person in the courthouse older than Marvin the Maven.

Judge Schwartz was propped on two pillows, either because his hemorrhoids were flaring up or because, at five foot three, he couldn't see over the bench. Known as King of the Curmudgeons when he was younger, his disposition had gotten even worse with age. He now had the title of "senior judge," meaning he was somewhere between Medicare and the mortuary. No longer permitted to preside over trials because of lousy hearing, a weak bladder, and chronic flatulence, he nonetheless handled bail hearings, motions, and arraignments.

At the moment, Judge Schwartz was peering through his trifocals at a teenager in baggy, low-slung pants. Skinny and round-shouldered, the kid had the vacant, openmouthed look of the terminally stupid. From what Steve could gather, the kid had just pleaded guilty to possession of marijuana and was getting probation.

"You're getting a second chance, you understand that, José?" Judge Schwartz said.

"My name's Freddy, Judge," the kid said. "You know, short for Fernando."

"Hernando? Like the county? I own thirty acres up by Weeki Wachee."

"*Fer*-nando!" the kid repeated.

"I don't give a flying fandango what your name is, José. You come back here for spitting on the sidewalk, I'm sending you straight to Raiford, where some big bucks are gonna use your candy ass for a piñata. You *comprende*?"

"*Viejo comemierda,*" the kid muttered.

Either the judge didn't hear him or didn't know he'd just been called a shit-eater, because he started absentmindedly thumbing through his stack of files.

Steve worked his way to the front row of the gallery and took a seat on the aisle. It took a moment to realize he was sitting next to Dr. Bill Kreeger.

"What the hell . . . ?"

"Good day, Steve."

"What are you doing here?"

"Surely you know that I testify on occasion. I'm considered quite an effective witness."

"Pathological liars usually are."

It couldn't be a coincidence, Steve thought. First, Kreeger popped up at Joe's. Then he started saying nice things about Steve on the air. Now he showed up in court, looking spiffy in a dark suit and burgundy tie. What was the bastard up to?

"And how's the gorgeous Ms. Lord?"

"Fine. How's your niece? Amanda, right?"

"Lovely young thing, isn't she?"

"*Woman,*" Steve said. "Lovely young woman. Only psychopaths see people as things."

"It's only an expression, Solomon. I assure you that no one in the world appreciates Amanda's qualities the way I do. She has an intelligence and understanding far beyond her years."

"What did you say her last name was?"

"I didn't."

"And just how is she your niece?"

"Too many questions, Solomon. Don't you know that curiosity killed the cat burglar?"

"State of Florida versus Stephen Solomon!" the clerk sang out.

Steve popped up and headed through the swinging gate into the well of the courtroom.

"Is the state prepared to proceed?" Judge Schwartz asked.

"The People are ready and holding steady, Your Honor."

The voice came from the back of the courtroom. Bouncing on his toes, a trim African-American man in a double-breasted pin-striped suit strutted toward the bench. Silver cuff links shaped like miniature handcuffs clinked as he walked. The man was in his mid-forties and still looked like he could fight middleweight, as he did in Golden Gloves when growing up in Liberty City.

What the hell? Pincher only showed up for cases that could get him face time on television.

Dumbfounded, Steve whispered to Pincher: "Sugar Ray, what's going on?"

"A special case that time won't erase."

"What the hell's so special about it?" Steve hissed at the prosecutor. "Are you backing out of the plea?"

"Relax, Solomon." Pincher turned his politician smile on the judge. "Your Honor, we've reached an agreement, but nothing vehement."

"You mean a plea deal?"

"Which now I'll reveal."

"Stop that damned bebop and get to the point."

Pincher gave a courteous bow to the judge, as if he'd just been complimented on the cut of his suit. "Your Honor, the state is prepared to dismiss the felony charges, and Mr. Solomon will plead nolo to simple assault with adjudication to be withheld pending completion of anger-management therapy."

Steve let out a breath. Okay, that was exactly what he'd agreed to with one of Pincher's deputies. But why was the boss here? What was so damn special about the case?

"Mr. Solomon?" The judge seemed to focus on Steve for the first time. "Aren't you that lawyer I throw in the clink every now and then?"

"I plead nolo to that, too, Your Honor."

"Okay, then. Let's put the stuffing in this turkey."

The judge started running through the plea protocol. Did Steve understand the charges against him? Did he know he had the right to a trial? Was he entering the plea freely and voluntarily?

Steve gave all the right answers, and in less than three minutes, the judge had checked off the boxes on his form and signed the order Pincher handed to him. Judge Schwartz leaned close to the document, showing the courtroom the crown of his bald head as he read: "The Court finds that the defendant is alert and intelligent and understands the consequences of his plea, which is accepted for all purposes. Adjudication of guilt is withheld pending completion of anger-management therapy under the auspices of William Kreeger, MD, board-certified psychiatrist."

What!? Did the judge say what I think he said?

"Dr. Kreeger will file a written report with the Court at the conclusion of said therapy."

Yes. He definitely said it. But that's nuts. There must be some mistake.

"At which time, charges will either be dismissed and all records expunged, or in the event of the failure to satisfactorily complete said therapy, the defendant shall be sentenced in accordance with his plea of nolo contendere."

"Hold on, Judge!" Steve shouted, loud enough for the old buzzard to hear. "Kreeger's a convicted felon."

"Not anymore," Pincher shot back. "His rights have been restored. Dr. Kreeger received commendations from the Corrections Department for his work with violent offenders, and the DPR restored his medical license. He's a model of rehabilitation."

"He's a model nutcase," Steve said.

"You heard my ruling," the judge rasped. "Now stop your bellyaching and go get your anger managed."

The judge hammered his gavel. "Clerk, call the next case."

"No fucking way," Steve said.

"What'd you say?" the judge demanded.

"No fun this way, Your Honor."

"It's not supposed to be fun. You're a criminal, aren't you?"

"No, sir. I'm a defense lawyer."

"Same difference. You're accused of assaulting

one . . ." The judge licked his index finger and thumbed through the court file. "Arnold Freskin, an employee of the great State of Florida." Judge Schwartz used his feet to pedal his chair away from his desk and toward the flagpole a few feet away. He grasped the edge of the state flag and pulled it taut. "What do you see, Mr. Solomon?"

"I see the state seal, Your Honor. A Native American woman is scattering flowers on the ground."

"Damn right. These days the squaw would be raking in chips at the casino." The judge dropped the flag and rolled back to his desk. "My point, Mr. Solomon, is that you offended the dignity of the great State of Florida, and Mr. Pincher has magnanimously decided to cut you a break."

"Yes, sir, but—"

"No 'but.' I just disposed of this baked turd of a case."

"I'm being set up, Judge. By Mr. Pincher and Dr. Kreeger."

"You're talking in riddles, Mr. Solomon. I called the next case, and by God, I'm going to hear the next case."

The clerk called out: "City of Miami Beach *versus* Weingarten Delicatessen. Violation of Kosher Food Ordinance."

Pincher grabbed Steve's elbow and whispered: "Just chill. See Bill. Ain't nothing but a fire drill."

"You sold me out, Sugar Ray." Steve turned to the judge. "Your Honor, I move to withdraw my plea."

"Are you still here?" Judge Schwartz was scowling. "I'm going to charge you rent, Counselor."

Steve felt a presence beside him. Kreeger had come through the swinging gate. "Your Honor, Mr.

Solomon's recalcitrance is a normal manifestation of his behavioral type. I'm sure he'll do fine with therapy."

"Like I give a rat's *tuches*," the judge said. "Where's that butcher who's selling *trayf* as kosher?"

"Judge, there's a motion pending," Steve insisted. "I've moved to withdraw my plea. I want to go to trial."

"Motion denied. It's time to clear my calendar, Mr. Solomon, and not the one with the Playboy bunnies on it."

"Your Honor, I have an absolute right to—"

Bang! The judge smacked the gavel so hard, Steve could feel his teeth reverberate. "I'm driving the Studebaker, Mr. Solomon, and you're the greasy speck of a horsefly on my windshield."

Steve had no intention of giving up or backing down. "Judge, I once represented Kreeger in a case. State Attorney Pincher prosecuted for the state. They've cooked this up. If Kreeger doesn't clear me, you'll sentence me to jail. Can't you see it, Judge? It's a conspiracy."

Judge Schwartz turned his bleary gaze on Kreeger, and for a moment Steve thought maybe he'd made an impression.

"Let's hear from the headshrinker," the judge said. "Doc, what do you say about these accusations?"

"Nothing to be alarmed about, Your Honor," Kreeger replied in his soothing baritone. "While I'm working on Mr. Solomon's anger, I'll check out that paranoia, too."

SOLOMON'S LAWS

6. A creative lawyer considers a judge's order a mere suggestion.

Seventeen

THE UNFINISHED BUSINESS
OF PARENTING

"What did you do to make the judge so furious?" Victoria demanded.

"Nothing," Steve said. "Nada. Bupkes."

"You must have done something."

"Why?" Steve had come home hoping for comfort and support. Instead he was being cross-examined in his own kitchen. "Why do you automatically assume it's my fault?"

"Because you have a knack for driving people crazy."

"Judge Schwartz was crazy decades before I met him. Can you believe I'm supposed to be counseled by that psychopath Kreeger?"

"Sociopath," Bobby corrected him. "With narcissistic tendencies and omnipotent fantasies." The kid had been reading psychology texts and checking out various medical websites. At least that's what he said when asked why his computer had bookmarked nymphomaniacs.com. Now Bobby gave the adults his wiseguy look from underneath the bill of his Solomon & Lord ball cap. Steve had formed a team in the lawyers' softball league, but desperately short of players, he recruited clients to play. Purse snatchers turned out to be excellent base runners; pedestrians knocked down by taxicabs were a little slow off the bag.

Outside the windows, fronds from a sabal palm swatted the stucco walls of the house. Inside, Steve was defending himself from Victoria's torrent of criticism.

"I didn't do anything wrong," Steve insisted. "Kreeger set me up, and Pincher was in on it."

"Why? What's Pincher have to gain?"

"More like what he has to lose. Kreeger threatened to go public, tell everyone our esteemed State Attorney used tainted evidence to convict him."

"Pincher told you that?"

"I figured it out. Pincher's up for reelection next year. Who'd he rather have pissed off at him? A defense lawyer or a guy with a radio show?"

"Aw, why make a big *tsimiss* out of it?" Herbert Solomon walked into the kitchen, carrying a tumbler filled with ice. "Do the therapy and get the charges dismissed."

"Not that easy, Dad. Having Kreeger as my therapist is like having a burglar in my bedroom."

Herbert had filled his glass so high with bourbon, he needed to slurp it out. "So don't flap your gums about family secrets. Stonewall his ass."

"Then he files a report with the court saying I'm hiding my lunatic impulses."

"If the judge ordered you to go to Kreeger," Victoria said, "you have no choice."

"That's the difference between you and me, Vic," Steve said. "I consider judges' orders as mere suggestions."

"That's the difference between civilization and anarchy. And in your life, anarchy rules."

"Anarchy rules," Bobby repeated. "ANY CRUEL RASH."

"No reason to be all tore up, son," Herbert said. "Maybe the more time you spend with that shrink, the better."

"How you figure, Dad?"

"Ah couldn't find hide nor hair of that boat captain. You need a new plan."

Victoria shot Steve a look. He hadn't told his father everything, and she knew it.

"Dad, it doesn't matter if you found De la Fuente or not. I just want Kreeger to know I'm looking."

Herbert's bushy eyebrows seemed to arch higher. "So you send your old man on a wild-goose chase. Fine son you are."

"But you're right, Dad. There's an upside to spending more time with Kreeger. His girlfriend, too, if I could get her alone."

"You still think you can convince her Kreeger's a killer?" Victoria said.

"No!" He slapped his forehead to signify what an idiot he was. No one disagreed. "I've got it backwards. I think she *already* knows his past."

"And you base this on what?" Victoria asked.

"Something Kreeger said to me about how much he appreciates Amanda's qualities. That she has an intelligence and understanding beyond her years. That sort of thing."

"Yeah?"

"She's the one he feels safe with, the one who comforts him. Kreeger could have told her about Beshears and Lamm. And who knows? Maybe there's—"

"A third murder," Victoria said.

"Exactly. If Amanda knows Kreeger's secrets, and I can drive a wedge between them, maybe I can get her to help me nail him."

"This 'wedge' of yours? How's that going to work, exactly?"

"I don't know yet, Vic. I'm just riffing here."

"And you don't think a guy as smart as Kreeger will catch on?"

"So he's smart. What am I? Chopped liver?"

"You don't exactly bend spoons with your mind, Uncle Steve." Bobby unscrewed two halves of an Oreo cookie and used his teeth to scrape off the vanilla filling.

"Thanks, guys," Steve said. "But Kreeger's got his weaknesses. He's so damn cocky, he'll figure there's no way I can take him down."

"The omnipotence fantasy," Bobby added. "Freud wrote about it."

"And if Kreeger wants to hang out, like Dad says, that's fine, too."

"Keep your friends close but your enemies closer," Bobby recited.

"Freud?" Steve asked.

Bobby winced. "Al Pacino. *Godfather, Part II.*"

"Don't you have homework to do?" Steve said.

"Nope."

"And where were you last night?"

"Nowhere."

"Physically impossible."

The boy tossed his shoulders, the adolescent symbol for "so what" or "whatever" or "who gives a shit?"

"You violated curfew, kiddo."

"Jeez, this is like a prison."

"Ease up on the boy," Herbert said. "When you and Janice were kids, Ah—"

"Was nowhere to be found," Steve interrupted.

* * *

Bobby wanted to tell Uncle Steve the truth.

"I was with Mom. We sat in her car down by the bay and talked for hours."

But he couldn't do it. Uncle Steve thought she was a really bad influence. But she didn't seem that way at all. She seemed kind of lost, like she needed Bobby more than he needed her.

Mom seems so lonely, like there's nobody for her to talk to.

So Bobby had listened as she talked about growing up in a house with a sick mother and an absent father, Grandpop always being off somewhere, and Steve out playing sports. Mom had been the outsider, or that was how she felt, anyway.

When Mom was talking about the man who picked her up hitchhiking—she couldn't remember his name, even though he might be Bobby's father—Bobby tried to decide whether he loved her. Yeah, he probably did in some weird way. But he was certain he felt sorry for her.

Now Bobby listened as Uncle Steve and Grandpop argued for the zillionth time about the past.

"Don't tell me you're still mad because I didn't come to your Little League games," Grandpop said.

"Or to my spelling bees, my track meets, or the hospital when I had my tonsils out."

"For crying out loud, you were only there a few hours."

"Because you wouldn't pay for a room. The doctor wanted to keep me overnight."

"Highway robbery."

Sometimes Bobby wished the two of them would grow up.

* * *

Victoria tried to decide who was more immature, Steve or his father. Clearly, they were equally argumentative and pugnacious. She tried to picture the Solomon home during Steve's childhood. It didn't seem to be a happy place. Certainly, it was not a quiet place.

They railed at each other another few moments, Herbert calling Steve an "ungrateful grumble guts," Steve calling Herbert a "tumbleweed father, gone with the wind." Then they seemed to tire, and Steve turned back to Bobby. "You still haven't said where you were last night."

"Probably with his little shiksa," Herbert said.

"Dad! That's a derogatory term."

"The hell it is."

Here we go again, Victoria thought. *These two could argue over "Happy Chanukah."*

"A shiksa's a gentile gal," Herbert continued. "Nothing derogatory about it. As for little Miss Havana-Jerusalem, her mother's a Catholic and that makes her a shiksa."

"So I'm a shiksa," Victoria said.

"Hell, no. You're Jewish by injection." Herbert laughed and took a pull on his bourbon. "Unless you two haven't played hide-the-salami yet."

"Dad, put a lid on it," Steve ordered.

Herbert grinned at Victoria. "How 'bout it, *bubele*? Stephen been slipping you the Hebrew National?"

Herbert cackled again and headed toward the living

room without waiting for an answer. "Hold mah calls. Ah'm gonna watch a titty movie on Cinemax, then take a nap."

Victoria whirled toward Steve. "Why do you have to bait him?" she demanded.

"I could tell you, Vic, but I'm not sure you'd understand."

"Try me, partner. I've been to college and everything."

"It's a Jewish thing. We love arguing, complaining, talking with our mouths full. You're Episcopalian. You love—I don't know—drinking tea, wearing Burberry, the Queen of England."

Victoria was not particularly pleased about being reduced to a stereotype. She would talk to Steve about it later. But right now Bobby was still there, fishing into the Oreo bag. "Steve, don't you have some unfinished parenting to do?"

"Parenting's always unfinished." He turned to the boy. "So, kiddo, was your grandpop right? Were you with Maria last night?"

"Jeez, it's like the Inquisition in here." Bobby pried off the top of a cookie. "No, I wasn't with her. Maria's stupid dad won't let me see her anymore."

Victoria spoke gently. "Bobby, what's happened?"

"Nothing, except Dr. Goldberg thinks I'm weird." The pain was audible in the boy's voice.

"You're weird?" Steve said. "He's a periodontist."

Victoria ran a hand through Bobby's hair. "Why would he say something like that?"

Bobby hunched his shoulders. "Lots of reasons, I guess. Dr. Goldberg's always cracking on me. Like, he hates the T-shirt Uncle Steve got me."

"What T-shirt?"

Steve shook his head in Bobby's direction, but the kid either didn't pick up the sign or didn't care. "*'If We Don't Have Sex, the Terrorists Win.'*"

Victoria shot a look at Steve. In the household of the three Solomon men, she now concluded, Steve clearly was the most childish.

"And Dr. Goldberg hated the poetry I wrote for Maria," Bobby continued. "I made anagrams of every line of 'The Rubaiyat of Omar Khayyam.'"

"Why, that must have been beautiful," Victoria said, trying to boost the boy's ego.

"Dr. Goldberg said the whole poem was smutty."

"Smutty!" Steve smacked the countertop.

Why was it, Victoria wondered, that men always needed to throw things, hit things, and make noise to express displeasure?

"Who uses words like 'smutty' anymore?" Steve railed. "What else did this tight-ass say to you?"

"Nothin'." The boy licked another open-faced Oreo.

"C'mon, Bobby. Don't hold out on Uncle Steve."

Without looking up from the table, Bobby said: "That I was a klutz. That he didn't want me hanging around Maria. And in case I thought she liked me, she didn't. She just wanted me to do her homework."

Steve smacked *both* hands on the countertop. "That asshole! I'm going over there and kick his butt."

"That would be very smart," Victoria said evenly. "Give Kreeger ammunition for the judge."

"Forget Kreeger. This jerk's got no right to talk to Bobby that way."

"It's okay, Uncle Steve."

"The hell it is!"

"Steve," Victoria cautioned. "Settle down. You're not going over to the Goldbergs'."

"Vic, this is between Bobby and me, okay?"

She stiffened. "What does that mean?"

"Nothing."

"Are you trying to put distance between us?"

"I have no idea what you're talking about."

"Then answer this. Am I a member of this family or not?"

Steve hesitated. Just a second. Then he said, "Sure. Sure, you are."

Victoria remembered an early boyfriend once saying he loved her. She had thought it over a couple seconds—one-thousand-one, one-thousand-two—and finally agreed, *"I love you, too."* But if you have to think about it, well, the feeling just isn't there.

"So you don't consider me a member of the family?"

"I just said I do."

"Let's examine the instant replay," Victoria demanded, "because you looked like you were moving in slow motion."

"I just like to think before I speak."

"Since when? You have an intimacy problem, you know that, Steve?"

"Aw, jeez, don't change the subject. Name one good reason why I shouldn't go over to Myron Goldberg's house and call him out."

"Because it's juvenile, illegal, and self-destructive," Victoria said. "Three reasons."

That seemed to silence him. Then he said: "Okay, I get it. I'm going to take care of my stuff first. Go to Kreeger. Get my head shrunk, get the case dismissed.

Then I'm going to see Myron Goldberg and ask politely but firmly that he apologize to Bobby."

"And if he doesn't? What then?"

"I'll kick his ass from here to Sopchoppy," Steve said.

SOLOMON'S LAWS

7. When you run across a naked woman, act as if you've seen one before.

Eighteen

SKIN SHOW

Halloween had come and gone, Thanksgiving was around the corner, but the air was washcloth thick with heat and humidity. The palm fronds hung limply on the trees, no ocean breezes drifted inland. Driving through the winding streets of Coral Gables, Steve wore green Hurricanes shorts and a T-shirt with the logo *"I'm Hung Like Einstein and Smart as a Horse."* On the Margaritaville station, Jimmy Buffet was singing "Off to See the Lizard."

Steve parked next to a pile of yard clippings in a cul-de-sac off Alhambra, next to the Biltmore golf course. Halfway down the block was the home and office of Dr. William Kreeger.

Steve hopped out and headed down the street on foot. He could hear a power mower churning away behind one of the houses, could smell the fresh-cut grass. Around the corner, on Trevino, the sounds of sawing and chopping, a city crew cutting back the limbs on neighborhood banyan trees.

He wasn't quite sure why he parked so far away. Kreeger's place had a driveway, and there was parking at the curb, too. Maybe it was the embarrassment,

going to visit a shrink. Or was Steve more like a burglar, stashing the getaway car out of sight? Didn't matter. The walk through the neighborhood of
Mediterranean homes with barrel-tile roofs gave him a
chance to plan. Should he bring up the subject of the
boat captain? He could try bluffing, tell a big, fat lie.

*"Say, Kreeger. I found the guy who was driving the
boat when you killed your pal Beshears. Oscar De la
Fuente. He's got some interesting things to say."*

No. Too obvious. Let Kreeger bring it up. By now,
he should know that Steve had been looking for the
guy. Herbert had dropped off Steve's business card at
every saloon and boat-repair yard in the Keys, linger-
ing longer in the saloons, no doubt. Steve had placed
ads in newspapers and on the Internet, promising a reward for anyone finding De la Fuente. No one came
forward.

Kreeger lived in a stucco house that dated from the
1920s. The walls had been sandblasted, giving them
the pallor of a dead man. Kreeger's office was around
back. Steve followed a path of pink flagstones between
hibiscus bushes and emerged in a yard surrounded by
a ficus hedge. A waterfall gurgled between coral rock
boulders and spilled into a rectangular swimming
pool.

Steve had been here before. A lawyer always visits
the scene of the crime. At the far end of the pool was
the hot tub where Nancy Lamm had drowned.

Nothing had changed since Steve was here seven
years ago, except that day, best he could recall, there
was no naked woman on a chaise lounge. But today,
reclining on a redwood chaise with thick patterned
cushions was a very lithe young woman wearing sun-

glasses and nothing else. Her body was slick with oil, and the scent of coconut was in the air.

"Hello there," he said jauntily.

She sleepily turned her head toward him. "You don't recognize me, do you?"

"Sure I do." In truth, he hadn't been looking at her face. "Amanda, right? The niece. But I don't know your last name."

"Is that important?"

"I was just wondering how Dr. Bill is your uncle."

She rolled onto her side. "It's an honorary title. But I think that makes Bill even more special, don't you?"

The random fortuity of life struck Steve just then. One sunny day, you're walking on the beach and a bird shits on your head. Or if you're really unlucky, a tsunami swamps you and drags you out to sea. But another day, you're going to see a homicidal guy who hates you, and *poof*, a naked woman appears directly in your path. A woman who could alter the course of several lives. Could do justice where justice has failed. And there she is, like the gatekeeper at a bridge in a Greek myth.

It's almost too coincidental. Okay, strike the "almost."

Kreeger always seemed to be one step ahead of him. If Steve had plans for Amanda, surely Kreeger did, too. Steve just wasn't sure what they were.

"Wanna go for a swim?" Amanda asked.

The question threw him.

"Uncle Bill's still with a patient," she continued. "We've got time."

She cocked her head in the direction of Kreeger's office, a converted Florida room facing the yard. Slatted wooden shades appeared to be closed, but it was possible someone on the inside was watching them.

"I don't have a swimsuit."

"Me, either."

"I see that."

Dumb. "I see that." Of course you see it, schmuck.

"Nice day for a swim, though," he said. "Hot."

"I love hot days," Amanda purred.

"I see that."

Again? "I see that"? Act natural. Act like you've seen a naked woman or two.

She stretched her arms over her head, yawned, and pointed her toes. The motion was graceful and catlike. Her breasts were small, round, and tan, the nipples the color of copper. She was thin but strong, with developed calves that flexed as she straightened her legs. Carved abs. Farther south, a thin triangular strip of pubic hair ran between two small tattoos, but he couldn't make them out from this distance.

"An arrow and a heart," she said.

"What?"

"The tats you're staring at."

"Oh. Well. I wasn't. Staring, I mean. Exactly."

In retrospect, "I see that" sounded more intelligent.

"I mean, I was looking at your . . . uh . . . landing strip. That's what you call it, right? My girlfriend asked me if she should get one. I guess, technically, you don't 'get one.' It's not like buying a purse, right?"

He was aware he was babbling. What was it about a naked woman that discombobulated a man?

Her nakedness, idiot! Right. I see that.

What happened to his plans? He had wanted to find out everything about Amanda. How long had she known Kreeger? Did he ever talk about Nancy Lamm or Jim Beshears? Would she help Steve? But confronted with a naked woman, logical questions tend to evaporate faster than coconut oil.

"You were Uncle Bill's lawyer, weren't you?" Amanda asked.

"Right."

Wait a second. I'm supposed to be asking the questions.

"You double-crossed him."

"He tell you that?"

"Uncle Bill tells me everything."

"I thought he might. Maybe we can get together and swap stories."

"Uncle Bill wouldn't like that."

"Not a date or anything. I just want to talk."

Amanda gave him a patronizing smile with just a hint of an eyebrow raised above the sunglasses. "That's what he wouldn't like. Talking about private stuff. Having sex with you he wouldn't mind. If that's what I wanted."

Oh.

"But I haven't made up my mind about you yet," she said. She swung her legs out of the chaise and walked toward him. It wasn't a seductive walk. More bouncy and athletic, like a cheerleader, her small breasts not even jiggling. She came up to Steve, as if daring him not to move out of the way. He took the dare, and she stopped six inches in front of him. She took off the sunglasses. Her eyes were a greenish gold. "I don't know if you'd be as good to me as Uncle Bill. He always puts me first. My pleasures. My desires. That's how he got his honorary title."

"That's some uncle," Steve allowed.

"Uncle Bill loves me. And he has for a long time."

She took a half step toward him, stood on her tippy-toes, and kissed Steve lightly on the lips. He didn't kiss back, but he didn't pull away, either. "But a girl can always have *two* uncles," she whispered.

She moved past him, one breast brushing his arm, giving him a last look at her from behind. Bouncing toward the house, calves undulating, her butt high and firm. And just above the crack between her cheeks, another tattoo: an iridescent jellyfish, beautiful and deadly, its tentacles streaming down each buttock.

Nineteen

SHRINK WRAPPED

Ten minutes later, Steve was settling into a brown leather chair in Dr. William Kreeger's home office. The floor was Dade County pine, the stucco walls painted a grayish-green color Steve didn't care for. He once read that shrinks used earth colors to calm their troubled patients. But no beige walls, no corn plant in the corner, no gurgling fish tank with parrotfish and lionfish frolicking through coral caves.

The only personal items were several framed photos on a credenza. Kreeger on a power boat, a big-ass sport fisherman in the fifty-foot range. Best Steve could tell, there were no bodies floating in the water. Then there were a couple of grainy shots taken from videotape: Kreeger on CNN, opining why husbands kill their wives or mothers kill their children, or maybe even why clients kill their lawyers.

"Did you see Amanda on your way in?" Kreeger sat in his own leather chair.

"All of her." Steve looked toward the wood-slatted windows. Now he was sure Kreeger had been watching them, had planned the whole thing.

"She's a remarkable young woman," Kreeger said.

"Tell me about her."

"We're here to talk about you, Solomon. Not her."

"Hey, you brought it up."

"All I'll say is this: When I was in prison, Amanda was the only one who wrote me, the only one who cared. And when I got out, she was waiting for me."

"Seems a little young to be one of those wackos who fall for murderers."

"You have much to learn, Solomon. And so little time to learn it." He used a handheld sharpener to grind a fine point on a pencil, then continued. "Now, what should we discuss first? Your violent temper or your sleazy ethics?"

"That's sweet, Kreeger. You lecturing on ethics is like the Donner Party talking about table manners."

"I detect antagonism in your voice. Still having difficulty controlling your anger?"

"Aw, shit."

Kreeger crossed his legs and balanced a leather-bound notebook on his knee. An open leather briefcase, the old-fashioned doctor-bag variety, was at his feet. A rattan table with a green marble ashtray sat between the two men, and a paddle fan whirred silently overhead. They had barely started, and already Steve felt like bolting. If the bastard asked if he'd ever wanted to kill his father and sleep with his mother . . . well, there'd be a second assault-and-battery charge in his file.

"Tell me about your childhood," Kreeger instructed, his voice clinical and distant. "Were you a happy child?"

"Screw you, Kreeger."

"Did you have a good relationship with your father?"

"And the horse your rode in on."

Kreeger scribbled something in his notebook.

"Let me guess," Steve said. " 'Patient is obstreperous, uncooperative, manifests antisocial tendencies.' "

"Let's get something straight, Solomon. You're not my patient. I'm not here to treat you. I'm here to teach you how to manage your anger. It's up to you whether you take my advice. My report to the court will state whether your penchant for violence is under control or whether you should be incarcerated as a danger to the community. Understand?"

"Yeah."

"Splendid. Now, you still want to fuck with me?"

Steve took a breath and tried to relax. This wasn't going the way he had planned. He'd intended to be cooperative, maybe drop a comment or two about Nancy Lamm, maybe something about Jim Beshears, see if Kreeger brought up Oscar De la Fuente.

"Okay, Doc. Let's get this over with."

Kreeger reached into the open briefcase. He pulled out a photograph and slid it across the rattan table. "When you look at that, how do you feel?"

Steve picked up the photo and laughed. It was black-and-white and grainy, but there he was, in his U.M. baseball uniform, bareheaded. He'd already tossed his cap to the ground. His arms were thrown out to the sides, frozen in an awkward position as if he were attempting to fly. His face was contorted into an expression that seemed to be equal parts anguish and anger. A vein in his throat stood out, thick as a copperhead. He was screaming at an umpire, whose face was just inches from his own.

"Championship game of the College World Series," Steve said. "Bottom of the ninth. Two outs. I was on third, the potential tying run, and I got picked off. At least, the ump said I did, but I got in under the tag." He shook his head. "How do you think I felt?"

Kreeger scribbled something on his pad. "You tell me."

"Angry. Cheated. Humiliated. Angry."

"You already said that."

"I was *really* angry, but I didn't hit anyone. Write *that* down."

"What about this?"

Kreeger slid a photocopied newspaper clipping toward Steve, who immediately recognized the story from the *Miami Herald*. The headline read: "Judge Quits Bench, Dodges Indictment." A photo—a prize-winning photo, as it turned out—showed Herbert T. Solomon, in shirtsleeves, carrying a cardboard box down the steps of the Criminal Justice Building. Clearly visible in the box were miniature scales of justice, tilted to one side, the chains tangled. The look on Herbert's face: abject shame.

"Dad on the worst day of his life. What about it?"

"How does that picture make you feel?"

"It hurts. A lot. Happy now?"

"Let's analyze your pain. Which was greater? Pulling a bonehead play and losing the championship? Or seeing your father disgraced?"

"That's easy. Watching Dad go down was way worse."

"Why do you suppose you hurt so much, when the disgrace wasn't your own?"

"Because I love my father. Is that concept a little tough for you to understand, Kreeger?"

"And if he were guilty, if your father had taken those bribes, would you still love him?"

"Sure. But Dad was innocent. He was falsely accused."

"Then why didn't the Honorable Judge Solomon fight the charges?"

"Maybe he was afraid of a bad call from the umpire, too."

"Fair enough. He'd lost his faith in the system. Like father, like son-of-a-gun."

"What are you getting at, Kreeger?"

Again Kreeger reached into his briefcase. Another photo. A police mug shot. The woman was in her thirties. Round, pasty face. The tattoo of a snake peeked out of her tank top. Greasy ringlets of hair seemed to be glued to her forehead. And the eyes, glassy and staring into some distant universe.

How long ago must it have been, Steve wondered, that she was a pretty, well-mannered girl living in an upscale house on Pine Tree Drive? With a posse of girlfriends that elicited remarkable electrochemical reactions in a fifth grader named Steve Solomon.

"My sister Janice. What's she have to do with this?"

"Your sister the thief. The drug abuser. The abusive mother."

"All of the above."

"Do you love her, too, Solomon?"

"I'm not doing this, Kreeger." Steve got up and walked to the windows. With an index finger, he lifted one of the wooden shades. Clear view of the pool, the hot tub, and the chaise lounge, now empty. Not a nude young woman in sight.

"I'm afraid you don't have a choice. You kidnapped your nephew from your sister, didn't you?"

"I *rescued* Bobby."

"You hit a man, crushed his skull with a stick of some kind. What was it?"

"A piece of oak. A shepherd's staff."

"Not quite as heavy as a gaff, I would think."

Ah, so there it was, Steve thought. The boat in the Keys. Beshears overboard. De la Fuente at the wheel. *Okay, now we're getting somewhere.* "We talking about my hitting a guy named Thigpen or you hitting a guy named Beshears?"

"You'd agree there is some similarity. Except, of course, I was trying to rescue poor Jim Beshears."

"Funny. I didn't kill Thigpen. But you killed Beshears."

"Tell me about Thigpen, and I'll tell you about Beshears. Nancy, too."

Steve didn't know whether to believe him, but there was very little to lose. "Janice kept Bobby in a dog cage, fed him gruel. She would have sold him for half a dozen rocks of crack. I got him out of there, and I had to hit somebody to do it."

Remembering a snowy night in the Panhandle. A commune where Janice and her brain-dead friends grew marijuana in the summer and ingested all manner of illicit substances the rest of the year. Remembering swinging the staff, fracturing a man's skull, and carrying Bobby to safety. Bringing him home, the boy's first real home.

"Your turn," Steve said. "Did you push Beshears overboard? Did you intend to bash him with the gaff?"

"Police report said it was an accident."

"That's it, Kreeger? That's all you have to say?"

"Jim Beshears was an oaf and a boor and insanely

jealous of me. He ruined a perfectly fine fishing trip with his incessant pestering."

"Sounds like he deserved to be killed."

"Draw your own conclusions, Solomon."

"You're boasting, aren't you? Letting me know what you're capable of."

"We should go fishing sometime, you and I, Solomon."

Steve laughed; he couldn't help himself. "Why? So you could use me for chum?"

Kreeger gestured toward the photos on the credenza. The big sport fisherman tied up at a dock, then another shot, the boat powering through a channel, a mangrove island visible in the background, and a third photo, a closeup of Kreeger at the helm. "I love my boat. Brings me peace in times of trouble. You know its name?"

Steve shook his head. He hated cutesy boat names. Once, in a divorce, he got the wife her husband's boat, which she promptly renamed *Ex on the Beach*.

"*Psycho Therapy*," Kreeger said. "Two words. You like it?"

"It fits."

"So anytime you want, call me. We'll take the boat down to Elliot Key."

"Not without a Coast Guard escort."

"With your history of violence, I should be afraid of you, not the other way around. Hypothetical question: Would you kill Janice to save your nephew?"

"What!"

"If your sister posed a threat to young Robert, would you kill her to save him?"

"If I say yes, you'll tell Judge Schwartz I'm a

homicidal maniac, a danger to the community. At least the community of worthless junkies."

"I can tell the judge anything I want. This is just between you and me. Now, there's such a thing as justifiable homicide, isn't there?"

"Yeah. Self-defense. Defense of others."

"So who could blame you if you resorted to deadly force to protect an innocent child? What difference should it make if the person is your sister?"

"What's Janice have to do with anything? She—" Steve stopped. Suddenly, it became clear. "You're not talking about me. You're talking about you."

Kreeger smoothed out a fold in his silk guayabera, then laced his fingers together on his stomach. "How so?"

"That bit about the umpire and me. And my father quitting the bench. *You're* the one who doesn't trust judges or the legal system."

"Keep going, Solomon. It's always rewarding to a teacher when a slow child gets the hang of things."

"All your questions about whether I would kill Janice to protect Bobby. You're saying you killed Nancy Lamm because she was a threat to someone. And you're implying that I would do the same thing."

"We all would kill to protect someone we love. You and I are in the mainstream there, but it goes deeper than that. We're a lot closer than you'd like to admit."

"You still stuck on that blood-brothers shit?"

"Where's your sister now?"

"Prison. She's got another eighteen months. But if I know Janice, she'll beat up an inmate or attack a guard and get more time."

"Nope. She's out."

"What are you talking about?"

"She's detoxed and rehabbed and ready for civilian life."

"You're shitting me."

"I examined her myself for the Corrections Department. Volunteered my services. Janice was quite credible when addressing the commissioners."

"You helped her get out. Why?"

Kreeger smiled. "To see how far you'll go to protect someone you love. Did I mention that your sister's goal is to start over? What did she call it? 'Form a new family unit. Me and my boy.' Not very grammatical, but extremely moving."

"I don't believe this. You helped her so she can come after Bobby."

"Is there anything as powerful as a mother's love?"

"You son-of-a-bitch. You killed Nancy Lamm. You killed Jim Beshears. And you want me to kill my sister to prove I'm just like you. Well, you're nuts! I'm not like you, Kreeger."

"We'll see about that, won't we? And why do you keep bringing up poor Jim Beshears? Is it because you've been looking high and low for that boat captain?"

So he does know!

But if Kreeger was concerned, he didn't show it. A bemused smile played at his lips. "Find Señor De la Fuente yet, Solomon?"

"As a matter of fact, I have. He's signed one hell of an affidavit. Maybe you'll get a chance to see it."

"You'll give it to the State Attorney, I suppose. No statute of limitations on murder. Get him to indict me, that your plan?"

Kreeger slid open a desk drawer, and Steve caught

his breath. If he came out with a gun, Steve would fly across the desk. Like sliding into third headfirst.

"If anything happens to me, my office is under strict instructions to deliver that affidavit to Ray Pincher."

"Strict instructions, are they?" Kreeger laughed heartily, like coins *ka-ching*ing out of a slot machine. A second later, he pulled an emery board from the drawer and began filing his nails. "So how is the good captain? I haven't seen him in a long time."

"Retired. Living a quiet life. But he's got a great memory."

Kreeger showed Steve a patient smile. "I'm sure he's retired. And I'm sure it's quite quiet. The 'great memory' bit, not too convincing. Last time I saw Oscar, he wasn't doing that well."

Steve felt a chill, even though it was warm in the small office. Suddenly, he knew exactly where Kreeger was headed.

"Oscar had quite a drinking problem, you know," Kreeger continued. "And when he drank, he talked nonsense. Kept telling tales about these two med students who'd had a fight on his boat and one of them ended up dead. A fight! Oscar must have been drunk that day."

"You say you saw him?"

"Floating facedown. Must have slipped hopping from the rail to his dock. Could happen to anyone."

"And I'll bet he had a dent in his skull, too."

"That'll happen if you hit a concrete dock on the way into the drink."

So there it was, Kreeger delivering a message. *Threaten me and I'll kill you.* Just like he killed Beshears, Lamm, and De la Fuente. Steve felt his jaw muscles tighten. Yeah, *Psycho Therapy* was the perfect name for this freak's boat.

"Three bodies in the water," Steve said, shaking his head.

"Is there a better place to die?"

"Meaning what?"

"I've never really believed in ashes to ashes and dust to dust. We all crawled from the swamp, so how fitting to return to a watery grave. From the swamp to the sea, Solomon. That's our journey. From the swamp to the sea."

Twenty

TALKING STUPID

"You kissed a naked woman?" Victoria said.

"No. Yes. Not exactly." Steve realized he was ker-flumping. He opened the stainless-steel refrigerator door and looked inside. Empty, but the cool air felt great. They were in the model kitchen of a model townhouse on a model block three hundred yards from the ocean. Casa del Mar. Or Mar Bella. Or El Pollo del Mar, for all Steve knew. He hadn't bothered to read the sign.

"You kissed a naked woman!" Her voice had taken on the accusatory tone of a sentencing judge: *"You strangled a helpless kitten."*

"You're focusing on that?" Steve couldn't believe it. He had scarcely started telling Victoria about his visit to Kreeger, and she couldn't get past the suntanned nude in the backyard. "What's important is that Kreeger pretty much admitted killing De la Fuente. That makes *three!*"

"Is she pretty?"

"How many does it take to be serial killer?" Steve mused.

"I'll bet she has a nice body. That night in the restaurant, she looked very fit."

"More than two killings, for sure. But are three enough?"

"The way she stared at you, I knew something was going on."

"You know what this means, Vic?"

"You're cheating on me."

"What! What are you talking about?"

"You kissed a naked woman."

"Actually," Steve said, wishing there were beer in the model refrigerator, "*she* kissed me."

"But you didn't resist."

"What was I supposed to do? Clobber her?"

"No. I'll do that."

"She says Kreeger tells her everything. I was working her."

"I bet you were."

Steve kept opening and closing the refrigerator door, just to have something to do with his hands. The kitchen had a thirteen-foot ceiling, black granite countertops, and a teak work island the size of a racing sloop. The townhouse also had a seven-figure price tag that Steve knew they couldn't afford. But Victoria had wanted to look at the place, so here they were. He knew that women often shopped for items they had no intention of buying. He didn't know why this was so, but just last week Victoria had dragged him to Bal Harbour, where he sat patiently while she tried on a variety of exotic outfits by Italian designers. Each flimsy little frock had a price tag somewhat north of a flat-screen TV, and, of course, Victoria didn't buy a thing. Men would never do that, though he could remember once taking a test drive in a Ferrari, just for the hell of it.

"Anyway, it was all business," he said, closing the refrigerator door. And, hopefully, the subject of the naked Amanda.

Victoria studied him a moment, her brow furrowed. Steve had seen the look many times, though usually when she approached a hostile witness on the stand. "For the record," she said, "did you become aroused?"

Man, she just won't let up.

"Nope. It was way too quick for that."

"So, had there been time for a second kiss, you would have become aroused. Isn't that true?"

"Jeez, why did I have to fall for a trial lawyer? Here I am, being honest, telling you everything, and you're like Ken Starr in front of the Grand Jury."

"You must have flirted with her."

"I just stood there, being my irresistible self, but you're missing the point, Vic. This gives me a great chance to try to flip her."

"Your choice of words is absolutely Freudian."

"Maybe she wants to break away from him. If I help her do that, maybe she'll help me nail him."

"So you and your irresistible self will have to spend time with her, I suppose."

"Amanda shares Kreeger's bed. Who better to get close to if I want to bring him down?"

"I liked your first plan better. The one where you get Kreeger to kill you."

"*Try* to kill me." Steve checked out the built-in microwave. It had more gauges than the control panel of a jet. "C'mon, Vic. I'm gonna need your help with her."

"How many hands does it take to lube a woman with suntan oil?"

"You can give me tips on how to get her to open up."

"What can I tell you?" Victoria said, so airily Steve thought she might float away. "You've already gotten her naked."

"Hiya, lovebirds!" Jackie Tuttle burst into the kitchen from the patio, armed with her BlackBerry and soft leather briefcase. Her shoes and blouse shared something in common, Steve thought. Both were see-through. The shoes seemed to be made of Lucite. The blouse was a flimsy black material. And her gold hoop earrings were so big, you could toss a basketball through them. "Did you see the Jacuzzi, Vic? I can picture the two of you sipping spritzers and watching the sun set over the ocean."

"The sun sets over the Everglades," Steve said.

"Hot tubs give me yeast infections," Victoria said.

"Ooh. You two are fighting."

"No we're not," they said in unison.

"Great," Jackie replied. "Did you see the his-and-her closets?"

Steve ran a hand across the cool granite countertop. "Jackie, we can't afford this place."

Jackie glared at him. "Did I mention the windows exceed the hurricane specs? Won't shatter, even if Tori throws something heavy at you and misses."

"Jackie, Steve's right," Victoria said. "It's too much money."

Shaking a two-tone fingernail in Steve's face, Jackie said: "This is *your* fault."

"Now what'd I do?"

"If you'd let Tori upgrade the practice, you could buy a place in Gables Estates or at least Cocoplum."

"We're not gonna whore for banks and insurance companies."

"I suppose defending strip clubs is a high calling," Jackie shot back.

"First Amendment issues always are."

"And those sweaty migrant workers and illegal aliens you represent for free?"

"When the Pilgrims landed at Plymouth Rock, they were illegal aliens."

Jackie scowled at him. "You don't get it, Steve. Unless you two start making some real money, you'll never be able to afford a decent pup tent. Not in this market."

"I won't compromise my principles. Vic knows the rules."

"Rules?" Victoria pounced. "Like you're laying down the law? Like you're the Chief Justice of this relationship?"

"I didn't mean it that way, Vic. But it's Solomon and Lord, not the other way around."

Victoria folded her arms across her chest. "Maybe it would be better if it was just Steve Solomon, flying solo."

"C'mon. I'm senior to you. You have to acknowledge that. I've tried more cases in more courts and—"

"Been held in contempt more times."

"But we're equal partners in everything else," he said.

Jackie Tuttle gathered up her briefcase and started for the door, pausing only for one last shot. "Steve, let me tell you what Tori won't. You've got a very thick skull."

"You're wrong, Jackie. She's already told me."

"Has she told you this? Sometimes you're a real jerk, and if you don't watch it, you're gonna lose the best woman in the world."

Steve turned to Victoria, waiting for her to disagree. He waited five seconds, or was it five years? Nothing. Then he said something stupid. No, stupid wouldn't begin to describe it, he thought later. Maybe it was that idiotic male need to appear cool and unconcerned. He didn't know the reason. But instead of professing his love and care for Victoria, he said, "Hey, we're all free agents. Vic can do whatever she wants."

Jackie headed straight for the door, and Victoria turned her back on him.

*　*　*

Victoria stayed silent on the drive down Collins Avenue. Steve tuned the radio to the Margaritaville station, all that annoying island music he loved and she found so juvenile. When Jimmy Buffet began singing, "Beach House on the Moon," Victoria leaned forward and turned the volume down. She'd been processing their latest conversations, starting with the other day when Mr. Sensitivity had basically told her to butt out, that he would decide what was right for Bobby, and if he wanted to go down to the Goldberg house and swing on the chandelier like a deranged chimpanzee, then by God, he would. Then, just now, Steve's "rules" for "his" firm. Followed by his invitation to take a hike. Even though she knew he didn't mean it, she was fuming. His interest—professional or otherwise—in Amanda the Naked Tramp wasn't helping, either.

So irritating. So aggravating. So condescending.

And he doesn't even know it.

He can hurt my feelings and put distance between us without even realizing what he's done.

As they passed through the dingy burg of Surfside,

she shot a look at him. "Steve, are you sure you really want to move in together?"

"Sure. Haven't we discussed this already?"

Shutting off discussion again.

"What are you saying? The court has ruled?"

"Still with that? I'm not ruling on anything. We made a mutual decision, and—"

"Face it, Steve. You're not ready for a real relationship." Then she was silent again.

* * *

Steve figured the best way to get out of the personal relationship funk was to talk business. With Victoria staring straight ahead, he summarized his session with Kreeger. Back at the townhouse, Victoria had gotten so hung up on Amanda, he hadn't fully debriefed her. Now he told her about the doc's hypothetical admission that *if* he'd murdered Nancy Lamm, he did it only to protect someone else. And then the news that Steve's larcenous and drug-addled sister Janice, a shoo-in for Worst Mother of the Century, was a free woman, thanks to Kreeger's intervention.

"Kreeger tried to bait me about Janice. Said I'd kill my own sister if she was a threat to Bobby. You think that's what he wants? To set me up to kill Janice?"

No response.

"Or maybe he kills Janice and pins it on me. That would appeal to the freak."

They passed the Eden Roc and the Fontainebleau, both undergoing major renovations, neither Frank Sinatra nor Sammy Davis, Jr., anywhere in sight. Traffic was backed up at the bridge leading to Arthur Godfrey Road, and Steve eased to a stop.

"What I can't figure," Steve rambled on, "is who

was Kreeger supposedly protecting when he killed Nancy Lamm? He doesn't have any kids. Who's this mythical person who's analogous to Bobby?"

"What did Kreeger say, exactly?" Victoria asked, breaking her silence.

Great. She can't resist a mental challenge.

"Best I remember, he said, 'Who could blame you if you resorted to deadly force to protect an innocent child? To protect the one you love?' "

"He's talking about you and him both. You see that, right?"

"Sure, he's saying I would kill to protect Bobby. But who's his kid? Kreeger doesn't have any children."

"Technically, neither do you."

"I have a nephew I love, and Kreeger knows that."

The light turned green and Victoria said: "You really don't see it?"

"No. That's why I'm asking for your help."

"If you'd stop looking for serpentine paths, you'd see how simple and straightforward it is."

"Okay, already. Tell me before the Everglades disappear."

"You're Bobby's uncle."

"Yeah?"

"So who calls Kreeger 'Uncle Bill'?"

"Amanda!"

"She'd have been what, about thirteen when Nancy Lamm was killed. A child."

Questions flashed through his mind, and he spoke them aloud. "But why'd Amanda need protecting? Who is she, anyway? And is Kreeger even telling the truth?"

"I'm sure you'll figure it out, Steve." She motioned toward the curb. "Drop me off on Lincoln Road."

"What! We're finally cracking this case here."

"I need new shoes."

"C'mon. This isn't about shoes. What's going on?"

"I choose to go shopping. Just the way you choose to reject a beautiful condo on Brickell and a beautiful townhouse in Bal Harbour."

"So you're pissed at me? That's why you're buying shoes?"

"Let's just say the Jimmy Choos are on the other foot now."

Twenty-One

A WOMAN'S RIGHT TO SHOES

Victoria didn't really need new shoes. What woman really *needs* hot pink Jimmy Choo strappies or black patent leather Dolce & Gabbanas? Or even gunmetal Via Spiga slides and a pair of beige snakeskin Miu Mius?

But *need* is a relative term, Victoria knew. Maybe she didn't require shoes the way she required oxygen. But just now, she needed to get away from Steve for a few hours to think. And trying on purple velvet Manolo Blahniks was free, even if the shoes themselves were not. She had no intention of buying something she couldn't afford, but just why the hell couldn't she afford them?

Was Jackie right? Was Steve holding her back? Jackie didn't put it that way, exactly. But isn't that what she'd meant?

After Steve dropped her off, Victoria began walking west along Lincoln Road, passing the shops and cafés. Tall, willowy young women sat with suntanned men, sipping lattes and whiling away the afternoon.

Who are these people? Don't they ever work?

The more she thought about the current state of her

relationship with Steve, the more upset she became. Moving in together now seemed like an idiotic idea. Where would it lead? Steve hadn't even mentioned marriage. And was that even what she wanted? Could they get along over the long haul? Was love enough to carry a relationship? Didn't there have to be some commonality in personalities?

So many questions.

Her thoughts returned to the house they couldn't afford and the shoes that were ridiculously expensive.

Why shouldn't I be able to splurge on some wafery Italian footwear that costs nine hundred bucks?

She thought about it a minute. Wasn't there a constitutional right involved here? A Woman's Right to Shoes. Ha!

Her thoughts kept returning to Steve. Right now, he was so embroiled with Kreeger, he'd let the practice slide. The key in any law firm is to keep the faucets flowing. It's not enough to just work on the cases already in-house. You have to prime the pump, constantly bringing in new clients. And what was Steve, the self-appointed rainmaker, hustling up these days?

City of Coral Gables v. *Fiore*. Defending a homeowner who, having been ordered to cut his lawn, mowed "FUCK YOU" into the three-foot-tall grass. Then there was the DUI case for the Zamboni driver at the Florida Panthers hockey games. And let's not forget Sheila and Max Minkin, suing their rabbi for showing up late to their wedding. Steve tried one of his old tricks with those two whiners.

He brings in a lousy case with obnoxious clients, then tries to palm it off on me.

She was so angry at Steve right now, she wished she knew one of Herbert's Yiddish curses. The one about having an onion grow in your navel. Yes, that would do quite nicely. Lacking that, she silently cursed her lover and partner in English, conjuring up the most wicked voodoo she knew:

Dearest Steve. May you have to spend the afternoon with Max and Sheila Minkin.

Then she said the hell with it and whipped out her American Express card. She was going to buy some damn shoes.

Twenty-Two

MOTIVE FOR MURDER

Steve walked into his reception room to find the Minkins waiting.

Oh, shit. They didn't have an appointment.

What lousy luck is this?

Cece Santiago was there, in Lycra shorts and halter top, lying on her back, bench-pressing a buck fifty-five, the bar *clank*ing into its brackets. And here were the Minkins, thumbing through copies of *Coastal Living* and *Architectural Digest* that had been a year old when Steve pilfered them from a doctor's office.

"Hey, Max! Hey, Sheila!" Steve pumped as much pleasure into his voice as he could fake. "How are my favorite newlyweds?"

"How's our case?" Sheila shot back. Max kept his face buried in a magazine.

"Rabbi Finsterman won't settle, at least not yet. His lawyer filed an answer to the complaint, so the issue is joined."

The issue is joined.

Trying to sound like a lawyer. Trying to justify his fee. It was not entirely bad news that Finsterman refused to settle. Now that they were in court, Steve's fee had just been hiked up from one-third of the recovery to forty percent.

"When do we go to trial?" Sheila demanded.

"There are pleadings to file and discovery to take," Steve said, trying to justify whatever fee might be at the end of this faded rainbow. "And it's no slam dunk. Finsterman's lawyer has filed several affirmative defenses."

"What the hell are they?"

"The usual. Assumption of the risk. Comparative negligence. Plus he claims the rabbi was delayed because a thunderstorm snarled traffic. Says it was an act of God."

"It was August! It rains every frigging day," Sheila said.

"I'll probably have to go to the expense of hiring an expert witness."

"Like who?"

"A Talmudic scholar." Thinking Herbert might be up for it, now that he'd started going to synagogue.

The phone rang, and Cece picked it up. "Solomon and Lord. Felonies and misdemeanors. Torts of all sorts." She listened a moment, then said, "*Jefe,* it's for you."

"Ah, probably Justice Brandeis returning my call." Steve gave Cece a sideways glance so she wouldn't say: "*No, it's the collection agency for the rented copier.*" Then he headed for his inner office, thanking the Minkins for dropping by.

* * *

Ten minutes later, Steve sat cross-legged on the floor, pawing through the file of *State of Florida* v. *William Kreeger.* The death of Nancy Lamm. He'd had the criminal file pulled out of storage and started by going through the autopsy report and medical records. So far, he hadn't found anything relevant. The witness statements didn't help, either. He plowed back in time, poring over the notes of his first meeting with Kreeger.

It all started with a divorce and child custody case. *In re the Marriage of Leonard and Nancy Lamm.* Leonard claimed that Nancy abused cocaine and was an unfit mother. The judge appointed Kreeger to serve as court-appointed psychiatrist. He was to interview both parents and their child and file a report with the court.

Some details started coming back to Steve. The Lamms had a single child. A daughter. He remembered her name. *Mary.* Steve recalled Kreeger saying he'd told Nancy her daughter better not have a child out of wedlock or she'd be teased: "Mary had a little Lamm." Steve didn't think it was funny at the time, and it hadn't gotten funnier with age.

Riffling through the files, Steve found a copy of Kreeger's written report. The doc soft-pedaled Nancy's addictions and seemed to blame Leonard for her problems. Her husband was cold and distant and uncommunicative. Nancy was sensitive and lacked self-esteem, a problem exacerbated by Leonard's verbally abusive conduct. There was even a hint of abuse toward Mary. Kreeger phrased this part very carefully. Without ever accusing the father of making sexual overtures, he referred to the man entering the bathroom while Mary was showering. Another episode involved Leonard asking his daughter to sit on his lap, something Kreeger deemed "age inappropriate."

Leonard's lawyer filed a blistering set of objections to Kreeger's report. The lawyer called the claims fabricated and scandalous and asked that they be stricken. There was one objection—a huge one—that could have been made but wasn't because Leonard was unaware of it at the time. Kreeger had become Nancy Lamm's lover and should have been disqualified from the case on that ground.

The custody hearing was two weeks away when Nancy Lamm drowned in Kreeger's hot tub. At virtually the same time a Grand Jury was indicting Kreeger for murder, the family judge granted Leonard custody of the girl.

Steve went through the Family Court pleadings one at a time. With Nancy Lamm dead, the custody hearing had been moved to the uncontested calendar. Nothing fancy. Just a form order: "It is therefore ordered and adjudged that the Respondent Leonard Lamm be hereby granted permanent custody of the minor child, Mary Amanda Lamm."

Mary Amanda Lamm.

Amanda.

"Uncle Bill loves me. And he has for a long time."

Suddenly, it all became clear. The state had gotten the motive wrong. Pincher had told the jury that Kreeger murdered Nancy Lamm because she threatened to file a complaint about the shrink seducing her. But shrinks get involved with their patients all the time. Sure, it was unethical, but it was slap-on-the-wrist material, hardly a reason to kill the accuser.

The truth—the secret, ugly truth—was far worse. Nancy must have found out that Kreeger had seduced her daughter, Mary Amanda. *That* was what she threatened to disclose, maybe to the State Attorney as well as the medical board. Kreeger was facing prison time for statutory rape. He couldn't let that happen.

He *didn't* let that happen. He killed Nancy Lamm and kept her daughter for himself. Even if he had to wait a while. Amanda went to live with her father, and Kreeger went off to prison.

"Amanda was the only one who wrote me, the only one who cared. And when I got out, she was waiting for me."

When Kreeger told him that, Steve thought Amanda was one of those wacko pen pals murderers sometimes attract. But that wasn't it. They had a history.

Steve tried to picture what went on during the years Kreeger was in prison. Amanda Lamm should have been hanging out at the mall, going to cheerleader practice, and buying a prom dress. But her development had been stunted at age thirteen by the half man, half goat named Kreeger.

Steve imagined the girl sitting at home, writing notes on pink stationery, carefully folding them into scented envelopes, sealed with lipsticked kisses. Dreaming sweet thoughts of the man who stole her childhood and replaced it with whispered lies. Living in some perverted fairy tale where two lovers are pried apart by the dragons of fate.

Sure, Kreeger loved her. Loved her in a way both twisted and vile. And she loved him right back. Loved the man who had murdered her mother. And that, Steve thought, seemed as sad and tragic as the murder itself.

SOLOMON'S LAWS

8. Love is chemistry and mystery, not logic and reason.

Twenty-Three

WE ARE WHO WE ARE

Women don't sweep into a room anymore, Steve thought. There are no more Scarlett O'Haras, their dresses hoisted by hoops and petticoats, whooshing into a room, putting on airs.

But then there was Irene Lord.

The Queen burst through the door of his office, her eyes taking in the police-auction furniture, her glossy, collagened lips pursing as she contemplated whether it would be safe to sit down, lest a palmetto bug crawl up her panty hose.

"We must talk," Irene breathed, those puffy lips barely moving.

"Vic's not here," Steve said.

"I'm not blind, Stephen. Old and decrepit perhaps, but not blind."

Steve knew the remark was intended to elicit the obligatory denials, and he semi-complied. "Irene, you're not decrepit or blind."

"And . . . ?"

"And you're not old. You're gorgeous and vibrant and men still come sniffing after you like skunks after sunflowers."

"Thank you, Stephen. I've always been quite fond of you."

That stopped him. "A little early in the day for your gin and tonic, Irene."

"I haven't been drinking. I've come to see you, not my daughter, and I'm making pleasant small talk. Haven't you one iota of decorum?"

"Now, there's the Irene I love."

"And the truth is, I am somewhat fond of you, despite how damned aggravating you can be."

"Thank you."

"I know you say things just to get a rise out of me, but sometimes you're so aggressive and pushy."

"Pushy? Dammit, Irene, that's an anti-Semitic slur."

"Oh, for heaven's sake. Not that again."

"We wanted to join your country clubs. We were being pushy. We wanted to attend Princeton. We were being pushy. Damn pushy Jews!"

"Don't raise your voice, Stephen. It's very unbecoming."

"Ah, so I'm loud, too. 'Loud' is another ethnic slur."

"Some of my favorite fiancés were Jewish, so please cease this harangue. It's becoming tedious."

"You never hear about those pushy Episcopalians, do you? Those loud Lutherans? Don't think so. What's next, Irene. How about 'greedy'?"

"You're not greedy. God knows, I wish you cared more about money. Now, would you please calm down and give me some legal advice?"

"Ask Vic. She knows more law than I do."

"I need someone who's more . . ." Irene clucked her tongue as if ticking off words until she found the right one. "*Flexible*. And forgiving. My darling daughter is somewhat . . ." *Cluck-cluck-cluck*.

"Rigid?" Steve helped out.

"Exactly. Can I count on your discretion?"

"Lawyer-client privilege trumps boyfriend-girlfriend. Who'd you kill?"

Irene rolled her eyes and reached into a soft leathery purse that seemed to be made of the belly skin of a baby alligator. She pulled out a document, slid it across Steve's desk, whisked invisible dirt from the cracked leather client chair, and sat down. Her hair, the color of corn silk, was swept up in a style that reminded Steve of Princess Grace of Monaco.

"First Dade Bank versus Irene Lord," Steve said, reading aloud. "Mortgage foreclosure?"

"They're after my condo, Stephen. You must help me."

"Says here you're five months behind on payments."

"At the moment, I'm cash strapped. What can I do?"

"What about those old boyfriends with all the money? Call that Australian shipping magnate who said you were his favorite ketch."

"He moved on to a sleeker sloop."

"What about the gold-bullion trader? He's loaded."

"Last year, when I turned fifty, he traded me in for two twenty-five-year-olds."

"C'mon, Irene. Last year you turned fifty-seven."

"So he traded me for three nineteen-year-olds. The point is, I'm with Carl now, and he doesn't have a dime."

It hit him then. Carl Drake. Alleged heir of Sir Francis Drake. Smooth talker with a trim mustache and a gold-buttoned navy blazer. "Is that where your money went, Irene? To Drake?"

"It's for my share of the expenses in the trust. I had to put up my money to stake my claim."

"The son-of-a-bitch. When I grilled him at Joe's, he said you didn't have to put up a cent."

"I know. I know."

"And you kept quiet."

"The way I was brought up, Stephen, a woman does not contradict her man."

"Too bad you didn't pass that along to your daughter." Steve shook his head. "Jeez, Irene. Drake's a con man."

"Expenses came up. It happens, Stephen."

"Oh, come on, Irene. Sir Francis Drake's money hasn't been sitting around for four hundred years waiting for you to claim it. It's a scam. A flim-flam. A con job."

"When it pays off, don't expect an invitation to my yacht."

But she said it with such a lack of conviction that Steve immediately sensed something else. Irene *knew* she'd been swindled. Maybe she even knew it when she was writing the check. And this from a woman who was always the recipient of money and jewelry and designer duds. Which could only mean one thing, and that was scariest of all.

"Irene, please don't tell me you're in love with this guy."

Her eyes, unnaturally wide open thanks to lid surgery, now brimmed with tears. "With all my heart, Stephen. The man fills me with wonder."

"Oh, jeez." Steve stood up. "C'mon, Irene. It's not too early. I'm gonna buy you a drink."

* * *

They sat at a sidewalk table at an Ocean Drive café. A woman lost in the deep and treacherous ocean of love, Irene Lord rejected every logical suggestion Steve made.

No, she wouldn't break up with Carl Drake; no, she wouldn't sue him and freeze his accounts; and no, she certainly wouldn't file charges with the State Attorney.

Steve said he would do what he could to slow down the foreclosure litigation. He'd hit the bank with endless discovery. He'd claim fraud and usury and violations of banking regulations, and anything else he could think of, including the Treaty of Versailles and the Nuclear Test Ban Treaty. He'd obfuscate and distort, muddle and confuse. He'd buy time with dilatory tactics, and if all else failed, he'd have Irene enlist in the army and seek protection under the Soldiers and Sailors Civil Relief Act. That was where The Queen seemed to draw the line, but otherwise she seemed to approve his strategy. And with each sip of Tanqueray, she appreciated Steve even more.

"I feel we're bonding here, Stephen."

"Aw, c'mon, Irene. The only bonds you know about are tax-free municipals."

She laughed. "I'm not going to pretend I'm your biggest supporter. Many is the day I've wished Victoria had found a man who was more traditional and less . . ."

"Pushy?"

"Reckless." She smiled at him, her veneers snowy white. "But you do have something going for you."

He waited to see if a zinger was attached to the compliment, like a stinging cell on a jellyfish.

"Victoria loves you. She loves you in a way she's never loved any other man. And that goes a long way with me."

Wow. The Queen had never said anything to him like that before.

"Stephen, this is where you say you love her, too."

"I do, Irene. A lot. More than I ever knew was possible. I fell for Vic when we were on opposite sides of a case, and it just grew from there."

"So. If there's anything I can ever do for you . . ."

It was an offer she'd never made before and might never make again. "To tell you the truth, I could use some advice right now. About Victoria."

"If you're worried, that's a good sign. Some men are so dense they never see it coming."

"It?"

"The three-inch heel of the Prada pumps as they're walking away."

Steve let out a sigh.

"Of course you have problems, Stephen. Every couple does. Nelson Lord was the love of my life, but boy did we fight." She used her fingertips to squeeze the lime into her gin and tonic. "With you and Victoria, it's even more difficult because you're so different."

In the next seventeen minutes, Steve summarized the current state of his relationship with Victoria, admitting that, yes, he had some second thoughts about moving in together, and sure, she'd picked up on it. Now she didn't seem to want to share a Coke with him, much less live under the same roof.

"She needs to know where the two of you are headed," Irene said.

"Why can't she just relax, go with the flow, see where it takes us?"

"Someone as highly organized as my daughter

needs certainly in her life. Let's face it. Spontaneity isn't her strong suit and predictability isn't yours."

"I can change."

"How's that, Stephen?"

He thought about it. On the sidewalk, the usual collection of wannabe models sashayed past their table. In the street, teenage boys drove by in their parents' SUVs, gawking at the girls, their CD players blasting unintelligible reggaeton, something with a lot of drums from Tego Calderon.

"I'm gonna tell Vic to choose where we should live," he answered. "I'm gonna go to the ballet with her. I'm even gonna join the Kiwanis."

Irene's laugh was a bit louder than necessary. Three gin and tonics will do that. "If The Princess wanted a man like that, she would have married Bruce."

Meaning Bruce Bigby, Steve knew. Real estate developer. Avocado grower. Chamber of Commerce Man of the Year.

Irene signaled for another drink. But the waiter must have been an out-of-work actor, because he seemed to be posing for a table of teenage girls in shorts and tank tops. "Victoria dropped Bruce for you," Irene continued. "Why do you suppose she did that?"

"Temporary insanity?"

"She loves you the way you are, despite your many peccadillos. So don't you dare try to change. Besides, it wouldn't work. We are who we are. You, me. Victoria. Carl. All of us. Our true natures will come out, no matter what we do to disguise them."

"That's your advice, Irene? Don't change?"

"That's it. Although . . ."

Here it comes, Steve thought.

"What's the Jewish word for money?" she asked.

"Yiddish word. 'Gelt.' "

Irene smiled at him and did her best impression of a Jewish mother. "Would it hurt you, Stephen, to bring home a little more gelt?"

Twenty-Four

DANCE FOR ME

It was dark, but the moon was three-quarters full—the waning gibbous, Bobby knew—so the yard was illuminated. Myron Goldberg spent a fortune on outdoor lighting, so the house was lit up, too. Bobby heard a whirring sound, followed by a *whoosh*. Below him, sprinkler heads popped out of the lawn like those aliens in *War of the Worlds*. A second later, water shot out, the spray chilling his bare legs. A dozen feet above the ground, Bobby was wedged into the crevice between the trunk and a gnarly limb of a mango tree.

Maria's mango tree. Bobby could smell the peachy aroma of the fruit, still green and hard. A wasp sat on one of the mangoes, antennae wiggling. Could the wasp smell it, too? It annoyed Bobby that he didn't know if wasps had a sense of smell.

Maria. Where are you?

While he waited, Bobby whispered to himself the names of the shrubs and flowers surrounding the Goldberg home. Even their gardener wouldn't know the real name of the honeysuckle with the flowers that looked like purple trumpets.

Lonicera sempervirens!

Then there was the bougainvillea vine with flowers so red, if you crushed them, the liquid would look like wine.

Maria! Where are you?

The wind picked up, rustling leaves. Bobby shivered and felt goose bumps on his legs.

If a goose gets cold, does he say to his mate: "Hey, take a gander at my people bumps"?

It was nearly midnight. Any minute now. The Goldberg house was dark except for the outdoor lighting that cast an eerie glow over the tree and the shrubs.

"When the clock strikes twelve, be there."

That was what Maria had said. As if he would be late. He'd been in the tree for at least an hour, and his butt hurt from the way he was wedged against the trunk.

"Should I throw pebbles against the window?"

"Totally old school, Bobby. At midnight, call but don't say who it is. Just say, 'Dance for me.' "

"What if your parents hear the ring?"

"I'll have the phone on vibrate, and I'll keep it between my thighs."

"Wow."

The conversation had pretty much left him breathless. Now he rehearsed his line several times, trying to lower his voice into a manly baritone, emphasizing the word 'dance' a few times, then the word 'me.'

"Dance for me." Definitely hit the "me."

The hottest hottie in the sixth grade was going to dance for him. She hadn't said "naked," but he had his hopes.

It seemed fair, Bobby thought. He had taught Maria how to divide decimals by whole numbers and how to change fractions into decimals. She had asked him if the quotient becomes larger or smaller as the dividend becomes a greater multiple of ten.

Duh.

He checked the time in the cell phone window. Oh, jeez, 12:03. He speed-dialed her number, listened to the *brrring,* heard her whisper, "What do you want?"

"Dance for me!" His voice cracking, but he got it out.

A light flicked on in the second-story window. Maria's bedroom. Bobby could make out a lamp near the window, probably on Maria's desk. A moment later, the light took on a reddish glow as Maria draped a red cloth over the lampshade. Ooh. This was gonna be good.

She stood in front of the window, her silhouette tinged reddish-black from the lamp, and she started dancing, moving her thin arms overhead in a motion that made Bobby think of someone drowning. If there was music on, he couldn't hear it. She slipped out of her top and turned sideways, her boobies the size of eggs.

Bobby heard his breathing grow deeper, and suddenly he wasn't cold anymore. He shifted his position between the trunk and the limb because of the tightness in his pants. But then new thoughts emerged, intruding thoughts, flowing like a river, breeching the dike his mind had erected.

That cloth over the lampshade. Is it cotton or polyester? What is its flammable rating?

And the lightbulb. He hoped it wasn't a halogen. Those babies throw off 250 degrees Celsius, which he calculated in about three seconds to be 482 degrees Fahrenheit.

Maria slithered out of her shorts, and judging from the angle of her elbow, her hand seemed to be in her crotch, but Bobby couldn't concentrate. He was certain that, any moment, the cloth would burst into flame. The curtains, the bedcovers, the wallpaper—everything would be ablaze. Would Maria even have time to run from the room? Was their A/C hooked up to natural gas? If so, he was sure it was leaking. The house was about to become a fiery inferno, and it was all his fault. In the window, Maria writhed from side to side and swiveled her hips. But in Bobby's mind, all he could see was an orange fireball exploding, tearing the house apart at the beams, incinerating Maria, her mother, and her father.

And that was when he screamed as loud as he could, "Fire! Fire! *Fire!*"

Twenty-Five

MOTHER LODE

Steve ran full speed along Kumquat Avenue, took the bend to the left, then another left on Loquat. The only sounds were his Nikes hitting the pavement and his own breathing.

The phone call had come just after midnight, waking him from a dream that involved stealing home in the College World Series—instead of being picked off third base—and getting carried off the field on his teammates' shoulders.

"This is Eva Munoz-Goldberg. My husband is Dr. Myron J. Goldberg . . ."

Doctor. As if I might confuse him with Myron J. Goldberg, garbage collector.

"Get over here and pick up your sicko nephew before I call the police."

Oh, shit.

Steve had grabbed the closest T-shirt—*"I'm Not Fluent in Idiot, So Please Speak Clearly"*—pulled on a pair of orange Hurricanes shorts, and took off down the street.

What now, Bobby?

As he ran, Steve envisioned his nephew being

caught in Maria's bedroom. What was it Herbert had called her? A harlot-in-training. But maybe they were doing homework and just fell asleep on Maria's bed. Thinking like a defense lawyer.

The yard lights were blazing when Steve huffed to a stop. Spots embedded in planters illuminating the sabal palms, floodlights under the eaves of the barrel-tile roof, Malibu lights lining both sides of a flagstone path, and matching lanterns on bronze posts at the front door. All in all, as bright as the Orange Bowl for a Saturday night game.

Swaying from side to side, Bobby stood with his shoulders hunched and his arms hugging himself. Steve wrapped an arm around the boy and whispered in his ear. "It'll be all right, kiddo. Uncle Steve's here."

Myron Goldberg, a small man in his forties, wore a bathrobe and bedroom slippers and a look of consternation. His wife, Eva, her long black hair asunder, wore a white silk robe that stopped at midthigh. She was a petite but large-bosomed woman around her husband's age, and even without X-ray vision, Steve could tell she wore nothing under the robe. Cradled in the crook of her right arm was a short-barreled automatic weapon.

"Mrs. Goldberg, tell me that's not an Uzi," Steve said.

"This is America. I've got the right."

Maria appeared in the doorway behind them. "Bobby didn't do anything!"

"Back in the house!" Eva ordered. "*Ahora mismo!*"

The girl muttered something Steve couldn't hear, then disappeared behind the front door.

"The thing is," Myron began hesitantly, "your

nephew is a peeper. We caught him in the tree outside Maria's bedroom."

His head pressed against Steve's side, Bobby whimpered.

"Doesn't sound like my Bobby," Steve said, giving the boy a squeeze.

"Ask him!" Eva insisted with a wave of her arm and the Uzi.

"Would you mind putting that gun down?" Steve said.

She gave a dismissive little snort. "Second Amendment. You're a lawyer. Look it up."

"I'm gonna take Bobby home and talk to him there," Steve said evenly. "I'll call you in the morning and we'll sort everything out."

"Not good enough," Eva said. "I want a police report."

"Let's not overreact," Myron said, so softly he could barely be heard over the neighborhood crickets.

"Overreact!" She swung around to face her husband, and for a second, Steve thought she might unleash a quick burst with the Uzi and cut him in half. "You want this little pervert to do it again?"

"Hey," Steve said. "Everybody's a little excited. Maybe we should all just go to sleep and—"

Screeching tires interrupted him. Steve turned toward the driveway, expecting to see a police cruiser, figuring Bobby's future had just turned to a pile of crud. His nephew was about to become his client. A date in Juvenile Court. Psychiatric testing followed by sex-offender registration.

But it wasn't a cop. It was a muddy green Dodge pickup truck, at least ten years old. A woman got out and headed their way. She wore a granny dress that came to her ankles and two-strap Birkenstock sandals. She was tall and stout, with a round face and hair pulled straight back and tied with a band. Even before she got into the light, Steve recognized her and immediately wished it had been the police.

"What the hell are you doing here?" Steve said.

"Bobby called me on his cell. What the fuck's going on?"

Bobby peeked out from behind Steve. "Hi, Mom," he said.

* * *

It was all happening too fast, Steve decided.

First, Bobby tangled in a mess that could toss him into the maw of the justice system. Next, Janice showing up, allegedly to help Bobby, the child she'd neglected and abused and abandoned.

"Bobby called me on his cell."

Meaning they'd been in touch, and the kid had never said a word.

Bobby, Bobby, Bobby. How could you?

"If I was you, I'd put that gun down," Janice said to Eva Munoz-Goldberg.

"And if I were you, I'd wash my hair and lose some weight," Eva fired back.

"Gonna ask you nice one more time. Put the fucking gun down before I jam it up your tight ass."

"Now see here—" Myron attempted.

"Janice, let me handle this," Steve said.

"You ain't doing so hot, baby bro." She turned to the Goldbergs. "The way I hear it, little Miss Hot Pants invited my boy to a peep show, so what's the big deal?"

"How dare you!" Myron said.

"Look, dickwad. I'm not throwing stones here. Hell, I was blowing guys behind the school gym when I was twelve. Don't get so self-righteous. Kids will be kids."

"I've heard about you," Eva said. "You don't even know who Bobby's father is."

"Hey, let's call it a night." Steve spoke up, not on his sister's behalf, but for Bobby. The kid had enough problems without these kinds of insults. "C'mon, everybody's nerves are frayed."

"*Chingate,* shyster," Eva hissed. "I heard all about you on the radio. And I know about your father, the dirty judge."

"Let's leave family out of this," Steve cautioned.

"Coke whore. Shyster. Dirty judge. A whole family of degenerates."

"Let the bitch who is without sin cast the first stone," Janice said.

Eva gestured with the gun. "What's that supposed to mean, *puta?*"

"Jesus loves you. Everybody else thinks you're a twat."

Eva took a step forward, but Janice swung first. A combination punch and lunge, astonishingly quick for a woman her size. The punch grazed Eva's cheek, and she probably wouldn't have fallen, except Janice plowed forward, head down. Janice's beefy shoulder caught Eva squarely in the chest. An *oomph*, and both women tumbled to the ground, the Uzi flying into a planter filled with impatiens. The two men were left looking at each other, wondering if they were supposed to throw some punches, too.

"Boob job! Boob job!" Janice screeched as she straddled Eva, the smaller woman's robe thrown open.

"Jesus, Janice, get off her!" Steve said.

"Don't take the Lord's name in vain," Janice scolded.

"*Requetegorda!*" Eva screamed. "Get off me!"

"Ladies, please," Myron begged.

It was all too surreal, Steve thought. Was he hearing things? Did his sister, who had had her bat mitzvah at Temple Emanu-el all those years ago, just call Jesus "the Lord"?

"How much those hooters set you back?" Janice demanded, holding Eva's robe open. "I was thinking about getting me a pair as soon as I have the liposuction."

"*Puta fea,*" Eva wheezed, Janice sitting on her gut.

"Christ Almighty," Myron Goldberg said.

"Yes, he is," Janice replied.

"Janice, what's all this religious stuff?" Steve asked.

"Jews for Jesus, little brother. In prison, I recognized the true messiah."

"No way."

"Cross my heart."

It just kept getting crazier, Steve thought. A father who'd gone ortho and a sister who'd Jesus-freaked. Just then he caught a flash of movement.

"Look out, Mom!" Bobby shouted.

Myron had picked up the Uzi.

A Jewish periodontist with an Uzi!

Unless the guy was in the Israeli Army, this was a prescription for disaster. Myron seemed to be trying to figure out how to wrap his hand around the pistol grip when Steve took a quick step and uncorked a right-hand punch. His fist caught Myron Goldberg squarely on the chin. Myron fell in a heap, dropping the Uzi.

Steve felt a throbbing pain in his wrist.

On the ground, Myron moaned.

Janice slid off Eva, who was cursing in Spanish. "You did good, little brother," Janice said. "Hey, Bobby. Me and Stevie make a great team, huh?"

"We are not a team." Steve shook his wrist, but the throbbing only increased.

"We're on God's squad," Janice said blissfully.

Myron shakily got to his feet, holding his jaw, saying something that sounded like "*law-shute.*"

A police siren drowned him out.

"Gotta split," Janice said, heading for her truck.

"Hey, sis. Stick around for the cops. I might need a friendly witness."

"He that leadeth into captivity shall go into captivity," she said, without emotion, like an evangelical zombie. "He shall have judgment without mercy that hath showed no mercy."

"Nice sermon. What's it mean?"

She dropped her bulk into the driver's seat of the muddy green pickup and started the engine. "You're on your own, little brother."

Twenty-Six

CALL ME IRRESPONSIBLE

Victoria thought she should be both delicate and diplomatic. She could say: *"I question your judgment in striking Myron Goldberg."* Or perhaps: *"For someone still facing assault charges, your conduct might be considered somewhat ill-advised."*

But she settled on: "You're a child! An undisciplined, self-indulgent child."

"C'mon, Vic. I was the peacemaker."

"You're probably guilty of trespassing. And definitely assault and battery."

"I handled it. The cops interviewed me, then headed off to Krispy Kreme."

"So you're not being charged?"

"They're still investigating."

"I should talk to Dr. Goldberg," she said. "Try to talk him out of filing charges."

"I should sue him." Steve held up his swollen right hand. "My wrist is sprained."

They were stuck in traffic on South Bayshore Drive on a muggy autumn morning. Thankfully, Steve had put the top up on the Mustang, or her hair would resemble a floor mop. They were trying to work their way out of Coconut Grove on the morning after the reappearance of Janice, the nabbing of Bobby, and the near-arrest of Steve.

Just another day in the saga of the Solomon family. Do I really belong here?

Steve was like a trapeze artist working without a net. Sooner or later, he would fall. Would she catch him or be squashed by him?

Okay, if Steve's a trapeze artist, what am I?

The gal in tights who rides the prancing elephant?

No, the poor gal following the elephant with the shovel and pail.

She had picked up the circus metaphors from Marvin the Maven, the octogenarian leader of the Courthouse Gang, an unabashed admirer of Steve. Marvin had once told her why he followed Steve from courtroom to courtroom. *"With Steverino, it's like the circus. You never know when a dozen clowns are gonna fall out of a little yellow car."*

But Steve's courtroom antics were usually planned and made some sense, even if they were borderline unethical. These latest actions—clobbering Arnold Freskin and now Myron Goldberg—made Victoria feel that Steve was out of control.

"How's Bobby doing?" she asked.

"Better, I think. He's calmed down."

"Do you want me to talk to him? About girls, I mean."

"Already did. A speech about being a gentleman, respecting girls. I also told him I was disappointed he didn't tell me about Janice the Junkie coming around."

She shot him a look.

"I didn't call her that," he said hastily. " 'Your loving mother' is what I said. 'How could you sneak off with your loving mother like that?' "

"Go easy on him, Steve. He's got a lot going on."

"Yeah, well, so do I."

Steve banged the horn at a Hummer that was trying to nose into traffic from the Grove Isle bridge. "Asshole! Guy thinks he owns the road 'cause he's got the biggest bumper."

Great, Victoria thought. Just what they needed. A road rage incident.

Steve slid down the window on the passenger side, leaned across, and shouted: "Hey, you! Big car, little dick!"

Victoria swatted his hand away and hit the button, closing the window. "What's wrong with you! Don't you know how many drivers in Miami are armed?"

He turned on the radio. "No, but I'm sure you do."

"Your conduct lately simply defies description."

"Oh, c'mon, Vic. Give it a try."

"For starters, you've been both irresponsible and reckless."

A sports talk station came on, the caller and host debating whether Shaquille O'Neal was a better player than Wilt Chamberlain. The consensus seemed to be that Wilt scored more points and more women.

"Could you change that, please?" Victoria asked.

Steve punched a button, and another sports station came on, the host asking callers to choose the sexiest cheerleader from the Dolphin Dolls.

"How can you listen to this garbage?" she asked.

"I like it. Is that being reckless or irresponsible?"

"Juvenile."

"I guess good old Bigby doesn't listen to sports radio."

"Where did that come from? What's Bruce have to do with anything?"

"I don't know. He sort of popped into my head."

Ahead of them, traffic started moving and they inched past Mercy Hospital on the way downtown. Strange, Victoria thought. Just last night, her mother brought up Bruce. Victoria had been complaining about Steve and his penchant for trouble. Weirdly, The Queen had spoken up for Steve. What had she said exactly? Victoria couldn't remember.

Steve gave the Mustang some gas and said, "Good old boring Bruce Bigby."

Omigod.

That was almost exactly what The Queen had said. *"Steve may drive you crazy, but you love him. And frankly, he's a lot more fun than good old boring Bruce."*

"Have you been speaking to my mother?"

"Why would I? She hates me."

Victoria reached over and changed the station. On came Steve's damn Margaritaville music, Jimmy Buffet singing "Growing Older but Not Up." Another of the beach bard's paeans to the good life.

Victoria hit another button, and a deep voice rumbled from the speakers: *"Now in its twenty-third printing,* Looking Out for Numero Uno. *So, log on to Dr. Bill's website and order the book today. With every purchase, get a free Dr. Bill ball cap with the logo 'Me First.' "*

"I'll change that," she said, reaching toward the radio.

"No. Let's see who he's blasting today."

"Now, a special treat. You've heard Dr. Bill pre-

scribe remedies for addiction before. Hard work. Willpower. Self-reliance. Forget groups and steps. Don't waste your time listening to other people's problems. Our guest today helped herself, and you can, too. Remember, folks, 'invincible' starts with 'i.' "

"What's he peddling now?" Steve asked.

"Today's guest is a woman who turned her life around. A woman who was mired in criminality and drug abuse and made the conscious decision to find the power that lies within. Welcome to the program, Janice Solomon."

"Oh, shit!" Steve slammed on the brakes and was nearly rear-ended.

"I couldn't have done it without you, Dr. Bill. You inspired me."

"That's generous of you, Janice. But I give you all the credit. Now, take our listeners through your life, from your upbringing in a dysfunctional family to your descent into drugs, to your rehabilitation . . ."

"What a load of crap," Steve said.

". . . and now your coming home to reclaim the son you love."

The words hit Steve like a one-two combination—jab-hook, jab-hook—and seemed to reverberate inside his brain.

"The son she loves?" Steve nearly spat the words. "She nearly killed Bobby!"

"The son who was illegally taken away from you."

Steve stomped on the gas and pulled through a U-turn, tires screeching.

"What are you doing?" Victoria said.

"We're going to the station. I'm not gonna let him get away with this."

"You can't play on his turf. Remember last time you went on the air?"

"Got no choice. Kreeger's setting the table for a custody fight. I've got to expose him as a fraud."

"He's taunting you. He *wants* you to come after him."

"Fine. He wants a fight, he's gonna get it. Janice, too."

Typical Steve, she thought. Rushing blindly into danger, never considering the consequences.

She sank back in her seat as the Mustang squealed around the turn at Seventeenth Avenue on the way to Dixie Highway. Steve was right about one thing, she thought.

He's not like Bruce at all.

Bruce carried an umbrella, even when the forecast was sunny and clear. Steve windsurfed in thunderstorms, mast pointed toward the sky, daring Zeus to toss lightning bolts his way.

Just now, good old boring Bruce doesn't sound so bad.

On the radio, Janice was going on about how much she missed her son when she was incarcerated and how, alone in her cell, she pledged to clean up her act so she could come home and raise the boy.

"My brother did the best he could while I was gone. But he's a bachelor, without any children of his own. He's actually quite immature himself."

"The Eva Braun of mothers is criticizing my parenting," Steve muttered.

"No way my brother can do what I can."

"Right. No way I'd abandon the boy and nearly let him freeze to death."

"Steve. Don't do anything stupid, okay?"

"*I'm the mother and there's nothing like a mother's love.*"

"I'm not going to do anything stupid," Steve said.

"*I'm so anxious to make up for all the lost time.*"

"But I'll tell you this, Vic. I'll kill her before I let her have Bobby."

Twenty-Seven

LET'S KILL ALL THE LAWYERS

When Steve and Victoria entered the control room, Dr. Bill Kreeger was just finishing his umpteenth commercial for one of his products, a seven-set CD collection entitled: "Stop Kissing Butt and Start Kicking It." Through the window, Steve could see Kreeger and Janice, earphoned and miked, engaged in the mutual stroking of egos.

"Welcome back Janice Solomon, a truly courageous woman who took control of her life," Kreeger said. "Janice, tell my listeners how you did it."

"Sitting in my jail cell, I read all your books," Janice answered. "*Looking Out for Numero Uno* made me realize I needed to love myself. When I finally put myself on a pedestal—that's chapter three—I realized how much my son needed a person as worthy as me."

"Attagirl," Kreeger enthused.

"Attagirl?" Steve said. "A sociopath high-fiving a child abuser."

"Let's get out of here," Victoria said.

"Tell us about your childhood, Janice," Kreeger coaxed.

"When I was a kid, I was in Girl Scouts, and I was a

candy striper at Mount Sinai. Really caught up in the pleasing-others game."

"Chapter four," Kreeger said. " 'The Pleasing Others Fallacy.' Altruism is for suckers. Pleasing others is a waste of time."

"That was me. I baked cookies for shut-ins and babysat for poor families for free. I never got in touch with my inner 'I.' Never learned to say, 'I am *numero uno*.' So naturally, the more I gave, the more I was taken advantage of. Especially by boys."

"Do-gooders do bad all the time," Kreeger agreed. "No good deed goes unpunished."

"Then there's my brother, Stevie."

"Regular listeners will remember Steve Solomon, another family member with a checkered past," Kreeger pointed out, helpfully.

"You got that right, Dr. Bill."

"Well, speak of the shyster." Kreeger gestured toward the window. "Here's your brother now. C'mon in, Solomon. Let's have a family reunion."

"Don't do it, Steve," Victoria said. "Please don't do it."

"I have to, Vic. My inner 'I' says so."

* * *

Twelve minutes later, just after a promo for Kreeger's new video game, "Shaft Thy Neighbor," Steve listened as the shrink prattled on about himself.

"I've been an expert in quite a few custody cases over the years," Kreeger said.

Yeah. The deceased Nancy Lamm's case, for one.

"And correct me if I'm wrong, Counselor, but doesn't the law favor mothers over fathers, much less uncles?"

"Only with very young children," Steve said. "And not when the mother is demonstrably unfit."

" 'Demonstrably unfit.' Now, there's a pettifogger's term for you. So, you don't believe in rehabilitation, Counselor?"

"We talking about Janice or you?"

"Do you really want to go there, Solomon? Because I'd be forced to ask if your shoddy representation of me proved you're a 'demonstrably unfit' lawyer."

"Janice is an unfit mother, and I can prove it."

"You'll have your chance, Counselor."

"Kreeger, why don't you just butt out of my family's personal matters?"

Next to him, Janice laughed. "Too late for that, little brother. Dr. Bill's testifying for me."

"I can't wait to cross-examine him," Steve said.

"More lawyer tricks?" Kreeger said. "Technicalities and obfuscations. No wonder Shakespeare said, 'Let's kill all the lawyers.' "

"Shakespeare had a villain say that," Steve replied, miraculously remembering a long-ago English Lit class at the U. "Dick the Butcher said it in a play, one of the Henrys. His pals were planning to overthrow the government, so the first thing they planned was to kill the lawyers to make the job easier. You're misconstruing the line, just like you're mischaracterizing my sister."

"More legalese?" Kreeger taunted him. "More fine print and sleight of hand. Yes, indeed. Let's kill all the lawyers before they kill all of us."

Janice leaned closer to the microphone. "I think Stevie's capable of murder. When he kidnapped Bobby, he broke Rufus Thigpen's skull."

"I didn't kidnap Bobby. I rescued him from the dog cage you locked him in."

"If I'd been the one in that shed instead of Thigpen, would you have cracked my head open, too?" Janice prodded.

"I'm not gonna answer that."

"Hear that, listeners!" Kreeger said happily. "The shyster invokes the Fifth Amendment."

"This is bullshit!" Steve slammed his hand on the table.

"Please refrain from profanity and violence, Counselor. Janice, should I call security?"

"I'm not worried," she said. "When we were kids, I used to beat the crap out of Stevie."

"Yeah," Steve said. "When you outweighed me by thirty pounds."

"You oughta thank me. How do you think you learned to run so fast?" Janice lowered her voice as if sharing a deep secret. "I used to make him eat mud pies."

"Hold that thought, and don't touch the dial," Kreeger instructed. "We'll be back right after this news break." He pointed toward the control room and took off his earphones. "This is great radio. Solomon, perhaps you can ask Ms. Lord to join us for a while. I'd love to ask her about you."

"Why don't we talk about you?" Steve said as a news announcer droned in the background. "About you and Amanda."

"What's to say? I saved the poor girl, just as you claim to have saved your nephew."

"No, you didn't. You killed her mother to get at her. You're a freaking pedophile."

"Delusions and hysteria. I'd better make a note to add that to your report."

Just then, two uniformed officers entered the studio from the control room. Steve had a disconcerting sense of déjà vu. He'd been arrested here once before, for slugging Arnold Freskin. But these two were City of Miami, not Beach cops. And he recognized them at once. They'd shown up at Goldberg's house last night and taken statements. Rodriguez and Teele. Hispanic cop and black cop, just like on TV. Rodriguez had a thin mustache and Teele sported a mini-Afro, again like a TV cop, circa *The Mod Squad.*

"Hello, Mr. Solomon," Rodriguez said. "Is this your sister?"

"Yes! Take her away, officers. What is it this time: drug possession? Parole violation? Did she rob a bank this morning?"

"Ms. Solomon," Teele said. "Last night, were you present when your brother struck a Dr. Myron Goldberg on or about the face?"

"Yeah. Stevie slugged him right in the kisser."

"Was your brother protecting you from Dr. Goldberg at the time?"

"What do you mean?" Janice asked.

"Was Dr. Goldberg threatening you with a firearm?"

A moment of silence.

"C'mon, Janice," Steve prodded. "Tell them about the Uzi."

"Mr. Solomon, please remain quiet," Teele instructed.

"Dr. Goldberg didn't do anything," Janice said. "Stevie just hauled off and sucker-punched him."

"That's a lie!" Steve was halfway out of his chair when Rodriguez grabbed him by a shoulder and spun him around. Teele had the handcuffs on before Steve could say he wanted to make a phone call.

Kreeger punched a button and yelled at his board operator. "Cut into the news. We're going live. State *versus* Solomon. Chapter two."

SOLOMON'S LAWS

9. Q: What do you call a judge who is old, cantankerous, and flatulent?

A: "Your Honor."

Twenty-Eight

GET THEE TO A SHRINKERY

A week after being booked for slugging Myron Goldberg and released for a second time in a month on his own recognizance, Steve was driving south on Dixie Highway, Bobby riding shotgun, when the pip-squeak said, "I don't want to go to Jewey school."

"To what?" Steve had never heard the expression.

"You know. Beth Am Day School."

"Who said anything about transferring?"

"Grandpop."

"Why, that *alter kocker.*"

Ever since Herbert had gone ortho, he'd been behaving strangely. Not only was he schlepping to temple every Friday night and Saturday morning, he seemed to be celebrating a new holiday every week, either a feast or a fast. Sure, Steve knew about pigging out—without the pig—at Sukkot and starving at Yom Kippur. But there was his old man, celebrating the Fast of Esther, the banquet at Simchat Torah, eating blintzes and cheesecake on Savuot but zilch on the seventeenth of Tammuz. Maybe his old man was acting weird because his blood sugar was riding a roller coaster.

"If your grandfather wants to discover his roots, fine," Steve told Bobby. "But you're staying in public school. It's good to mix with kids of different backgrounds."

"That's what I told Grandpop. I can say 'fuck off' in five languages."

Steve pulled into the left-turn lane and waited for the light to change. Only way to cross traffic during morning rush hour was to wait for a yellow light turning red. To his right was the University of Miami and the baseball stadium where once he won a game by scoring from first on a single. Looking back—the high-fives, the cheers, the late night with a Hurricane Hottie—he wondered if that was the high point of his life.

Just examine the facts.

Victoria, the woman he loved, was stewing over their relationship. All talk of moving in together had ceased. Even staying together seemed problematical. Jeez, they hadn't had sex in an eternity.

Kreeger was pulling his chain like a puppeteer with a marionette. Taunting him with Janice and the threat of a custody fight. Nothing had changed. Every step Steve took, the bastard was one step ahead of him.

Gotta stop playing defense, start playing offense.

And Bobby? If Victoria was Steve's heart, the boy was his soul. Steve would do anything for his nephew, make any sacrifice. Just watching Bobby smile clutched at his heart. There had been damn few smiles and laughs those first months after Steve brought the boy home from the commune. Half-starved, locked up, deprived of social contact, Bobby had withdrawn into a shell. In Steve's house, he would sit cross-legged in a corner, swaying, speaking gibberish, if anything at all. Now, seeing Bobby's growth, watching in awe as his brain sizzled and snapped with electrifying speed, well, it brought tears to Steve's eyes.

So how could you betray me, Bobby? How could you sneak off to see that woman who loved crack more than she loved you?

"Because she's still my mom."

That was Bobby's defense. The night Steve clobbered Myron Goldberg, Steve took Bobby home and made him a smoothie. They talked until dawn, Bobby crying and saying he was sorry he hadn't been honest. A few weeks before, when Janice got out of prison, she had started coming around the neighborhood. At night, she'd sneak into their yard and sometimes look through Bobby's window just to catch a glimpse of him.

Sure, Steve thought. Even with her brain cells burned out by twenty years of narcotics and hallucinogens, Janice had known better than to knock on the door and give her baby brother a big hug. So she'd hung out at the park on Morningside Drive like a regular mom and one day called out to Bobby when he rode by on his bike.

"Why didn't you tell her to fuck off? In five languages."

"Because she's still my mom."

Steve couldn't understand it. And knew he couldn't fight it, either. If he forbade Bobby to see his mother, he'd be the villain. The two of them would sneak around behind his back, make a game of it. He was in a lose-lose situation.

The light blinked yellow, and Steve honked at the Beemer in front of him to *turn the hell left so we don't sit here another fifteen minutes*. The light was red when Steve followed onto Augusto Street, pulling up to the entrance of Ponce de León Middle School. A sea of urchins in shorts, T-shirts, and backpacks was surging toward the front door.

Steve reached over and squeezed Bobby's shoulder. He wouldn't kiss the boy, not when his pals might be watching.

Bobby made no move to open the door. "I don't want to go to school."

"Why not?"

"First period is P.E. Second is Study Hall. Third is Civics, and I've got permission for independent study off-campus."

"Independent study? You getting your master's degree?"

"I can go to court with you today if you want me to."

"You have anything in writing to back up this story?"

"Jeez, Uncle Steve. Don't you trust me?"

"About as far as I can throw Shaquille O'Neal. Now, what's going on?"

"You've got to go in front of some judge, right?"

"Yeah. The Honorable Alvin Elias Schwartz. So what?"

"Grandpop says a defendant should always look as sympathetic as possible. That's why serial killers bring their mothers to court."

"Yeah?"

"I can make you look more sympathetic. I'm Exhibit A in your trial stratagem."

"What kind of word is that for a twelve-year-old? 'Stratagem'?"

"Don't you always say, 'If the law doesn't work, work the law?' "

"Not like this. I won't use you as a prop."

"C'mon, Uncle Steve. If the law doesn't work, work your nephew."

* * *

Victoria paced in the corridor outside Judge Schwartz's courtroom. Morning calendar, the place overflowing with defendants, their wives, girlfriends, and mothers. Bored cops and sleazy bail bondsmen, overworked probation officers and perjurious witnesses—all the jetsam and flotsam of the criminal justice system.

It was a familiar place to Victoria, but still she felt ill at ease. This was the venue of her greatest professional embarrassment. Ray Pincher, the State Attorney, had fired her in Judge Gridley's courtroom, not twenty yards away. She could remember her face reddening, the tears welling, and opposing counsel—Steve-the-Shyster Solomon—hitting on her. An inauspicious beginning to their tumultuous relationship.

Now, hustling down the corridor were two judges—Stanford Blake and Amy Steele Donner—robes flying, chatting away. She nodded to them in the way lawyers do, being polite, but not too familiar. His Honor and Her Honor smiled back.

What were they saying? She could only imagine.

"There's Victoria Lord. She got suckered into a mistrial by Steve Solomon, ended up sleeping with him."

Riding the escalator moments before, Victoria had encountered the head of the state's Major Crimes Division. They exchanged hellos. The man asked what brought her across the bay. Expecting a murder trial, maybe. White-collar crime. Something to ring the cash register at Solomon & Lord, Attorneys-at-Law.

Not... *"Defending my partner in his second assault and battery case in a month."*

No wonder she was embarrassed. The humiliation didn't stop with Ray Pincher sacking her. Her partner and lover could be counted on for continuing acts of mortification.

Down the corridor, the elevator door opened and out walked Steve.

With Bobby!

She watched as Steve cruised toward her, slapping pals on the back, howdying prosecutors and defense lawyers alike. Smiling and laughing, a glide to his stride. He could be strolling along a sun-dappled country path on his way to pick strawberries, instead of heading to his own arraignment. He paused a moment to buttonhole Ed Shohat and Bob Josefsberg, two of the top defense lawyers in town. Just Steve's way of letting them know he wasn't in jail, and if they had any cases or clients beneath their dignity, he could use the work.

"Yo, Vic," he called out.

"Yo, yourself. Bobby, why aren't you in school?"

"This is my class project," he replied.

"Bobby's my stratagem," Steve said.

She gave him her *don't bullshit me* look.

"It's true. Bobby's going to stand by my side."

"Just let me do the talking," she said. "All you have to say is—"

"Not guilty. I know, I know."

"Not guilty, *Your Honor.*"

"Okay. You're the boss." He turned to Bobby.

"Look, kiddo, you'll sit next to me and get up when I stand to enter my plea."

"That's your stratagem?" Victoria asked.

"And our theme for the case. I was protecting Bobby that night when I inadvertently struck Myron Goldberg. I stand with Bobby, and he stands with me. We're sending a message."

"With Judge Schwartz's eyesight, I doubt he'll see either one of you."

"He can see okay. It's his hearing that's off." Steve turned to Bobby. "And if His Honor cuts loose a fifty-decibel fart, try not to laugh."

Bobby giggled. "He does that?"

"The old goat passes wind and blames it on the court reporter. So be cool." Steve turned back to Victoria. "Let's go do it. And trust me. 'Not guilty, Your Honor.' Not a word more."

* * *

Judge Schwartz, irascible, aged, and flatulent, was running through his morning calendar of motions, bail hearings, status reports, arraignments, and other procedural gimcracks of the criminal justice system.

Steve, Victoria, and Bobby took seats in the front row of the gallery. Steve spotted Ray Pincher sitting across the aisle. Next to the State Attorney sat Myron Goldberg. The periodontist was sporting a fat lip the color of an eggplant and wearing a soft neck collar for no reason Steve could figure except possible civil litigation.

"Oh, my aching neck."

Goldberg wasn't needed at the arraignment. No testimony would be taken. Why the hell was he even here?

The clerk, a young woman with dreadlocks and no apparent facial expression, called out: "State of Florida versus Stephen Solomon."

The judge peered over the tops of his trifocals as everyone made their way past the bar. "You again?"

"Guilty, Your Honor," Steve called out. "Of being Steve Solomon. *Not* guilty of the charge."

"Didn't ask for your plea."

"I know, Judge, but I promised my lawyer that's all I'd say." Steve and Bobby took their seats, leaving Victoria standing to do the real work.

"What now?" the judge demanded.

"New case, Your Honor," Pincher said. He wore a burgundy three-piece suit. Pincher's trademark miniature handcuffs clinked as he gestured, bowing slightly as if he were a maître d' welcoming diners to his overpriced restaurant. "Mr. Solomon has again committed assault and battery."

"Allegedly," Victoria broke in. "Victoria Lord for the defense, Your Honor."

"Say, aren't you that lady lawyer who got shat on by a bird down in Gridley's courtroom?"

Victoria reddened. "A talking toucan, Your Honor. Mr. Solomon fed it prune Danish."

"Used to eat poppyseed myself, but the damn seeds stick to my dentures."

"Your Honor, Mr. Solomon will enter a plea of not guilty."

"Already did," the judge said.

"In that case," Victoria continued, "the defense waives reading the information and requests trial by jury."

"Fine and dandy. The clerk will set a trial date not

to conflict with the Florida Derby. You like the ponies, missy?"

"Not particularly, Your Honor. We also move to withdraw Mr. Solomon's nolo plea in the earlier case."

"On what grounds?"

"My client was not represented by counsel when he entered the plea."

"Motion denied. Your client's a lawyer. Who'd he hit this time, Pincher?"

"Dr. Myron Goldberg, a neighbor," the State Attorney said. On cue, Goldberg rose stiffly, a pained look on his face. "Dr. Goldberg caught Mr. Solomon's nephew peeping in his daughter's window. In the ensuing confrontation, Mr. Solomon assaulted Dr. Goldberg."

"Not true, Judge." Steve leapt to his feet, and so did Bobby. "I was defending my nephew and my sister."

"Sit down!" Victoria hissed.

"I wasn't peeping!" Bobby insisted.

"First a peeper," the judge said sternly. "Then a flasher. Next thing you know, you're pulling down girls' panties and having your way with them. You know what they did to rapists in ancient Rome?"

"Crushed their balls between two rocks," Bobby said.

"The little perv knows his history, I'll grant him that."

"I'm not a perv!"

"Pipe down, son. You'll have a chance to prove that."

"The boy's not on trial," Pincher reminded the judge.

"Maybe he should be," Judge Schwartz shot back. "He's really starting to torque my tail."

At that, an unmistakable *pop-pop-pop* came from the bench, a Gatling gun of rapid-fire flatulence.

Bobby giggled and said, "Who blew the butt trumpet?"

"That's enough, you little rascal."

"Because it sounded like a bench burner," Bobby continued.

Steve put a hand on Bobby's shoulder, trying to quiet him.

"Are you trifling with me, boy? Do you know who I am?"

"Alvin Elias Schwartz," Bobby replied, scrunching his face in concentration.

"No, Bobby!" Steve ordered. "No anagrams."

"Alvin Elias Schwartz," Bobby repeated. "WAS A SNIVEL ZILCH RAT."

The judge hacked up some phlegm. "I ought to send both of you straight to clink."

"Your Honor," Victoria spoke up. "Mr. Solomon has yet to be tried, and there are no charges against his nephew."

The judge whirled around in his high-backed swivel chair. One revolution. Two revolutions. Three revolutions. The judge disappearing from sight, then reappearing, white fringes of hair above his ears blowing in the breeze. When the chair slowed to a stop, he said: "I question Solomon's mental competence. Where's that shrink's report from the other case?"

Pincher answered, "Not filed yet, Your Honor. Mr. Solomon missed his last appointment."

"If that happens again, he's going straight to jail. Do not pass Go. Do not collect two hundred shekels."

"Judge, don't send me back to that quack," Steve pleaded.

"Get thee to a shrinkery!" Judge Schwartz ordered. "What's the name of that head doctor?"

"William Kreeger," Pincher said.

"That's the one. Go see him. Both Solomon and the kid. I want to know if Solomon's a menace and the little rapscallion's a sicko."

"Your Honor doesn't have jurisdiction over the minor child," Victoria said.

"He's in my courtroom, missy. My fiefdom. It's in the Magna Carta. You can look it up."

"But Your Honor," Victoria pleaded. "Due process precludes—"

The judge rapped his gavel. *Bang!* "That's it, Ms. Lord. Both of your clients go see the shrink." Another *bang*! "Ten-minute recess. My bladder ain't what it used to be."

SOLOMON'S LAWS

10. You won't find it in Darwin, Deuteronomy, or Doonesbury, but it's an essential truth of human nature: We'll all kill to protect those we love.

Twenty-Nine

THE CON ARTIST BLUES

Carl Drake's suite at the Four Seasons was pretty much what Steve expected. Beige sofas with thick pillows in the living room, gray marble in the bath, a curved desk of blond wood in the tidy office. The windows looked across Biscayne Bay, glistening turquoise in the midday sun. Key Biscayne was a green atoll in the distance, a dozen sailboats visible on the far side of the causeway. Just what you would demand for twelve hundred bucks a night.

But who was paying for it? Before he even settled into the sofa, Steve was struck with the notion that The Queen would never get a shilling out of Carl Drake. No matter how much money Drake stole, he seemed to be the kind of guy who enjoyed spending every last cent.

Steve had filed the usual dilatory motions to slow down the mortgage foreclosure, but that could buy The Queen only so much time. Today, he intended to shake some money out of Drake. It was the first of two unpleasant tasks on his calendar, the second being a court-ordered appointment with William Kreeger, M.D.

"What'll it be, Steve?" Drake asked pleasantly, standing at the gleaming marble-topped bar. "Champagne? Cristal."

"No thanks, Carl."

"Wait. I'm good at this. I know from dinner that you drink tequila after dark. Now, as for the daytime . . ." Drake fingered a bottle of single-malt Scotch, then eyed a bottle of Maker's Mark. "I'm betting you're a bourbon man."

"Hemlock, if you have it. Drano on the rocks if you don't."

"Been a rough week, has it?" Laying on a bit of a British accent. Stopping just short of saying "old chap."

"Carl, this is uncomfortable for me," Steve said.

Drake poured himself a Scotch over ice, walked to a facing sofa and perched on the arm. He wore linen slacks the color of melted butter and a shimmering blue shirt, the fabric so soft, it invited petting. "Did Irene ask you to come?"

"She ordered me not to."

"Do you frequently disregard your clients' instructions?"

"All the time. I figure if they were so smart, they wouldn't need my counsel."

Drake gave him a pleasant smile. It seemed to be a well-practiced gesture from a well-mannered, well-accented smoothie.

Steve took a breath and surveyed the room. A portrait of Sir Francis Drake sat on an easel. A map of the seven seas, circa 1550, was pinned to a display board. A polyurethane block embedded with gold coins—Spanish doubloons, Steve supposed—sat on the desk, a seductive tease for any possible heirs of the sixteenth-century privateer. A calfskin briefcase bulged with papers.

Steve turned back to Drake and said: "What do you have in the pockets of those fancy pants you're wearing?"

"I beg your pardon?"

"Wallet? Keys? Take them out."

"Are you robbing me?"

"When I hang you off your balcony by your ankles, I don't want you to lose anything."

Drake laughed, the Scotch jiggling in his glass, a golden whirlpool. "I guess that's called a 'shakedown,' isn't it? But from what I hear, you can't afford any more dates in Criminal Court."

"You're gonna give Irene back her money."

"Oh, would that I could. The money's already gone to pay expenses in the administration of the estate."

"Like room service at the Four Seasons?"

"As a matter of fact, my travel expenses are included. But the payoff to Irene will far exceed—"

"At dinner, you said there were no fees."

"I'm afraid I wasn't totally forthcoming. But I was loath to discuss business on Irene's birthday, and my little deception seemed a good way to short-circuit the conversation."

"You're good, Drake. You're what my father would call 'slick as owl shit.' "

Drake hoisted his glass. "A toast to your father, then."

"Did you know the bank foreclosed on Irene's condo?"

Drake's suntanned face froze momentarily. "The hell you say."

"She's too embarrassed to tell you. Just like you're

too embarrassed to tell her you're a con man. There's no estate of Sir Francis Drake. You're just pulling a scam. I'm guessing that ritzy briefcase of yours holds a first-class ticket to wherever scumbags go when the Grand Jury starts issuing subpoenas."

Drake stood, walked to the bar, and poured himself another Scotch. "Foreclosure? I don't understand it. Irene led me to believe she had millions."

"It's a role she plays."

Drake gave a little rueful laugh. "Seems I'm the one who's been conned."

"One difference, Drake. Irene didn't steal your money."

"I never intended to hurt her. She's very special to me."

"I'll bet you say that to all the widows."

"This is different." He took a long pull on his drink. His crisp British accent seemed to have been replaced by flatter tones—Chicago, maybe—and his shoulders slumped. Losing some of his polish, Drake seemed uncomfortable and out of place, like Vice President Cheney in a Speedo.

Drake nodded toward the briefcase. "The plane ticket's there, all right, Solomon. Rio de Janeiro. I'm usually gone by now. I stayed only because of Irene. The damn truth is, I'm in love with her."

"Great. Invite me to the wedding. After you pay her back."

"I wish I could. Truly. But the money's gone."

Steve considered himself a human polygraph machine. Looking at Carl Drake at that moment, the man's mask slipping away, his brow furrowing, his voice choked with regret, the machine said the con artist was telling the truth. For some reason, that only made Steve angrier. "Dammit, Drake. You say you love her, but you stole the roof from over her head."

"Are you going to hang me off the balcony, then?"

"I would, but I sprained my wrist hitting a guy. I'd probably drop you."

"Then what shall we do?"

"Let's have that drink," Steve said. "Bourbon will be just fine."

* * *

Cabanas—tents of flowing white cotton—blossomed like sails in the breeze. At poolside, Steve and Drake sat in the shade of a sabal palm and sipped their drinks, a soft breeze scented with suntan oil wafting over them.

"You could still go to Rio," Steve said. "There's nothing I could do to stop you."

"Too depressing," Drake said. "That's where Charles Ponzi went."

"The Ponzi pyramid scheme?"

"That's him. Fled to Italy, then Rio. Became a smuggler."

"Must be your hero. Like me following Rickey Henderson. A's to Yankees to Padres to Mets. Stealing bases wherever he went."

"Charles Ponzi died in the charity ward of a Brazilian hospital." There was a touch of sadness in Drake's voice. "I don't want to end like that."

Steve took a second to admire two sun-worshipping young women in bikinis. "Rickey Henderson ended up back in the minors."

"The shame is, I'm quite good at my work," Drake told him. "When I find a mark, I always look for the weakness that lets me pry loose the money."

"Greed, I would think."

"Sure, with the traditional cons. But I was always drawn to people who yearned to be something larger than themselves. You tell people they're descended from Sir Francis Drake, all their defenses evaporate. They dream that their current lives were destined to be greater or more meaningful. Then I turn a seemingly harmless conceit into a way to relieve them of their money."

"You don't sound particularly sorry about being a thief."

Drake shrugged. "We are who we are."

Echoing Irene's words. An incontrovertible fact of human nature.

"So what happened to the money, Drake?"

"I paid off debts. Gambling losses. A real estate investment trust that went belly-up. Even a gold mine that tapped out. I'm broke."

"Why not stay until you rip off enough people to get ahead?"

Drake sniffed at the suggestion. "That's what an amateur would do. A professional knows that it's better to bail out a month early than a day late. I had my usual story ready. Complications with the estate. Must fly to London. That buys a few weeks, and by then, I'm setting up shop in South America."

"And the reason you're not on the beach at Impanema is that you fell in love?"

Drake tipped his glass forward, the ice cubes clinking, the drinker's signal of affirmation. "I wanted to tell Irene everything. Beg for forgiveness. Promise to go straight so she and I could start a life together."

"Where? In the condo that's being foreclosed?"

"As I have no residence of my own, that was a distinct possibility." Drake emitted a laugh that was more of a sigh. "It's turning out rather like an O. Henry story, isn't it?"

"I wouldn't know. Henry Aaron, I might know."

"Oh, I think you understand me quite well. You're a good deal smarter than you let on. And you're an excellent judge of character."

"When I was a kid, I'd go to my father's courtroom and watch trials. For a while, I'd close my eyes and just listen to witnesses. Then I'd cover my ears and just watch. I'd put everything I'd seen and heard together. It was a game I played to figure out who was lying."

"It serves you well to this day. You saw through me in an instant."

"Wasn't that hard. I'm just surprised Irene came to me for help. I'm not on the list of her five hundred favorite people."

"Oh, you're wrong about that. Irene likes you. Worries about you because of that Dr. Bill character. She thinks you're playing with fire there."

That stopped Steve. "What does she know about that?"

"What you say to Victoria she repeats to Irene, who then tells me."

Of course. Mothers and daughters.

"Jeez, next you'll be telling me the last time we had sex."

"Two weeks, Tuesday. Right after *Sports Center*."

"During. The hockey highlights gave us a window."

"I've listened to Dr. Bill on the radio," Drake said. "All that psychobabble to sell worthless books and tapes."

"Do you know about his theory of evolutionary

psychology? We're all hardwired for murder. We're programmed by millions of years of evolution that favors survival of those who slaughter their enemies."

"And all this time, I thought we were just programmed for larceny."

"It's a pretty simple theory. Our genes carry the same murderous impulses as Paleolithic man."

"Interesting," Drake said. "If our DNA instructs us to kill, why fight it? The ideal rationalization for murder."

They each sipped their drinks, mulling it over. "Kreeger says I'm just as much a killer as he is," Steve said, after a moment. "For a while, I thought he was planting that seed in my brain, trying to set me up to kill my sister."

"And now?"

"Some days, he says we're both killers. And some days, we're both heroes. Kreeger claims he rescued a girl the way I rescued my nephew. But what Kreeger really did was sick and twisted."

"It sounds like a game to him. Putting you through the wringer like that."

"Whenever the bastard mentions Bobby's name, a chill goes up my spine."

"He's found your weakness, then."

"My nephew?"

"Your *love* for him. If Kreeger wanted to hurt you, he'd go after the child. Isn't that apparent?"

Too much so, Steve thought.

The way to cripple me, the way to inflict pain without end, would be to hurt Bobby.

What kind of man would do such a thing? Bill Kreeger would. The man who sees himself as the product of millions of years of evolution.

But then, so am I.

Kreeger was wrong about most things, but he was right about something. It's an essential truth of human nature that to protect those we love, every one of us will kill.

Thirty

OF NYMPHS AND NUDNIKS

With Bobby riding shotgun and Jimmy Buffet singing about "Changes in Latitudes, Changes in Attitudes," Steve drove north on Alhambra in the Gables. The Biltmore golf course peeked out from between the sprawling Mediterranean and Colonial homes. They crossed the bridge over the waterway at Taragona and slowed near at the intersection of Salvatierra Drive.

Kreeger's place was a block away, and Steve was edgy. All his plans had been shot to hell. First, he had tried to simply warn off Kreeger. A tough-guy routine. *"If you come after me, I'll land on you like a ton of concrete."* Yeah, real impressive. Then he'd tried to spook Kreeger with tales of searching for—and finding—De la Fuente. But with the boat captain dead, Kreeger had nothing to fear. Trying to enlist Amanda as an accomplice hadn't worked, either. She'd been lying in wait for Steve. Naked and flirtatious. Clearly put up to it by Kreeger. Maybe to sabotage his relationship with Victoria. Who knew? The bastard was after him on multiple fronts.

And today's plan? A speck of an idea, totally lacking in sophistication.

Illegal, yes. Dangerous, yes. But sophisticated, no.

Judge Schwartz had ordered him to bring Bobby to Kreeger for evaluation. As long as they had to be in Kreeger's house, why not snoop around? Why not burgle the place and see what he could find?

"We're early," Bobby said. "Twenty-one minutes and thirty-four seconds early."

Steve pulled up to the curb and stopped. "I want you to wait in the car. I have something to do."

"What?"

"Can't tell you. And when we see Kreeger, don't mention our showing up early, okay?"

Bobby took off his glasses and cleaned them on the front of his Florida Marlins jersey, his lips pursed. His Solomon & Lord baseball cap was turned around backwards. "Are you gonna get in trouble, Uncle Steve?"

"Why would you say that?"

"Because you're wearing a tool belt and you're not a carpenter."

"It's a jogger's fanny pack, not a tool belt."

"Then why'd you put those lock picks and master keys in it?"

"You ask a lot of questions, squirt."

"Florida Statute eight-ten-point-zero-six," Bobby said. "It's a crime to possess burglary tools with intent to trespass or steal."

That damn echolalia, Steve thought. Bobby had been hanging around the office the day Steve signed up Omar Ortega, a kid charged with possessing a metal ruler suitable for breaking into parking meters. Ortega professed his innocence, even while paying his retainer in quarters and dimes.

"We're invited into Kreeger's house, right, Bobby?"

"Yeah, the judge says we gotta go."

"So I'm not trespassing. I'm just arriving early. If there are any locked doors or cabinets, I might just want to poke around a bit."

"Mom says if you go to jail, I can come live with her."

"Very hospitable of her."

"She said even if you don't go to jail, she's gonna get a judge to give her custody."

"How do you feel about that, kiddo?"

"I know she treated me really bad, but she was so messed up then, I don't think she could help it. I don't hate her or anything, and she kind of needs me because she's all alone. I mean, she doesn't even have any friends."

They sat in silence a moment and Steve felt his stomach knot with fear. In a few moments, he'd be sneaking through Kreeger's house like a cat burglar, but the only thing frightening him was that his nephew seemed ready to desert him. "What are you saying, Bobby? You want to live with your mom because you feel sorry for her?"

Tears formed in the boy's eyes "I know you hate her because of what she did to me."

"I don't hate her. She's still my sister, so somewhere deep inside, I suppose I still have feelings for her."

"And she's still my mom."

That again.

There was a river of sweetness that ran through Bobby that Steve didn't share. Truth be told, those *feelings* he claimed to still have for his sister were mostly homicidal in nature.

"I just want to do what's best for you," Steve said, fighting the urge to yell: *"If I hadn't taken you away from her, you'd be dead by now!"*

"I want the two of you to stop fighting."

"Okay. What else?"

"I want to see my mom, but I want to live with you, Uncle Steve. You and me, we're tight, right?"

Steve felt his muscles unclench. "Okay, I'll see what I can work out with Janice. I'd rather know where you are than have you sneaking out to see her. But I want some proof she's cleaned up her act. Deal?"

"Deal." Bobby reached over and they pounded knuckles.

Steve opened his door and had one foot out of it when Bobby added, "Please be careful, Uncle Steve. If you get in trouble, what will happen to me?"

* * *

A Lexus SUV sat in Kreeger's driveway. Steve figured the owner was a patient, midway through a head-shrinking session. Steve walked along the pink flagstone path that followed the hibiscus hedge toward the backyard. For all he knew, Amanda was sunning herself again, all toasty warm and naked in the midday sun. But before rounding the corner of the house, which would have brought him in line of sight from Kreeger's office window, Steve ducked into the vestibule. The side door to the kitchen was open, and he walked in.

The kitchen could use updating, but it was clean and airy. A pot of coffee sat in its place, still warm.

"Just came in looking for a cup of java, Doc."

Planning his alibi.

An interior door led to a corridor that opened into a living room. Traditional furniture, windows shaded with Bahamas shutters, a seldom-used fireplace. Above the fireplace, a painting. An idealized portrait of Kreeger at the helm of his big boat, *Psycho Therapy*. The shrink appeared a bit taller and thinner. Tanned and fit, one hand on the wheel, one on the throttles. A man in control.

Steve always thought portraits should be reserved for dead ancestors. Wasn't it an act of unbridled ego to commission a painting of yourself? Maybe Kreeger's boat should be renamed *Narcissist*.

Steve took a set of stairs to the second floor, stepping lightly.

Now, just what the hell are you looking for, anyway?

He didn't know. He didn't expect to find a framed document on the wall: *"I killed Jim Beshears, Nancy Lamm, and Oscar De la Fuente. Sincerely, Dr. Bill."*

But you never knew. A diary. An unfinished memoir. Steve once defended a case where his client wrote a to-do list reminding himself to buy a mask and listing the address of the bank he intended to rob.

Steve felt he needed to do something. Find something. Not just wait for Kreeger to make another move.

At the top of the stairs, a corridor. A door was open at the end, and he entered the room.

Master bedroom.

King-size bed. A four-poster. Lightweight duvet, silvery color.

He surveyed the room, trying to pick up vibes from the guy who lived here. In the corner, on a pedestal, a bronze sculpture, the torso of a boy. On the walls, Caribbean art. Brightly colored paintings of partially clothed islanders working on boats and tending fields. Young girls carrying produce.

On a credenza, a man's jewelry box. Steve opened it

without need of master key or pickaxe. Two men's watches, expensive. Several pairs of cuff links. Gold, onyx, jade. Steve ran a finger across the felt lining of the box. Nothing hidden underneath.

Somewhere in the house, pipes rumbled. Steve checked his watch. Another ten minutes before he would get Bobby from the car.

He had been hoping for a computer. Who knew what would be buried in there? Criminals who would never leave fingerprints at a crime scene drop trails of bread crumbs in the "history" window of their laptops. A guy who tried to kill his wife by dropping a roaring hair dryer into her bathtub was found to have electrocution websites plastered all over his hard drive.

But no computer in Kreeger's bedroom. Steve had to look for clues the old-fashioned way. He opened a drawer in the bedside table. A holstered nine-millimeter Glock. Okay, pretty normal for South Florida. In the lower drawer, an old photo album. Yellowing pictures from college and med school. Steve thumbed through the plasticized pages.

A *bang*ing of pipes again from inside the walls.

He stopped at a page of snapshots. A handwritten date on the page, seven years ago. Photos of a woman, late thirties, and a girl who looked to be roughly Bobby's age. On the beach, in swimsuits, smiling at the camera, squinting into the sun. The photographer's shadow crept across the sand toward them. The woman was Nancy Lamm. Steve had seen enough photos during the murder trial to recognize her immediately. The girl was Amanda—Mary Amanda, in those days. Her hips hadn't rounded out, and her bustline was practically invisible, but the features were hers.

Steve sat down on the edge of the bed and turned

the page. Six more photos. No Nancy this time. But there was Amanda. On Kreeger's pool deck.

Naked.

Just as naked as Steve had seen her two weeks ago. But these photos were taken when she was perched on the fence between girlhood and womanhood. A variety of poses, a naked nymph stretching this way and that, arching her back in one, jutting out a bony hip in another, throwing her shoulders back, turning sideways to reveal breasts that were barely buds, then facing the camera head-on, legs spread, unashamedly showing a small tuft of hair, strawberry blond in the sun. Smiling goofily in one shot, seemingly innocent. Pouting seductively in another, a child's parody of pornography. A close-up, just a head shot, showed something else. A glassy-eyed stare.

Stoned. She was high on something.

Twelve or thirteen. Naked and stoned. There was something both sad and horrifying about it. As for Kreeger, could there be any doubt? He was both a killer and a pedophile. For a moment, Steve imagined himself as Amanda's father. What would he have done? Beaten Kreeger with a baseball bat. For starters. Crushed every bone in his body, starting with the ankles, working his way up to his demented skull.

Yeah, Kreeger, we're all capable of killing. And maybe we're all capable of justifying it, too.

One of the photos jogged something in Steve's mind, but what was it? He studied the shot. Amanda, her arms thrown back and shoulders leaning forward, like a swimmer, on the blocks at the start of a race.

The bronze statue in the corner of the bedroom.

It wasn't a boy at all. It was Amanda, cast in bronze, her thin torso boylike. Kreeger had chosen to freeze his memory of her at her prepubescent stage. And those paintings on the walls. The Caribbean islanders. Those young girls carrying the produce. Naked from the waist up.

Getting creepy in here.

He heard a sound, and an interior door opened. The bathroom.

Out walked Amanda, her hair wringing wet, a white towel wrapped around her body. Her startled look melted instantly into a playful smile. "Good morning, sir. You must be the handyman."

He had expected a scream. Not role-playing.

"My mommy and daddy aren't home," she continued in a little-girl voice. "But you can fix anything you want."

Was the childlike tone the way she spoke to Kreeger? Then and now. In this very room, on this very bed. Creepy had just become downright base and vile.

"Nothing here I could fix." Steve dropped the album back in the drawer. "Too big a job."

"Don't you like my pictures?" She giggled. When he didn't answer, she unwrapped the towel and dropped it to the floor. "Which do you like better, the old me or the new me?"

Steve hadn't moved from the corner of the bed. She stepped closer, spreading her legs, pressing her inner thighs against his knees, pinning him in place. Her skin was burnished red from the hot shower, her breasts at eye level, nipples taut. If she moved any closer, he could suffer a detached retina.

"Uncle Bill likes the old me better." Her tone one of mock sadness. "When I was thirteen, I could lock my ankles behind my head."

"You should have tried out for the Olympics."

"Uncle Bill says my boobs are too big now, but I mean, I'm not exactly a cow, right?" She moved her shoulders from side to side, her breasts barely jiggling just inches from his nose.

"Your breasts are fine, Amanda."

"Uncle Bill likes them small. Little tulips, he calls them." She plopped into his lap, her legs spread, facing him, straddling his thighs. "You sure you like mine?"

"What's not to like?" Sounding like his father. Feeling like a schmuck, a real nudnik.

"So why don't you touch them?" A whiny child's voice. "You can, you know. You can kiss my boobies and do anything you want."

He didn't move.

She turned sideways so that one breast slid across his cheek, smooth and warm against his skin. She made a humming sound and said, "You need a shave, but it feels good."

"You're a bad girl."

"So spank me." She slid sideways across his lap and flipped over, arching her back so that her bottom was hoisted just above his knees. He saw the jellyfish tattoo again, tentacles streaming down each buttock.

"If I spank you, will you be good?"

"I'll be so-o-o good." Another girlish giggle. "Unless you want me to be so-o-o bad."

He hesitated, weighing the options.

"What are you waiting for, Uncle Steve?"

Uncle Steve.

The name sounded repulsive on her lips.

He drew back his arm and slapped her butt as hard as he could with an open palm. A one-handed *smack* as loud as a marlin hitting the water.

"Ow! What the fuck!" She leapt off him, yelping,

all traces of jailbait vanished from her voice. "You bastard! That hurt like hell!"

"Sorry, Amanda, but I'm not your Uncle Steve." He got to his feet and started for the door.

"I'm gonna tell Uncle Bill what you did."

"What'd I do?"

"Raped me."

"Right. Gave you a candy bar and had my way with you."

"He'll believe me. And then you know what he'll do?"

"Hit me on the head and dump me into the Jacuzzi? Like he did to your mother."

A laugh came from her mouth, but her eyes were hard, narrow slits. "Is that what you think happened?"

"The jury called it manslaughter. But you and I know better, don't we, Amanda? We both know Bill killed your mother so he could be with you."

"That's crazy." Another laugh, sharp as barbed wire. "You've got everything backwards."

Steve longed to ask the question: *So what happened, Amanda? What happened the night your mother drowned?* But sometimes the best cross-examination is silence—the best question, the one unasked. Leave a moment of dead calm, and the witness might just fill in the gap.

"Uncle Bill didn't kill my mom, silly," Amanda Lamm said. "I did!"

* * *

Jogging toward the car, Steve played back what Amanda had told him. She and her mother were spending the weekend at Kreeger's house. Her mother found her on the pool patio, smoking some weed. They had a blistering argument, Mom screaming she'd lose custody if Amanda didn't clean up her act, the girl screaming back that she gave Bill more pleasure than Mom did, and the only reason he kept the old lady around was to be close to Amanda. Her mother slapped her. Amanda picked up a skimmer pole—the "pool thingie," she called it—and hit back. Somehow, her mother ended up in the hot tub and drowned. Later that night, after the paramedics had carted Mom away, with the police investigating, good old Uncle Bill tucked Amanda into bed with warm milk, a handful of pills, and the promise that he would cover for her.

But that's not what really happened. Amanda was lying.

No. Lying is the wrong word, Steve thought. Amanda could pass a polygraph exam because she believed her own story.

But Steve felt sure she hadn't killed her mother: Kreeger simply convinced her that she had. How hard could it have been for him? Amanda was a thirteen-year-old with a drug problem. Her parents were going through a horrific divorce. An older man had started paying attention to her. A devious and manipulative man who preyed on her insecurities and took her to his bed.

Steve tried to picture the end of that horrific night, Kreeger leaning over Amanda's bed. What did he whisper to her? How did he shape her memories?

"I took care of everything, Amanda. Don't worry."

"What happened, Uncle Bill?"

"I told them your mother slipped and hit her head. It'll be all right."

"What will?"

"You never intended to hit her."

"I hit my mother?"

That was the only version of events that made sense to Steve. Nancy Lamm, who had her own addiction problems, discovered Kreeger was drugging her daughter and having sex with her. Nancy argued with Kreeger, threatening to blow the whistle on him. Kreeger killed Nancy, then convinced Amanda that she'd done it.

But there was no way to prove it.

Now Steve slowed to a walk. The morning air was heavy with humidity. The golf course was quiet. Not even a "fore." Steve approached his Mustang, parked in the shade of a banyan tree. No one inside.

Where's Bobby!

Had he wandered off? He could have sneaked over to the golf course to watch duffers flail away in the scrubby roughs.

Janice! Where the hell's my worthless sister? She could have followed us here. She could have waited, and—

No. No need to do that. All she had to do was call, and the little stinker would sneak out and get ice cream with her.

Kreeger!

Steve whirled and ran back toward the house.

FIRE OF MY LOINS

Laughter was coming from the ground-floor office. Bobby's laugh. Childlike and innocent, a bird's song on a summer breeze. Steve threw the door open. Kreeger was behind his desk, Bobby sitting cross-legged on a leather chair.

"Hey, Uncle Steve. We started without you."

"Come in, Solomon." Kreeger's smile seemed sincere, as sincere as a wolf smiling at a lamb.

"What the hell's going on?"

"Your nephew is regaling me with his wizardry powers. Shall we try another one, Robert?"

"Go for it, Doc."

"How about my name? 'William Kreeger.' "

"Easy, 'cause it's got so many vowels, and I can make four words." The kid thought a second, then boomed: "WIRE ME RAGE KILL."

"Utterly delightful." Kreeger turned to Steve. "Robert was just telling me about the lovely Maria and the unfortunate incident that led to his coming here."

"She's a fox," Bobby said.

"Indeed, she is." Kreeger picked a wallet-size photo from his desk. "Lovely, isn't she, Solomon?"

"Where'd you get that?" It was a shot of Maria Munoz-Goldberg preening for the camera. Shorts and a sleeveless T-shirt that stopped north of her navel. Her back was arched in a way that showed off her small butt. Except for the clothing, she could have been Amanda, posing for Kreeger seven years earlier.

"I gave it to Dr. Bill," Bobby said. "He's giving me advice on bagging Maria."

"Great. I'll come visit you in Youth Hall."

"Nothing bad or anything. The doc says to just be myself. Don't try to be cool or imitate the guys on the football team, because it won't work. We all have to be ourselves, because if we fake it, smart people see right through it, anyway."

"That's good advice," Steve admitted, leveling his gaze at Kreeger. "Sooner or later, the phonies get caught. And then all their lies, all their deeds come back to haunt them."

"How true," Kreeger said. "Now, Robert, what were we talking about when your uncle walked in?"

"You asked if I thought Maria was a little prosti-tot."

"What!" Steve was halfway out of his chair. "What kind of question is that for a twelve-year-old?"

"Oh, come now, Steve," Kreeger crooned. "You've seen those nubile little cock teasers around the Grove, haven't you?"

"Hey. I don't talk that way in front of Bobby."

"Obviously, you haven't read my essay on verbal honesty. Now, Robert, does Maria have any piercings?"

"A shiny thing in her navel," Bobby answered.

"And I take it she wears clothing that reveals her bare abdomen?"

"Sure.

"As I thought." Kreeger beamed. "A little prostitot."

"That's ridiculous," Steve said.

"We'll see. Robert, have you ever seen Maria's breasts?"

"Not unless you count looking through the window in the dark."

"Well, if you don't try something, she'll think you're gay."

"That's nuts!" Steve thundered. "Bobby, don't listen to him."

"I'm not gay," Bobby said.

Kreeger smiled. "I know that, Robert. But does Maria?"

"Hope so."

"Sounds to me like she really wants you to do her."

Steve leapt to his feet. "That's it. We're out of here."

"In that case, Robert will be detained at Youth Hall, pending mandatory testing."

Steve sank back into his chair.

"Maria never said anything about wanting to do it," Bobby said.

"She won't," Kreeger said confidently. "See, Robert, man is the hunter. For millions of years, man killed the game and took the female of his choice. The female always yields to the strong man. When she says no, she means maybe. When she says maybe, she means yes."

"Wrong!" Steve turned to Bobby. "No means no. Maybe means no. Yes *still* means no because you're too young."

"Bobby, why don't you let your uncle and me talk

for a bit?" Kreeger suggested. "There's a bowl of fruit in the kitchen. And a box of chocolate chip cookies on the counter."

"Awesome. I'll bounce."

Bobby unspooled his legs and headed out.

After the office door closed, Steve got to his feet and leaned over Kreeger's desk. "You can tell the judge anything you want, but I'm not going to let you poison Bobby's mind."

"Relax, Solomon. I'm just testing the boy. I'm worried how Robert might react if Maria rejects him."

"What are you talking about?"

"The way Robert handles stress." Kreeger scribbled a note on a pad. "I'm quite concerned that the boy could become violent with her."

"What the hell are you writing down there?"

"Do you remember that girl who went missing down in the Redlands a few months ago? A boy in the neighborhood had a developmental problem similar to Robert's. The girl's body was never found, and the police lacked evidence, but I feel quite certain the boy was involved."

"Bobby's not violent. In case you forgot, you're the homicidal one, Kreeger."

"So you keep saying." Kreeger rested his hand on the desk, on Maria's photo. "Do you think Robert would mind if I kept this?"

"Yeah." Steve walked toward the window. "And so would I."

Kreeger slipped on a pair of reading glasses and studied the photo. Five seconds. Ten seconds. Way too long. Finally, he said: "Juicy one, isn't she?"

"Sick, Kreeger. Sick and twisted."

Kreeger closed his eyes and murmured: " 'Lolita,

light of my life, fire of my loins. My sin, my soul. Lo-lee-ta.' "

Quoting Nabokov's famous opening lines, admitting his own predilection for pubescent girls. Almost as if he were the patient and Steve the psychiatrist. Did he want help?

"You need to talk about it, is that it?" Steve said, coming back to the desk. "All these years, you've carried this around. Maybe you needed to talk about it when I defended you. Maybe I missed the signs."

Kreeger chanted, as if praying: "Lo-lee-ta. A-man-da. Ma-ri-a." Then he laughed, the cackling laugh of a rooster. "You think Robert's popped Maria's cherry yet?"

Steve didn't even try to hide his disgust. "You don't want help. You just want to wallow in the filth."

"Or have you beat him to it, Solomon? Bird-dogging your nephew's little hoochie?"

"They should send your sick ass to Raiford. You killed Nancy Lamm so you could be with her daughter."

"You know better than that." Kreeger's smile was as sharp as a knife blade. "Or don't you believe a naked woman? Amanda killed her mother, and I took the fall for her. Just as you would have done."

"What does that mean?"

"Let's say that young Robert got rough with Maria and the poor girl died."

"What sick fantasies are you working on now?"

"Just a hypothetical question, Solomon. If Robert killed Maria, wouldn't you do anything to keep him out of prison? Wouldn't you even take the rap for him?"

"That's not what happened with Nancy Lamm. That's just the story you sold a thirteen-year-old girl to keep her in your bed. What drugs did you have her on when you convinced her she killed her mother?"

"Now that I think about it," Kreeger mused, "there is one big difference between the two of us. I admit who I am, and you pretend to be someone completely different than who you are."

* * *

Back in the car, Bobby knew he was in for a goofy lecture. Uncle Steve seemed petrified that any day Bobby would be knocking boots with Maria and she'd get pregnant, which was weird, because so far he had kissed her exactly three times, including once when he missed and ended up with her earlobe in his mouth.

"You know I'd never steer you wrong?" Steve said, before they'd driven a block.

" 'Course I do."

"So you'll listen to me and not that freak Kreeger?"

"Yep."

"You remember what I told you about girls and sex?"

"Have I ever forgotten anything, Uncle Steve?"

"So say it."

"C'mon, it's so dorky."

"Say it, kiddo."

No way around it, Bobby thought, firing out the words. "It shows maturity to keep your purity."

"Attaboy."

"Did you, Uncle Steve? Keep your purity?"

"None of your business."

"That's what I thought."

The "purity" line was so unlike his uncle, Bobby figured he got it from one of those books piled up in the living room.

Raising the Adolescent Boy. Problems with Puberty.
Teenagers: An Owner's Manual.

As if I'm a puppy.

Uncle Steve always seemed scared something bad
would happen to him.

As if I'm breakable.

Probably because of Mom and the dog shed and a
bunch of stuff he didn't even remember.

"Be home before dark."

"Don't put that can of beans in the microwave."

"If your mother calls, I want to know about it."

Sometimes, Bobby wanted to shout: *"I'm not a
baby, Uncle Steve."*

Just now, Dr. Bill treated him like a man. Talking
about booty like that. Not trying to game him with
"purity" and "maturity."

Of course, Uncle Steve hated the guy. Which was
weird, because Uncle Steve fessed up that he was the
one who cheated back in the murder trial. Driving
over here today, he said the doc was dangerous. But he
said the same thing about Mom, and Bobby didn't see
that at all. Uncle Steve was just so mixed up about all
of this. So Bobby decided to keep some secrets. He
wouldn't tell Uncle Steve all the things Dr. Bill said.
Especially the last thing, right before Uncle Steve came
into the room.

*"Be a man, Robert. Take what you want. Maria
will love it. Trust me. I know."*

SOLOMON'S LAWS

11. I won't lie to a lawyer's face or stab him in the back, but if I have the chance, I'll look him in the eye and kick him in the *cojones*.

Thirty-Two

DEFROSTING THE
FROZEN CHOSEN

"You spanked a naked woman?" Victoria couldn't believe this was happening again.

"Not in the way you mean," Steve replied. "It wasn't a *Story of O* deal."

"She rubbed her breasts in your face?"

"Technically, only one breast."

"And you did absolutely nothing to invite the attention?"

"Not a thing, Counselor."

"Your mere presence provokes women to fling off their bath towels and squash their breasts in your face?"

"One woman, one breast," he specified, as if a court reporter were taking it all down.

They were in Steve's Mustang, the radio tuned to the sports talk station. Steve turned up the volume, intending to cut off her questioning, she figured. Victoria listened a moment as a caller complained in grave tones that the University of Miami's touted new wide receiver might, in fact, run the forty-yard dash a tenth of a second too slowly.

She punched a button, turning off the radio. "You were crazy to sneak around in Kreeger's bedroom."

"I was hunting for evidence and I found it."

"You mean the naked pictures? Or the naked woman?"

"I'm gonna nail Kreeger for sexual battery. Amanda was a minor. Extended statute of limitations, relaxed rules of evidence. I can get him, Vic!"

"And how will you persuade her to cooperate? Shower with her next time?"

"All I have to do is convince her that she didn't kill her mother."

"That's all?"

"And that Kreeger's not protecting her. She's protecting him."

"And how exactly will you do this?"

"I'm working on it."

He cut across two lanes and headed up Brickell Avenue, instead of taking I-95 to the Miami Beach fly-over.

"Where are we going?" Victoria asked.

"I've got a settlement conference. You can take the car."

"What settlement conference? There's nothing on the calendar."

"Sachs versus Biscayne Supermarkets. The butt-sticking case."

"They're willing to settle, even with an intervening tortfeasor?"

"No one says 'intervening tortfeasor' as sexily as you. In fact, no one else says it at all."

Something wasn't ringing true, she thought as they drove through the canyon of high-rises, home to

Miami's cliff-dwelling lawyers and bankers. "So what's the offer?"

"Nothing yet. But I'll have *mucho dinero* by noon."

So unlike Biscayne Supermarkets, Victoria thought. They fought every slip and fall, no matter how long the banana peel had been rotting on the floor. And this case had even trickier liability problems. Harry Sachs, one of Steve's "repeat customers," as Cece called him, had used the supermarket's rest room and ended up stuck to the toilet seat, which had been coated with Krazy Glue by a prankster. Paramedics used a blow-torch to melt the glue, and the seat peeled off, along with a semicircle of Sachs' butt skin.

"I'm surprised you're getting any offer."

"You know how persuasive I am, Vic. Rolly Ogletree will write me a check before lunch."

Funny, Victoria thought. She'd seen Rolly at motion calendar last week and he'd talked about a fishing trip he had planned for this week. Costa Rica. But she kept quiet. Why would Steve lie about something like that?

He pulled the car to a stop in front of the State Trust Building, a high-rise at Calle Ocho and Brickell. "Wish me luck." He leaned over and kissed her. As he opened the car door, ready to hop out, she said: "Where's your file?"

"You know me, Vic. I don't need no stinking files."

"Uh-huh."

"I keep everything right here," he said, pointing to his head.

He was lying about the Sachs case, she decided. Lying about a conference with Rolly Ogletree. For someone who twisted the truth so often, he wasn't very good at it.

"Good luck, Steve."

Victoria came around to the driver's side, taking her time, watching Steve bound up the steps of the State Trust Building. Sure, that was where Ogletree & Castillo, P.A., maintained its office, defending an array of tight-fisted insurance companies. But something was wrong. She pulled out into traffic heading toward the bridge that would take her downtown, and then across the MacArthur Causeway to Miami Beach. But on impulse, she hung a right onto Brickell Key Drive and parked against the curb.

Okay, Victoria, what are you doing? Surveillance on your boyfriend?

It seemed ridiculous. But with Steve interrogating a naked woman—twice—then his ham-fisted lie just now, what was he up to? Then she saw him in the rear-view mirror. Hurrying across Brickell, crossing to the west side of the street.

Superquick settlement conference, partner.

She watched as he turned north, heading toward the bridge. When he disappeared from sight, she got out of the car and doubled-timed it back to the intersection, a task not so simple in her velvet-toed pumps with the two-inch heels. She stayed on the east side of the street, keeping Steve in sight, staying half a block behind him. It only took a minute. Steve crossed the intersection at Seventh Street, and then ducked into the archway of one of the oldest buildings on Brickell.

The First Presbyterian Church.

Well, at least there wouldn't be a rendevous with a naked woman. But what was he doing there? Steve never even attended synagogue. Why the old church? She jaywalked, dodging traffic, and approached the sturdy building, a four-story Mediterranean Revival structure of stucco and keystone with a copper roof.

She entered through one of the archways, pausing before opening the heavy door to the sanctuary.

What if Steve sees me? How do I explain what I'm doing here? But then, what's he doing here?

She took a breath and walked inside, entering the cool darkness of the vestibule. The place smelled of old wood and wet stones. She took cautious steps, careful to make no sound. The light, a golden hue, filtered into the sanctuary through stained-glass windows. Simple oak pews, walls of bare plaster, a ceiling of acoustical tiles. A spare, clean Protestant look to the place.

Two elderly women sat in a back pew. Then she saw Steve. He sat in a pew at the aisle, one elbow propped on the side rail, his chin in his hand.

Thinking? Praying? Repenting?

At the very least, seeking solitude. Why couldn't he have told her? She had thought Steve lacked the capacity for quiet introspection. But maybe this was where he came for meditation and spiritual guidance. Not making a big deal out of it, just searching for peace in his own way. A flood of warm feelings swept over her. This was, after all, the man she loved. Surely she must have sensed this part of Steve's personality, even though he kept it hidden. She fought the urge to rush down the aisle and throw her arms around him.

No, he deserved this quiet time. She turned and left the sanctuary, wondering if perhaps a house with a yard might be perfectly fine for them after all.

* * *

Steve looked at his watch. He was on time, which meant that opposing counsel was late. It gave him time to think. Had Victoria seemed suspicious? God, how he hated to lie to her. Maybe that was why he'd told a half-truth. This *was* a settlement conference. But it had nothing to do with Harry Sachs and his sticky butt. This was far more personal. Steve had promised Irene Lord that he would get her out of a jam—save her condo from foreclosure—without Victoria ever knowing.

The legal task seemed impossible. Mortgage foreclosures had damn little wiggle room.

"Has the mortgagor paid the mortgagee?"

"No."

"Judgment for mortgagee."

Irene was five months in arrears, and the bank had demanded acceleration of the loan, meaning the entire balance—more than four hundred thousand dollars—was now due. No way Steve could allow the case to go to court.

He heard the *click*ing of leather heels on the tile, turned, and saw Harding Collins moving toward him. Tanned. Tall and trim, with a fine head of gray hair that had been expensively cut. A charcoal suit that shouted Brooks Brothers, and a white shirt with tasteful blue stripes. If Collins weren't a real bank lawyer, he could play one on TV.

"You must be Solomon."

"Sit down, Collins." Steve slid over to give the man room.

"Why on earth did you insist on meeting here?" Collins said.

"I like historic buildings. The wood in here came from the first Presbyterian church in Miami, the one where William Jennings Bryan taught Sunday school."

"I'm very well aware of that."

"Right. Because you're a deacon."

"Not here, of course." A hint of condescension. No, Harding Collins wouldn't attend what amounted to an inner-city church.

"I'm deacon at Riviera Presbyterian. On Sunset Drive."

A Suburban Presbyterian.

Steve considered himself a City Jew, though he had so little faith, he doubted he was entitled to the title. Basically, he'd come up with his own concept of Unintelligent Design, his belief that if a divine entity created humankind, He (or, heaven help us, She) was either dim-witted or a sadist.

Not knowing much about Presbyterians, Steve had enlisted Bobby and Cece for research and investigation. Cece came up with some dirt on Collins, and Bobby announced that "Presbyterian" could be rearranged to spell "Best in Prayer."

"My secretary caught a talk you gave at your church last week," Steve said.

Collins smiled, softened a bit. "Your secretary's a Presbyterian?"

"More like a parolee. But she liked your speech. Something about sympathy and service."

"Gifts of the deacons. Next week, I'm speaking about redemption. Feel free to attend."

"Actually, I play for another team."

"All are welcome," Collins said with a pinched ecumenical smile. "Now, what can I do for you?"

"First Dade Bank has sued to foreclose the condo of my client, Irene Lord. One of your junior associates filed the papers. Unfortunately, Irene's in a bit of financial trouble and could use a break."

"I've heard all the sob stories, Solomon. The family

breadwinner died. The kid's in the hospital. The roof blew off and there's no insurance."

"Yeah, a bunch of whiners out there."

"I represent the bank. My obligation is to the shareholders, not the poor slobs who take on too much debt."

"What about practicing what you preach? Charity, sympathy, gifts of the deacons."

"Religion is one thing, the practice of law is another. You, of all people, must know that."

"Why me of all people?"

"I asked around about you, Solomon. You give sharks a bad name."

"My rules are simple. I don't lie to opposing lawyers or stab them in the back. Head-on, I'll kick you in the *cojones*."

"From where I sit, you're a low-rent lawyer with bargain-basement scruples."

"Actually, I'm a *no*-rent lawyer, but I catch your meaning."

"My answer's the same to you as to anyone else," Collins continued. "No negotiation. Pay up or hit the pavement." His tone had changed. From principled humanitarian to icy defense lawyer in the blink of a time sheet. "So, unless you have a legal defense to the foreclosure . . ."

"Now that you mention it, there's a problem with the papers the bank had Irene sign," Steve said. "The disclosures about the adjustable rates aren't in boldface. Violates the Banking Act."

"Nice try, Solomon. But every borrower initials the rates clause. That proves actual notice that the rates may go up. And just so you know, we've been hit with lots of consumer lawsuits. I haven't lost one yet, and frankly, I was up against lawyers a helluva lot better than you."

"Different," Steve said.

"I beg your pardon?"

"You were up against lawyers *different* than me. Not better."

Collins laughed as heartily as a poker player who filled an inside straight on the river. "If that's your best shot, I really have to be going—"

"Got one more. I sent my secretary over to the Justice Building the other day. You've had seven parking tickets in the last year."

"I've also jaywalked quite a few times and I might have failed to put out the garbage cans on pickup day." Collins got to his feet.

"Three of the tickets were issued within one block of the Shangri-La Motel on Seventy-ninth Street. You know the neighborhood, Collins? The one the cops call 'Hooker Heaven.' As for the motel, it's what, thirty bucks for thirty minutes?"

Collins sank back into the pew. He shot looks left and right, as if the saints might be eavesdropping.

"Can't blame you for not parking that Mercedes convertible in the motel lot," Steve continued. "But you ought to feed the meters."

"What is it you want, Solomon?" His voice still in even-keeled lawyerly mode.

"The bank gives my client a grace period of eighteen months. Stay all principal and interest during that time. Then she'll resume payments without penalty."

"And if I don't agree?"

Cool and aloof, as if representing someone else. But then, didn't they call Presbyterians the "frozen chosen"?

"Maybe you didn't notice, but the Shangri-La Motel has that camera above the front desk," Steve said. "When you pay for the room, they take excellent digital video. A two-shot of the guy paying and whatever debutante is standing next to him."

Collins' suntan seemed to fade one shade. "You son of a bitch. It's sleazy bastards like you who give the profession a bad name."

"And I suppose foreclosing mortgages is doing God's work?"

"Bastard," Collins repeated.

"Maybe you'd like one of those videos for your talk about redemption."

Collins stayed quiet for a long moment. No more curses. The savvy lawyer seemed to be tallying up the odds. One measly condo mortgage against his life getting sucked down the drain.

I would never, ever follow through on the threat, but you don't know that, do you, Collins?

The bank lawyer barely registered a blip on Steve's personal chart of bad guys. Sure, Collins was a hypocrite. But that ranked pretty far down on Steve's sliding scale of sins. Collins' church work seemed real, and apparently was deeply felt. Maybe his way of repenting for his personal flaws.

So who am I to judge this man?

Florida Bar. Chamber of Commerce. Presbyterian church. Wife and kids and a house in Snapper Creek. In earlier times, Steve thought, Collins would have been called a pillar of the community. Steve wouldn't turn the pillar to salt; the guy simply didn't deserve it.

But I will bluff him till the hookers come home. C'mon, Collins. I'm not robbing the bank. I'm just asking for time.

Collins let out a soft hiss. "It will take a day or so to draw up the papers," he said. Then without a "Good day" or "Screw you," Collins shot one look toward the altar, stood, and walked out.

Steve sat alone, watching dust motes float in the light of the stained-glass windows. He was not particularly pleased with himself. Though it was cool in the sanctuary, he felt his shirt sticking to the pew. He wanted to splash cold water on his face.

Years ago, he had asked his father what the profession was all about.

"Lawyerin's like playing poker with ideas," Herbert Solomon had drawled.

It sounded both romantic and exciting. Like telling a kid that being a cowboy was about riding horses, leaving out all the shit-shoveling. Lawyering, Steve concluded, was more demolition derby than Texas Hold 'Em, and there was at least as much shit-shoveling as at the rodeo.

Thirty-Three

FEELINGS . . . WHOA . . . OH . . . OH . . . FEELINGS

Victoria sipped her Chardonnay and began crumbling blue cheese for the salad. Then she stopped. Steve liked grated Parmesan. She would go with that. But first, she checked the oven. The sweet potatoes—Steve's favorite—were coming along nicely, emitting a syrupy aroma.

This should be his night, she thought. A special night. No arguments, not even a debate over whether figure skating qualifies as a sport. Earlier today, Steve had said he wanted to talk. Not about work. Not about the Dolphins. But about them.

"I want to open up, talk about my feelings."

Yep, he used the dreaded "f" word, the two-syllable one. And this just one day after she spied him sitting in church. A quiet, contemplative Steve. Meditating or praying. Or maybe just thinking about their relationship. So rare in men these days.

She sensed a turning point. And just in time. Everything had become so strained between them.

Maybe it was her fault. Steve had been under so much pressure with Kreeger creeping back into his life. Then there were the two assault-and-battery charges.

And Janice, lurking in the background, threatening to file a custody action.

"You should be more understanding and less demanding, dear."

Amazingly, that's what her mother told her last night. She and The Queen had had dinner at Norman's in the Gables, and over mango-glazed snapper and a bottle of Zinfandel, her mother had expressed warm-and-cuddly sentiments for Steve.

"Stephen has a good heart. Sometimes, I fear you're too harsh with him."

"Me? Harsh?"

"And judgmental. And if I may so, a bit fussy and priggish."

"What!"

"I thought I'd raised you to be a bit more fun."

"And when did you do that, Mother? When you were off in Gstaad or Monaco?"

"Don't get huffy. All I'm saying, a woman has to support her man. Steve's in a real pressure cooker right now. And to throw a hissy fit because he happens to chat with an unclothed girl—well, if you ask me, that's a bit priggish."

Victoria had been too stunned to be angry. The Queen seldom spoke about anyone at great length, other than herself. And it was practically unheard of, a solar eclipse of an event, for her to say anything nice about Steve. But this was the second time in a matter of days that she'd taken his side. So what was going on? Bewilderingly, from the crab cake appetizer to the banana crème brûlée, her mother practically oozed affection for Steve.

"When are you moving in together, dear?"

"What's the hurry?"

"I have my eye on a charming housewarming gift."

"So, suddenly, you think Steve is right for me?"

"Trust me where men are concerned, dear. Despite that thorny exterior, deep inside, Stephen is a loving, caring man who adores you."

Just what were they putting in the sparkling water, anyway?

But the more Victoria thought about Steve, the more she thought her mother was right.

Meaning I've been right, all along. Beginning that night in the avocado grove—Bruce's avocado grove—when I sneaked off with Steve.

He had so many good qualities. His love for Bobby. His quest for justice, even if the road he took was usually off the beaten path. His quirky sense of humor. And, of course, one more thing, something her mother nailed as she sipped her after-dinner cognac.

"May I assume Stephen's good in the sack?"

"You may assume anything you wish, Mother."

"I always liked lanky, wiry men. Stephen looks pretty limber to me."

Right now, Mr. Limber was in the backyard, squirting fluid on the charcoal, lighting a fire for the steaks. T-bones, sweet potatoes, tossed salad, followed by a discussion of feelings, along with Key lime pie. Yes, this was going to be a special night.

Five minutes later, Steve came into the kitchen and headed straight for the refrigerator. What shoes and purses were to women, Victoria thought, the fridge and the TV were to men. He poked around a second and pulled out a cold Sam Adams.

He liked cold beer and rare steak. She liked white wine and grilled salmon. But tonight none of that mattered. Tonight they would get closer than ever. She just knew it.

"How long until you put the steaks on?" she asked.

"A while. You know I like the coals to be glowing. The secret to a great steak—"

"Is the hottest possible fire. Sear the outside, keep the inside juicy. I know, I know. Make mine well done?"

He made a face. "If you say so. Where's the Bobster?"

"In his room, studying."

"Alone?"

She gave him a bittersweet smile. Bobby had been moping around ever since he'd been exiled from the Goldberg house, and Maria had been forbidden from even setting foot on Kumquat Avenue. All by royal decree of the Munoz-Goldbergs.

Complicating the situation was Janice. Steve had begun allowing her to visit Bobby at home, but so far refusing to let her take him anywhere alone. He'd been afraid Janice would snatch him and run.

Now Steve picked up the salad bowl and shook it, shuffling the lettuce, tomatoes, and cucumbers, everything sliced thin, the way he liked it.

"You make a great salad," he said.

"Thanks." She sipped at the wine to let him go on without interruption. When a witness is ready to talk, best to keep quiet.

"You're really terrific in the kitchen," he continued. "A lot of women these days just don't take the time. But the way you balance work and everything else— well, it's pretty impressive."

She picked up the cheese grater and went to work. In truth, her culinary skills were limited to a couple of dishes, but she sensed this was just a warm-up, Steve taking a few practice swings. He looked a little nervous. Apparently, stalking a serial killer was not as scary a task as plumbing his own emotional depths.

"You're good at so many things," Steve went on. "You're amazing with Bobby; the kid adores you."

"It's mutual."

Okay, now we're moving in the right direction, though at the speed of a manatee. C'mon, Steve. Let's go from the nephew's feelings to the uncle's feelings.

"Maybe you and I can talk a bit while Bobby's still in his room," Steve said. "About personal stuff."

She stopped grating the cheese in midstroke. "Sure."

"There are things I've wanted to say to you for a long time, but you know how it is. . . ."

He plucked a tomato slice out of the bowl and let the words dangle in the air. Tongue-tied. Not his usual state. His dark hair was messed, and there was a smudge of charcoal on his cheek. He looked like a kid, she thought, in part perhaps because of his T-shirt: *"I Am Not Infantile, You Stinky Butt Poophead."*

"Go ahead, Steve. It won't hurt."

"So why does it feel like opening a vein?"

"When you're in a relationship, you've got to trust the other person. You can share feelings, expose your fears, your weaknesses." She reached over and wiped the smudge from his face.

He took a breath and sighed, as if to say, *"Here goes."*

She picked up her wineglass and waited. It was a two-sip wait. There was so much she wanted to hear. Words like "love" and "plans" and "future," and even "marriage" and "children." Sure, she knew he was conflicted. Men were like that. They yearn for the love of a woman, and then when they get it, they break into a cold sweat.

"You remember how I always told you about the College World Series?" Steve said.

That puzzled her, but she went with it. "U.M. down by a run in the ninth inning. You got picked off third base to end the game."

"What else? What do I always say?"

This must be some sort of metaphor, she thought, but what could it be? Steve was bringing back the most humiliating day of his life. He'd let his teammates down. So maybe he wanted to say: *I want us to be a team forever, Vic, and I'll never let you down.*

"You always say you got in under the tag," she replied. "The ump blew the call."

"Yeah, maybe the photos make it look that way. But the thing is, I felt the third baseman's glove swipe my hand when I dived for the base. All this time, Vic, I've been lying to myself and everybody else. The damn truth is, I was out."

Okay, Steve, you were picked off. Your team lost. What's it have to do with us?

But she didn't want to appear critical. What was it her mother had said?

"A woman must support her man."

She wrapped both arms around his neck and moved so close, their noses nearly touched. "I understand, sweetheart. You feel your life has been a lie."

"Well, not my whole life. But I feel so much better telling you what really happened."

"So that our relationship can move to a new level?" Prompting him, trying to make it easier.

"What level is that?"

"I thought you wanted to open up, discuss feelings, remember?"

"Yeah. I was feeling bad and now that I told you the truth, I feel better."

"*You* feel better?" She took a step back, astonished. "What about us? What about words like 'love' and 'plans' and 'future'? Where do I fit into your life now that we know you were picked off fair and square?"

Steve seemed startled. He took a gulp of his beer, then moved toward the window. In the yard, white smoke billowed from the hibachi. Either a new pope had been selected, or it was time to put on the steaks.

He turned to face her. "Vic, all these years, I never told anyone else what really happened in that game. I couldn't have told you if I didn't love you."

"Keep going, partner. What else?"

"I'm sorry I've been such a jerk about moving in together. I figured everything was good the way it was. We each had our own space, and I was afraid that if something changed, we'd be headed for the great unknown. So I guess I was scared."

"And now?"

"Life is the great unknown, isn't it? If we shy away from risks, we're running from life."

"So you do have plans? For us, I mean."

"My mind's full of plans, except I call them 'hopes.' When we met, I didn't dare *plan* you'd want to be with me. But sure, I hoped you would. Even when we got together, my hopes all came with fears. The biggest one, you'd wake up one morning and realize you'd made a gigantic mistake. So I couldn't talk about any of this. Even now it's hard for me to believe you want to live with me and help me raise Bobby. As for the future—well, I've got hopes there, too."

She didn't know how far to push him, but she couldn't leave that hanging. "What sort of hopes?"

"You know, permanent stuff."

"Yeah?"

"Marriage. Kids." His voice a whisper.

"Is that what you really want, Steve?" Asking ever so gently, trying not to frighten him.

"Someday," he said quickly. "If all goes well."

Okay, a tiny retreat. But he'd moved a mile forward and only one step backward. Once you say "marriage," the word can't be erased.

Victoria took both Steve's arms and wrapped them around her waist, because the poor guy seemed incapable of movement. Then she cupped his face in her hands and kissed him. As their lips touched, she murmured, "Those are my hopes, too."

She kissed him again and their bodies folded into each other, the contours fitting perfectly, a yin and yang of man and woman. "And by the way, I've studied those photos from the game. You did get in under the tag."

"No, Vic. I remember the glove hitting my hand."

"You remember wrong, lover. You were safe. You've always been safe."

Thirty-Four

A THUMP IN THE NIGHT

Several hours after the words "marriage" and "kids" tumbled from his mouth like skydivers leaping from a plane, Steve Solomon took stock of his life.

I'm a happy man.

Strike that, Madam Court Reporter. "Happy" doesn't quite say it. I'm a living beer commercial. I'm playing volleyball on the beach with the woman I love.

He had shared his feelings with Victoria and it hadn't hurt. They loved each other and had recommitted. They were about to take the giant step of buying a place and moving in together. Steve, Victoria, and Bobby. A ready-made family.

Bobby seemed happier at dinner, too. Steve made him laugh, and the kid worked up his first anagram in a week. Who knew that "President George Bush" could be rearranged to spell "The person is buggered"?

Now Victoria lay alongside Steve in bed. They had eaten their steaks and polished off an entire pie. They had talked some more in the bedroom, had made love, talked some more, made love again, and talked even more.

Steve was just drifting off to sleep, thinking he wouldn't trade places with anyone else in the world, when he heard the *thump*. There was a steady breeze, and sometimes a giant palm frond would break loose from the tree and sideswipe the house on the way to the ground. But that sound was different. He felt too tired and content to get up, but he did, anyway.

The house was dark, and he was naked. He reached under the bed, grabbed an aluminum softball bat, and padded out of the bedroom. In the kitchen, he peered through the sliding glass door. The backyard was an ominous greenish black, the foliage backlit by a neighbor's powerful anticrime spotlights. Something seemed different, but what was it?

It only took a second. The grill cover was on the ground. A metal lid, it should have been leaning against the house, where he'd left it. But it had been moved, maybe two feet, as if someone walking along the house in the dark had stumbled over it.

Steve unlocked the glass door, slid it open, and slipped outside, gripping the bat in his right hand. It was light and whippy. He could crush someone's skull with it, no problem.

He smelled something burning. What the hell?

Cigarette smoke.

Then a woman's voice, out of the darkness. "You've gotten bigger since you were nine."

Heart racing, Steve wheeled around, ready to swing the bat.

"Over here, Stevie."

He wheeled the other way and saw the glow of the cigarette and a heavyset figure reclining on the chaise lounge.

"Jesus, Janice! What are you doing here?"

"Here. Take this." She sat up in the chaise and tossed a towel at him. "You remember how Mom always made me give you a bath when you were little? You hated it."

Steve wrapped the towel—wet and cold—around his waist. "You stoned, Janice? What the hell's going on?"

"Clean and sober. I came to see Bobby."

"In the middle of the night?"

"It's the only time we can talk without you hovering over us like a wicked stepmother. Or stepuncle, or whatever the hell you are."

"I'm his caregiver. I'm his father and his mother, and I'd rather see him raised by wolves than by you."

"You're so great at it, where the hell is he?"

"In bed. Sleeping."

"Yeah, well, I just rapped on his window for ten minutes and he ain't there."

Steve's first thought was that Bobby was sleeping so soundly, he didn't hear Janice at the window. But no, the kid was a nervous sleeper. A car door slamming down the block, a police siren on Douglas Road, a teakettle whistling . . . everything woke him up.

A second later, Steve raced into the house and down the corridor. He threw open the door to Bobby's room and flicked on the lights. The bed was messed. And empty.

"Bobby!" Steve yelled. "Bobby! Where are you? Bobby!"

Thirty-Five

ON BEING A MAN

Steve paced in the living room. Victoria made coffee. Janice smoked.

"Here's what we know," Steve said, straining to be analytical, fighting the fear. "Bobby's bike is gone. That's a good sign. If he'd been snatched, he wouldn't be on his bike."

Steve wanted to believe he was right. When he'd seen the empty bed, his first searing thought was that Kreeger had kidnapped the boy. But no, the bike changed all that.

"That Juban princess," Janice said. "Maybe he went over to her house, and we'll find him up a tree."

"The Goldbergs live a block away," Steve said. "He wouldn't ride his bike. But we gotta check it out anyway. I'll walk over there."

"Not with the restraining order." Victoria came out of the kitchen, carrying a pot of coffee on a tray. "You can't go near their property. I'll do it."

"I'll go along," Janice said.

"No. You'll just start a fight," Steve said.

"Me? You're the one who busted the guy in the mouth."

"Stop it, both of you!" Victoria said it with such authority that they both clammed up. "Time's wasting. I'll go alone. Call me on the cell if anything—"

The doorbell rang. At this time of night, it was a sound as chilling as a scream. Steve's imagination took flight. He pictured a police cruiser, a young officer gnawing his lip, a sorrowful look on his face.

"*Are you the next of kin of a boy named Robert Solomon?*"

Steve hurried to the door and threw it open.

Myron Goldberg stood there in his bathrobe and sneakers. His wife was half a step behind him.

"Maria's missing!" Eva shoved her spouse aside. "*Desaparecida!*"

Steve's spirits soared. "That's great, Eva!"

"What!"

"Is she here?" Myron asked.

"No. Bobby's missing, too. But that means they're together. It means they're okay."

"But where?" Myron said. "Where could they be?"

Eva pushed through the open door. "If you put them up to this, Solomon—"

"Back off, bitch." Janice walked into the foyer.

"I should have known," Eva said. "Are you behind this?"

"What's the big frigging deal? They'll be back when they're done." Janice gave Eva a double-chinned grin. " 'Course, they ain't gonna be virgins no more."

"*Puta,*" Eva snarled.

"Okay, everybody relax," Steve said. "Let's work together on this. Myron, is Maria's bike gone?"

"I don't know. We didn't look."

"I'm betting it is and they're within a couple miles of home. Where does Maria usually ride?"

"The two of us go down Old Cutler," Eva said. "The path to Matheson Hammock."

"Bobby knows the place, too. That's a start. I'll drive down there, but we'll need people at each of our houses."

"Janice and I will stay here," Victoria said.

Meaning the Goldbergs should head home. Smart, Steve thought. Otherwise, Janice and Eva would surely end up mud wrestling before daybreak.

It only took Steve a minute to step into his running shorts and a T-shirt. He was headed to the door when Janice said: "I need a drink, Stevie. You got any liquor?"

"Bottle of Jack Daniel's above the bar."

"Looked there. Didn't see any Jack."

Steve wasn't about to start searching for whiskey for his sister. But as he got into the Mustang, he wondered about it. What happened to that new bottle of Jack Daniel's, the expensive one, Single Barrel?

* * *

"Ooh, that's strong," Maria said, sipping at the golden liquor. She took another swig, then passed the bottle to Bobby. "Bourbon, right? My dad drinks it."

"Sour-mash whiskey," Bobby corrected, "but people call it bourbon." He raised the bottle to his lips, took a gulp. His eyes watered as the liquid seared his throat.

They were walking at the edge of a mini–rain forest inside Fairchild Tropical Garden, navigating a tangle of woody vines thick as high-transmission wires. It was spooky in the dark, especially if you've seen those movies where killers in hockey masks jump out from behind trees.

Bobby screwed the top back on the bottle and they

continued through the forest. They wound their way past towering ficus trees, giant ferns brushing against their knees, sneakers sinking into the moist earth. Bobby carried a flashlight, but that only made the shadows deeper and scarier. He slipped and nearly fell. Totally uncool, but Maria didn't laugh. Then, hopping over a slippery log, he lost his grip on the flashlight. The beam skittered off to one side, and for a split second Bobby thought he saw the shape of a person, someone looking their way. But when he picked up the flashlight and pointed in that direction, no one was there.

He shook it off. This was maybe the best night of his life, and it was just beginning. An hour earlier, when they had gotten on their bikes, Maria took the ball cap from Bobby's head and put it on, tucking her hair in. The gesture, so feminine, made Bobby's heart ache. Maria was wearing short-shorts and a pink sleeveless T-shirt that had *"Spoiled"* spelled out in rhinestones with a glittery heart dotting the "i." In the light of the street lamps, her complexion was the color of café Cubano, heavy with cream.

They had ridden their bikes along the Old Cutler path, going airborne where the roots of banyan trees poked up through the asphalt. In the moonlight, Bobby watched the gentle curve of Maria's calves as she pedaled, could see a line of smooth caramel skin above her shorts. She was hot, so totally hot. He couldn't believe he was here.

"The next full moon. The rain forest at Fairchild. You'll score, I promise you."

Dr. Bill had told him that. He knew so much that Uncle Steve didn't. Or maybe Uncle Steve knew but wouldn't tell him. Like girls getting hot at the full moon, even girls who weren't hoochies to start with.

They'd ridden down Old Cutler to Matheson, crossing a marshy hammock, inhaling the salty smells, listening to the croaking frogs and the creaking insects. Then, standing alongside a tidal pool, a full moon dangling over the bay, they'd kissed.

The kiss was tentative, Bobby leaning in, waiting for Maria, hoping she'd join the action. She did, smelling of oranges and vanilla, her mother's perfume. The second kiss was softer, slower, wetter, deeper. He'd gotten a raging boner.

Slammin' idea, Dr. Bill.

They'd started hitting the Jack Daniel's then. Rocket fuel, ninety-four proof, according to the label. Bobby's stomach was a little queasy, and his forehead felt sweaty. What they needed was something to eat.

"Bring along something to drink. Vodka or rum or bourbon. The higher the proof, the better. Loosen her up."

But Dr. Bill hadn't said anything about food. Pretzels and chips would have been good. Maybe a blanket, too. And condoms?

But where would he get condoms, anyway? Uncle Steve didn't use them. Bobby had seen Victoria's birth control pills in the bathroom, looking like little candies in a Pez dispenser.

After three swigs of bourbon, two hiccups, and five wet kisses, Bobby and Maria got back on their bikes, rode back through the hammock, then down the path to Fairchild. The gates were locked, so they hid their bikes in a hibiscus hedge and climbed over a fence. Now they were headed through the rain forest toward the tropical fruit pavilion to find something to eat.

The pavilion was a giant greenhouse with a roof shaped like a pyramid to accommodate large trees.

The door was unlocked, and once inside, Bobby set about picking fruit. The lichees and passion fruit he recognized, but he needed to read the little signs stuck in the ground for the rest: jackfruit, langsat, sapodilla, and a bunch of others, scaly and unappetizing.

They sat on a grassy patch, nibbled the fruit, and drank more of the whiskey, kissing between nibbles. The passion fruit was tart, the tiny black seeds crunchy. The jackfruit was spicy hot and the lichees sweet like grapes. None of it went that well with the whiskey. Bobby lay back on the grass, looking at the treetops that seemed to be swaying in the breeze, but there was no wind here.

I'm dizzy. Dizzy from whiskey and kisses that taste like passion fruit.

Maria was talking about a girl at school, a total slut, who after P.E. used a banana to show her posse how to, you know, go down on a guy, but she gagged on it, then spit it up so that it squished out her nose.

"Totally grossed everybody out," Maria said. The story didn't make Bobby's stomach feel any better.

Maria was giggling, going back over details of the banana episode. Bobby was half listening, when he thought he heard the door to the pavilion squeak open, but maybe not. A moment later, Maria leaned over and kissed him again. Then, he wasn't quite sure how it happened, they were lying on the grass, their legs wrapped around each other, kissing and moaning and rubbing their bodies against each other.

Bobby let a hand slip under Maria's T-shirt, but she latched on to his wrist and pushed him away. A second later, he feinted with that hand, then sneaked the other hand under the shirt—*If Pickett had used a similar zigzag, the Battle of Gettysburg would have turned out way differently*—and a second later, he had hold of her bra. The fabric was cottony soft, and he could see the top of it peeking out of her shirt.

Pink brassiere. The letters rearranged themselves in his brain. BARE PENIS RISK.

He tugged at the bra.

"Bobby, don't."

Remembering what Dr. Bill had told him. *"Man is the hunter. Man kills the game and takes the female of his choice."*

"No, Bobby." She pushed his hand away again. Firmly, the way mothers teach them, Bobby figured.

"C'mon, Maria. You want it. I know you do."

Hearing the doc's voice now, as if he were right here watching. *"When she says no, she means maybe. When she says maybe, she means yes."*

"Bobby, I like you. I really do. But let's just kiss for now."

Sweat poured out of him, and his stomach heaved. But his boner was so hard, it had started to hurt. He took her left hand in his right hand and pinned it to her side. Then he slid his left hand around her back and tried to unfasten her pink bra.

"Bobby! No!"

She wriggled left and right, but maybe she just wanted to excite him more.

"The female always yields to the strong man."

He couldn't unsnap the damn thing, so he yanked the bra, and it slipped halfway around her torso.

"Ouch! Bobby, what are you doing?"

"Be a man, Robert. Take what you want. Maria will love it. Trust me. I know."

"You'll love it, Maria," Bobby said, deepening his voice. "Trust me. I know."

Thirty-Six

WHAT GIRLS WANT

The air should not smell so sweet on a night like this, Steve thought.

Top down on the Mustang, the scent of jasmine in the moist air, a full moon ducking in and out of clouds, he drove down Old Cutler Road, more worried than he had let on to the others.

With all the chaos swirling around—Janice and Kreeger, Victoria and Irene, Freskin and Goldberg—Steve wondered if he had been spending enough time with Bobby. Had he let his own problems distract him from the number one priority in his life?

Stop worrying. Bobby's okay.

Steve kept telling himself that. The boy hadn't run away from home; he hadn't been kidnapped. Maria's the first girl who showed him the rhinestone in her navel, so he's experimenting. They're probably necking somewhere under a palm tree, and they'll show up at dawn, sweaty and mosquito-bitten. It's normal.

He's okay, dammit. Stop worrying.

Steve had already checked out Cocoplum, driving down to the bay, then coming back up to the circle at the Gables Waterway. Now he hung a left at Matheson

Hammock. He passed the deserted picnic area and drove parallel to the bicycle path, which wound through a tangle of black-and-red mangrove trees. He stopped at the saltwater pond. No cars in the parking lot. Bicycle rack empty.

No Bobby. And no Maria.

Steve got out of the car and walked around the pond, just yards from the open bay. The tide was out, and a marshy smell hung in the air. A passel of herons tracked across the wet sand, seeking an early breakfast. Across the bay, a few lights twinkled in the condos of Key Biscayne. To the north, the downtown skyscrapers were dark.

The silence was broken by a Boston Whaler chugging out of the channel, an early start for a day of fishing. Over the ocean at the horizon, flashes of lightning brightened a ribbon of clouds. The wind was kicking up, rippling the water. The full moon was obscured by a growing cloud cover but still bright enough to light the sky, like a lamp through a shade. The forecast was for rain, a band of squalls in advance of a cold front.

Steve got back in the car and drove farther south on Old Cutler, pulling into Fairchild Tropical Garden. He'd brought Bobby there a few times, the boy enjoying the peacefulness of the place. Noises still tightened him up. Tranquillity seemed essential to his therapy.

Steve parked at the gate. Everything locked. He got out of the car, leaving the headlights on. Crouched down on a narrow dirt path that ran up to a perimeter fence near the entrance. Next to a hibiscus hedge, bicycle tracks. Two bikes had been here.

Okay, so what?

Well, for starters, the tracks were fresh. It had

rained briefly in late afternoon, and the tracks would have been made after that.

Great. Give yourself a Boy Scout badge, but like I said before, so what?

Well, you couldn't ride past this point. The dirt path dead-ended at the fence. So the bikers must have stopped and parked their bikes here. Maybe they went inside.

Yeah? So . . .

Steve didn't know. Except . . . in the reddish dirt two sets of tire tracks approached the fence, but only one left. So what the hell happened to the other bike?

Just then, Steve's cell phone rang, the sound jarring in the stillness. On the screen, he recognized his home phone number.

"Yeah, Vic?"

"Bobby just rode up."

"Great. Maria at her house?"

"No." He heard the tension in her voice. "Steve—Bobby doesn't know where she is."

* * *

Just before dawn, Steve slid the Mustang to a stop in his driveway and someone screamed.

He hadn't seen Eva Munoz-Goldberg running toward his front door. She nimbly leapt to one side and the front fender just missed her. In great shape from step class or tai chi, Steve figured. Good thing, or he'd be facing vehicular manslaughter charges.

Eva's momentum carried her toward the flagstone path leading to the house. She hopped over a small shrub, then lost her balance on the dew-slick flagstone. The second scream came when she pitched forward, scraping a knee. Steve admired the way Eva scrambled to her feet and headed for his front door without stopping to curse at him.

Bobby's bike was leaning against the pepper tree. Meaning the boy was inside. Steve heard the shouts before he made it to the front door. He found Eva in the living room, her knee bleeding, hair a mess, shrieking at Bobby. "Where is she! Where's my daughter!"

Janice slung a protective arm around Bobby's shoulder and kept her considerable girth between her son and Eva. "Back off, bitch, or you're gonna need some more plastic surgery."

"Thank God you're here, Steve," Victoria said.

Steve wasn't sure which was more disconcerting, Eva screeching or Janice holding on to Bobby. "C'mere, kiddo." He pried the boy away from his mother, hoisted him up by the armpits, and worked both arms under his butt. It's easy to do with a toddler, not a twelve-year-old, even one as gangly as Bobby.

Bobby was trembling and pale and he smelled sour. He looped his legs around Steve's waist and put his head on a shoulder.

"You stink, kiddo."

"Threw up."

He carried Bobby into the kitchen, just to get away from the others. He could hear Victoria telling the two women to give them some space, let Steve handle this.

"I'm sorry, Uncle Steve."

"It's okay. Where's Maria?"

"Dunno. We were at Fairchild. She got mad at me and left."

"What made her mad?"

"I was stupid."

"Yeah?"

"I tried what Dr. Bill said . . ."

Steve felt his jaw clench and a wave a heat flared through his gut. "Dr. Bill?"

"He said I should take Maria there at the full moon because that's when girls get really hot. And then she'd want to do it."

"But when you got there, Maria said no?"

"Yeah."

"And what'd you do?"

"At first, I sort of pushed her. But then I stopped. 'Cause of that dorky stuff you taught me. 'No means no. Maybe means no. It takes maturity to keep your purity.' All that stuff."

"Good boy. But Maria was still mad at you?"

"I guess. I got sick and hurled chunks all over some bromeliads. I went over to the lake to clean up, and when I got back she wasn't there. I got my bike, but hers was gone. I thought she was riding home."

"Did you try to catch up with her?"

"Yeah. How'd you know?"

"Because that's what I would have done. Ride really fast. If she only had a few minutes' head start, you would have caught her."

"That's what I tried. But I never saw her."

Because she was snatched! When she came to pick up her bike, someone was waiting.

It came back to him then. That day in Kreeger's office.

"Just a hypothetical question, Solomon. If Robert killed Maria, wouldn't you do anything to keep him out of prison? Wouldn't you even take the rap for him?"

Steve felt his arms involuntarily tighten around his nephew. Conflicting emotions. Thankful Bobby was safe. But absolute horror at the thought that his girl-friend could be dead by now. Maybe Bobby heard

Steve's breaths quicken or felt his heart thumping. Whatever it was, the boy whimpered.

A second later, Victoria was alongside, running a hand through Bobby's hair. He stretched his neck like a cat that wanted to be petted. A second after that, Janice was there, too.

"Bitch went outside," Janice reported. "How's my boy?"

Bobby shrugged. His arms tightened around Steve's neck.

"Stevie, can I have my son, please?"

"Yes."

"Because you've got no right to keep him away from—" Startled, she stopped. "Did you say yes?"

Steve put the boy down. "We gotta all be on the same team, Jan."

"Why? What's going on?"

"Take Bobby to bed and we'll talk."

Puzzled, Janice draped a meaty arm around the boy and walked him toward his bedroom.

"What's happened, Steve?" Victoria asked.

He could barely get out the words. "Kreeger. He's got Maria. He's going to rape her and kill her. And frame Bobby. All to punish me."

Victoria blinked twice. Then she swiftly recovered. "I'll talk to Eva. You call the police."

Just then, a woman's scream. Steve recognized it immediately. It was the third time he'd heard it that morning.

Steve and Victoria raced outside. Eva was standing next to Bobby's bike. The zipper on the vinyl bag attached to the seat was open. Eva clutched something to her chest. A moment later, when Steve realized what it was, a feeling of dread spread through him like a poisonous tide.

"Where is she!" Eva ran toward Steve, flailing at him. "Goddammit!" Her voice broke between spasms of sobs. "What did he do to her?"

Punches landed on his chest, his shoulder, his arms. One wayward blow glanced off his temple. Steve made no effort to ward off the punches. He was already in such pain, it simply didn't hurt to be hit by a petite woman, her face wet with tears, a small pink brassiere wrapped around her fist.

Thirty-Seven

FROM THE SWAMP TO THE SEA

The cop had a familiar face.

A mini-Afro. A name tag that said *"Teele."* A skeptical look.

Sure, the guy who arrested me at the radio station. The second time.

Bad break, Steve thought. They were standing in Steve's driveway just after seven A.M. Janice was inside, sacked out on the sofa. Bobby was asleep in his bedroom, Victoria sitting watch alongside. Myron and Eva were back in their house on Loquat, giving statements to Teele's partner, Rodriguez.

"Dr. Kreeger is canoeing on the Suwannee," Teele said.

"Canoe-ing on the Su-wan-nee?" Steve used his best derisive tone, dragging out the words. "That is the worst fucking alibi I've ever heard, and my clients have used some doozies."

Teele lowered his voice into serious cop mode. "You're saying Dr. Bill kidnapped this girl and planted evidence to incriminate your nephew, but you've got no proof. Now, I listen to Dr. Bill's radio show . . ."

Oh, great. A fan.

". . . and I think he makes some good points. As for the girl, she could be sleeping in somebody's backyard, and any minute she'll come riding up the street on her bike."

Cops usually assumed the worst because they see the worst. But this guy was an optimist, Steve thought. "So you reached Kreeger on his cell?"

"Couldn't get him. He's up the river past Hatchbend, where there's no service."

Up the river past Hatchbend? Jeez, I'm in Mayberry with Deputy Barney Fife.

"What the hell's he doing up there?" Steve demanded.

"Fishing for largemouth bass, the way we hear it."

"Lemme guess. The woman living at Kreeger's house gave you this cock-and-bass story."

Teele checked his little cop pad. "Mary Amanda Lamm. That's correct."

"Kreeger brainwashed her. She'd say anything he wanted her to."

"Was she lying when she said both you and your nephew are patients of Dr. Kreeger?"

"Not patients, exactly."

The cop made a note on the pad. "So you're not under court order to see Dr. Kreeger?"

"Okay, technically true, but—"

"For sexual deviancy."

"No!"

The cop used his pen to scratch his scalp through the mini-Afro. "I pulled the report, Solomon. The boy's a peeper. And Ms. Lamm claims she came out of the shower one day and found you lurking in her bathroom."

"*Bedroom,*" Steve corrected, a lawyer slicing the

bologna too thin. "I was lurking in her bedroom. But that's got nothing to do with the court ordering me to see Kreeger."

"Right. That would be for your violent streak."

"Look, Teele, Maria's missing. The clock's ticking. By the time you guys get off your butts, she could be dead."

"I hope not, sir. For your sake. Because your nephew was the last person to see the girl. By his own admission, he made unwelcome advances to her while inebriated, and her brassiere was found in his belongings. The way I see it, the only evidence points straight at him."

* * *

Victoria was the first one out of the Mustang when Steve pulled to a stop in front of Kreeger's home. The morning had turned windy and gray and smelled of rain. They'd left Bobby with Janice, but Cece was on the way there to chaperone.

On the drive to the Gables, Victoria had asked Steve if he had a plan.

"Amanda's going to tell us where Kreeger is," he said flatly.

"And betray her lover?"

"There's a glimmer of something good inside her. We just have to tap into that."

Victoria wasn't so sure. "And how do we do that?"

"Good cop, bad cop."

"I assume I'm the good cop."

"Which means you go first. If you don't get anywhere, I'll take over."

Victoria remained skeptical but kept quiet. No use in chipping away at Steve's confidence.

Amanda answered the door, for once wearing clothes. Two articles of clothing, to be exact: a red tank top and tight white short-shorts. No bra and clearly no panties, judging from the outline of her taco. No makeup. Hair tied in pigtails. A twenty-year-old trying to look fourteen.

She smiled and said, "Goody, more visitors. Hey, Ms. Lord, did you get that bikini wax yet?"

Victoria shot a look at Steve, who shrugged as if to say sorry.

"Cutie here really admired my landing strip." Amanda gave Steve a flirtatious tilt of the chin.

"Cut the bullshit, Amanda," Steve said. "We've got to talk."

She ignored him, focused on Victoria. "I offered Cutie a closer look, but he said he'd have to think about it."

"How unusual," Victoria replied. "*Cutie* so seldom thinks before acting."

One minute later, they were all inside. A nondescript living room with a sofa and two facing chairs. An old fireplace. A floor of Dade County pine. A coffee table with a bowl of slightly overripe fruit. No personal items, other than the oil painting of Kreeger on a power boat.

"Amanda, we really need your help," Victoria said, her tone pleasant.

"Like I told the cops, Uncle Bill's canoeing upstate."

"We don't think so." Still soft, still pleasant. "We think he kidnapped a twelve-year-old girl. We're afraid what he'll do to her if we don't stop him."

"That's silly," Amanda said, sounding like a preteen herself. She picked up a green apple from the bowl, tucked both legs under herself, and started munching.

Amanda didn't seem overly concerned, Victoria thought. A missing girl. Her lover accused. And here she was, nibbling away on a Granny Smith. Was it possible, Victoria wondered, that Amanda was as much a sociopath as Kreeger?

"Uncle Bill's a lover, not a killer," Amanda added with a sly smile. "And I ought to know."

"Dammit, Amanda!" Steve said, breaking in before he was supposed to. "Kreeger killed a guy named Jim Beshears. He killed a boat captain named Oscar De la Fuente. And he killed your mother."

"Now I know you're lying," Amanda said. "I'm the one who killed the witch."

She said it with a certain amount of glee that Victoria found unsettling. "You were thirteen, Amanda. Kreeger was giving you drugs when he seduced you. Your memory can't be trusted."

Steve picked up the story and they tag-teamed her: "Your mother found out about the two of you and they had a big fight. Kreeger hit her with a skimmer pole and pushed her into the hot tub. Then he convinced you that you'd done it."

"Like I said before, you have everything bass ackwards." Amanda giggled. "I seduced Uncle Bill. I was smoking a little weed, but that's it. Bill gave me some Valium after I killed Mom because I was freaking out. I wanted to call the cops and confess, but Bill said he'd take care of everything."

"He's brainwashed you, goddammit!" Steve said.

Amanda took a dainty bite from the apple. "Where was Mom hit, Cutie?"

"Right side of the skull."

"Uncle Bill's right-handed. If they were having a fight, wouldn't he have hit her on the left side?"

"Pincher covered that. Your mother must have turned and started walking away when Kreeger hit her."

Amanda's *"ha-ha-ha"* seemed contrived, like everything else about her, Victoria thought.

"That's not how it happened," Amanda said. "Me and Mom. We were facing each other. She called me a little whore, said she was gonna send me away to some school for fuckups and I'd never see Bill again. I picked up the pool thingie and hit her as hard as I could. She fell into the hot tub, and I just stood there and watched her drown."

Amanda picked up another apple from the bowl and flung it—*left-handed*—at Steve. He caught the apple and exchanged looks with Victoria.

"Uncle Bill got rid of the pool thingie," Amanda continued. "He came up with the story that Mom slipped and hit her head. The jury didn't believe him. Why should they? It wasn't true."

"I don't believe you," Steve said.

"But I do." Victoria stood, grabbed the apple from Steve, and tossed it from hand to hand as she spoke. "And if I'm right, if you're telling the truth, you owe your life to Kreeger. I'll bet you stayed faithful to him all those years he was in prison."

"I was a good girl. I promised I'd wait for him, and I did."

Victoria nodded in agreement. "After what he did for you—covering up a murder you committed—how could you do anything else?"

"You got it, Ms. Lord."

Victoria took a step toward Amanda. "Which means you'll never betray him, no matter what he's done in the past, no matter what he's doing now."

Amanda winked at Steve. "She's smarter than you are, Cutie."

"I know," Steve admitted. He turned to Victoria, looking defeated. "So if Amanda killed her mother, I lost a case for an innocent man. No wonder Kreeger hates me."

"But you were right about everything else." Still tossing the shiny green apple from hand to hand, Victoria paced in front of the sofa where Amanda sat cross-legged. "Kreeger killed Beshears and De la Fuente, didn't he, Amanda?"

"I'll never tell," she sang in her little-girl voice.

"You know one difference between Steve and me?" Victoria asked.

"I don't know and I don't care."

"Steve would never hurt a woman. It's not in him. But me . . ."

And before Steve saw it coming, Victoria drew back her right arm and threw a punch as hard as she could. Not a jab. And not a hook. A fist that had an apple in it and all her weight behind it.

The Granny Smith smashed squarely into Amanda's nose.

There were three sounds, coming a second apart. The *crack* of cartilage, the *thump* of Amanda's butt hitting the floor, and a *yelp*.

* * *

Steve heard a *yelp*ing sound, realized it had come from him. A stream of blood ran down Amanda's face; a pink bubble emerged from her lips as she exhaled through the torrent.

Did I just see what I think I saw? Did Vic just TKO Amanda with a Granny Smith?

"Fucking bitch!" Amanda bleated, her hands covering her face. "You broke my nose."

"Put your head back till it stops bleeding," Victoria ordered, suddenly the Nurse Ratched of the law business.

"Jesus, Vic. Why'd you do that?"

He was flummoxed. In all their time together, the most violence she'd ever shown was a wicked backhand on the tennis court.

"Don't you get it, Steve? We can plead and beg and try to find that glimmer of humanity you think is inside this sick puppy, but it won't do any good."

"And punching her will?"

"You're a Democrat and I'm a Republican."

"Yeah?"

"You're suspicious of the use of force. But the only way we're gonna get anything from her is to go Abu Ghraib."

"No way."

Victoria had strayed off script. Steve was supposed to be the bad cop, but apparently he hadn't been bad enough.

Still bleeding, Amanda got to her feet. She reached for a cell phone from the coffee table, but Victoria grabbed her wrist and twisted her arm behind her back.

"Ow!" Amanda rasped. "What are you, a dyke or something?"

Victoria snatched the phone with her free hand and threw it hard toward the fireplace. Her aim was high—not enough follow-through—and the phone sailed into the painting of Kreeger aboard his boat. It left a gash in the canvas.

"Bill ain't gonna be happy," Amanda said, no more little girl in her voice. "He loves that picture."

Still hanging on to Amanda's wrist, Victoria used a foot to kick the woman's leg out from under her. Amanda fell to her knees, Victoria tightening the grip and bending Amanda's arm like a chicken wing. Blood flowed from her nose and puddled on the pine floor. Victoria used the woman's arm like a crowbar, pushing higher and higher, until the back of her wrist lay flat against her neck.

"Fuck! That hurts."

"Vic, what are you doing?"

"Trying to save a girl's life. Bobby's, too. Now, make yourself useful and find something to tie her up."

Steve thought it was possible that his lover and law partner had quite suddenly gone insane.

"Where is he, Amanda?" Victoria demanded. "Where'd he take Maria?"

"Fuck you."

Victoria pulled higher on Amanda's wrist until it passed over the shoulder blade. There was a *pop*. And a scream.

"That was your elbow dislocating," Victoria said. "I've done that in tae kwan do. Hurts like the dickens, doesn't it?"

Amanda lay prone on the floor, her wailing interrupted only by her pained breaths.

"Hey, Vic, could you ease up a minute?"

"We don't have a minute. If we don't find Kreeger, that child's going to die. Isn't that right, Amanda?"

No more "fuck you"s. Just some sobbing.

"Let's work on the other arm," Victoria said.

"Wait." Amanda got to her knees. "Bill likes little girls."

"No shit," Victoria said.

Who is this woman?

"He takes them, sometimes. I don't know what happens to them."

"Sure you do," Victoria said flatly. "If they can ID him, he kills them."

"I don't ask him. There was a girl from the Redlands. About twelve or thirteen."

Oh, shit, Steve thought.

"That girl who went missing down in the Redlands . . ."

Kreeger had tried to blame the disappearance on a boy with disabilities. No wonder the bastard knew so much about serial killers. His knowledge fell into the forensics category called "It takes one to know one."

"Where's he go?" Steve now, getting with the program. "Does he have an apartment somewhere? A cabin in the Glades? Where!"

Amanda didn't answer, and Victoria reached for her other arm. This time, it didn't take a snapped tendon. Amanda flinched, then surrendered. She turned her head toward the painting above the fireplace.

Steve focused on the painting, Kreeger and his big-ass sport fisherman, the *Psycho Therapy.* "The boat! He's got her on the boat."

Amanda didn't say a word, but her look told Steve he was right.

"Where's he keep it?" Victoria said.

"Grove Marina," Amanda whispered.

"C'mon, Steve. Let's get going."

"No."

"No?"

"Something's not right. You torture people, they always lie."

He remembered the photos of the boat in Kreeger's office. A dock, a channel, a mangrove island. The island was distinctive, and he remembered seeing it before. It provided a windbreak for the boats anchored away from the dock.

The island. The island. The island.

It wasn't at Grove Marina. Where was it? He tried to focus the way Bobby would. What could he remember? A breakfast. No. A brunch. That restaurant on the Rickenbacker Causeway on the way to Key Biscayne. From the restaurant, you look out over the channel, straight at the mangrove island.

"Crandon Park Marina. On Key Biscayne. That's where Kreeger keeps his boat."

"Then go!" Victoria ordered. "I'll make sure Amanda stays put."

"You're too late," Amanda said. Neither pleasure nor regret in her voice. "They'll be in open water by now."

"Where?"

"Don't know. The ocean, somewhere. Bill does the girls after he gets out to sea. Then he weights their bodies and chucks them overboard. Something about the water's all mystical to him."

Again Kreeger's words came back to haunt Steve. The guy didn't believe in ashes to ashes and dust to dust. He believed in a watery start and a watery finish. What had he called it?

"From the swamp to the sea."

Thirty-Eight

PSYCHO THERAPY

Great sheets of rain pounded the pavement, the winds clocking around to the north. The Mustang sloshed across the causeway, shuddering in the gusts at the top of the bridge.

Steve passed the Seaquarium, the steering wheel in one hand, his cell phone in the other. The 911 operator told him to call the Coast Guard. The duty officer at the Guard base said no, they could not dispatch a flotilla of patrol boats, cutters, and choppers to parts unknown on a citizen's hunch that a crime was being committed somewhere at sea.

He tried the police again. After two transfers and seven minutes listening to recorded crime-stopping tips, Officer Teele came on the line. "Funny you called, Solomon. We've been looking for you."

"Why?"

"Got a bench warrant to pick you up. Seems you didn't show up for anger-management therapy."

"That's bullshit!" Sounding like he needed his anger managed.

"Got Dr. Kreeger's affidavit right here."

"It's Kreeger you should be after. He's got Maria on his boat. He's—"

"You really got to get over this thing about Dr. Bill."

"Goddammit, listen to me! Kreeger killed that girl in the Redlands. He's gonna kill again."

"Okay, Mr. Solomon. Why don't you just come downtown? Then you can tell us all about it."

"Why? So you can arrest me?"

"You're sounding a little paranoid, Mr. Solomon. So tell me, where are you right now?"

Steve clicked off the phone just as he turned into the marina. The car splashed to a stop. Steve jumped out and jogged toward the dockmaster's office, leaping over puddles. A red triangular flag whipped on a pole atop the small building. Small craft advisory, the winds hitting twenty-five knots.

Steve figured Kreeger had a several-hour head start. The *Psycho Therapy* would be in "open water," according to Amanda, but where? He needed to find someone who knew where Kreeger liked to cruise. Maybe someone saw the boat leave the dock. If they could pinpoint the time, it would be possible to calculate the range. Steve needed something—anything—to go on.

Soaking wet in his jeans and T-shirt, he was ten yards from the dockmaster's office when he caught sight of another flag. One pier over. A row of gleaming power boats in the forty to fifty-foot range. Flying from the top of an antenna was a flag imprinted with the image of a bearded man in an old-fashioned suit. The man looked familiar.

Sigmund Freud.

Now, who else would fly a flag with a picture of Freud?

Steve tore across to the pier toward the boat flying the flag. On a concrete piling, a stenciled sign in yellow paint: *"The Freudian Slip."* And on the transom of the white-and-blue sport fisherman tied at the dock: *"Psycho Therapy."*

Bow and stern lines taut, fenders in place. In the cockpit, both fighting chairs encased in their blue weather covers. Same for the console on the fly bridge. No sign that anyone was aboard or had been lately. So, Kreeger hadn't brought the girl here just before dawn. And now, in broad daylight, he surely wouldn't.

Amanda lied! Victoria had twisted her into a pretzel and she still lied.

Steve looked around. Lots of boats, but here not one person on this lousy nor'easter of a day. The rain pounded at the concrete, moving across the dock in seemingly solid walls, then stopping a few moments and starting again. The boats groaned in their moorings. Two seabirds flew overhead, battling the wind. On a nearby piling, a bleary-eyed pelican seemed to be staring his way.

Steve stepped from the dock into the cockpit. A teak deck, weathered and bleached by the sun, channeled the rainwater out the scuppers at the stern. He opened a freezer used for bait. Empty. Moved to a bait prep station, opened drawers. Fish hooks, pliers, knives, some spools of fishing line.

He slid a cushion off a bench and opened the lid to a storage compartment underneath. Fishing gear, deck shoes, life jackets.

No twelve-year-old girls.

Opened the lid on another compartment. Life rings.

An old fishing rod. Three metal buckets, brand-new, the kind you might use to mop the floor. A shovel, not new. It looked like a garden spade, a crust of mud along its curved sharp edge. And a canvas bag, maybe eight feet long, unzipped. Big enough to haul fishing rods or scuba gear . . . or a ninety-pound girl. Steve rooted around, running his hands over the canvas, half hoping to find something, half hoping not to.

What would be better? Evidence that she'd been here? Or nothing at all?

But the bag was empty. No little-girl barrettes, no little white socks, no notes saying, *"Help!"*

Then he caught the fragrance. What was it? He stuck his head into the bag and inhaled. Citrus. As if the bag had once held a couple dozen oranges.

Or a girl who borrowed her mother's perfume!

The fragrance Steve remembered from Bobby's room.

He tossed the bag aside and raced to the salon door. Glass in a metal frame. Locked. He grabbed the pliers from the bait station and shattered the glass. The sound startled him. But no alarms sounded. No one shouted. The only reaction was from the pelican, which flapped its giant wings and took off for quieter surroundings.

Steve unlatched the door from inside the jagged glass and let himself into the salon. Dripping water on the polished teak deck. A galley to one side. Stove, stainless-steel refrigerator, microwave, a built-in banquette and table anchored to the deck. On the walls, certificates attesting to the capture of a number of innocent fish in various tournaments. "Hello!" he yelled. "Maria!"

Nothing.

He went down several steps, his waterlogged running shoes squeaking. He checked out the staterooms. Beds made, neat and clean. No one home. He went into the head. A beach towel draped over a shower door. The towel was wet.

She's here! Or she's been here.

He went back into the salon.

"Maria!"

Still nothing. Water sloshed, the fenders squeaked against the hull. In the channel, a fifteen-foot outboard *putt-putt*ed toward open water, a couple of kids ignoring the weather warnings. From somewhere belowdeck, something creaked and something else rattled. Boat sounds. Meaningless.

"Maria!"

He heard a *clunk*. Metal against metal? No, a duller sound. It could be anything or nothing.

"Maria!"

Clunk. Clunk.

Again, belowdeck. He found the hatch in the deck, opened it, took a flashlight from a bracket, and crawled down the ladder into the pitch-black engine compartment. Moved the light over tanks and pipes, stringers and beams, and the two huge diesel engines. Shadows flashed across the bulkhead.

And there, on her knees, tape covering her mouth, ankles and wrists bound with a line attached to an engine mount, was Maria Munoz-Goldberg. Her eyes were closed as she banged her forehead against the deck. *Clunk. Clunk. Clunk.*

Thirty-Nine

RESCUE PARTY

Heart pounding, Steve ripped the tape from Maria's mouth and winced as she cried out in pain. She had red marks above and below her lips, and her forehead bled from where she'd banged it against the deck. Her entire body trembled, starting at her shoulders and running all the way down to her legs and feet. She sobbed, great streaks of tears tracking across her cheeks. Her wrists were bound behind her back with quarter-inch line.

Steve worked at the line, but her chest heaved as she sobbed, and her arms shook, and it took a while to undo the knots. They weren't slipknots. They were knots never intended to come loose.

When the line finally came free, he gave her a moment to rub out the stiffness in each wrist, both raw and bleeding.

"Thank you. Thank you. Thank you." She seemed to be chanting it between sobs. Steve wrapped his arms around her, could feel the tremors shaking her from the inside out.

The air was greasy and stale, and Steve felt the sweat drip down his arms. He tried to untie the line around her ankles, but it was too tight and she was bleeding where it had cut into her. The other end of the line was fixed securely to an engine mount.

"There's a knife in the cockpit. I'll be right back, Maria."

"No. Don't leave! Please."

Steve sat down with her. He'd give her a minute. "Where's Kreeger?"

The name didn't seem to register. Apparently, kidnappers don't introduce themselves. "The man who took you. Where'd he go?"

She shook her head. She didn't know.

Steve wondered if she was in shock. But then the words poured out. She started at the beginning. Bobby was acting up, and she decided to ride home without him. When she got to her bike, a man was waiting. He grabbed her and threw her into his car. A BMW, she noted. He reached up under her shirt and pulled off her bra, touching her. She thought he was going to rape her, but he just crumpled the bra and dropped it in Bobby's bike bag.

"Then he put my bike in his trunk. And I thought this was good. Like, no matter what he was going to do to me, he'd let me go, let me ride my bike home. But after he tied me up and we drove a little bit, he took my cap and put it in my bike bag."

"Your cap?"

"Well, Bobby's cap. That Solomon and Lord one he always wears."

Including the day we went to Kreeger's office.

"Then the man threw my bike in some bushes."

"Near the road?"

"Yeah. A few feet away."

Where the bike would be found. With strands of

Bobby's hair in the cap, his prints and DNA all over it.
Another piece of evidence, another nail in the coffin.

"Then he put me in the trunk inside a big bag, and I could barely breathe. I might have passed out, because the next thing I knew, I was down here, all tied up."

She started crying again.

"Did he say anything?"

"Only that we were going for a cruise, but he needed to wait for a store to open. I asked if he was getting sandwiches and drinks, and he just laughed."

A store? It made no sense to Steve, but there was no time to figure it out. Kreeger would be coming back. Steve put a hand on the girl's shoulder. "Maria, we need to get you out of here. I'm going up to get a knife. Is that all right?"

She nodded. "But come right back, okay?"

Steve scrambled up the ladder, climbed through the hatch, and took one step before the lightning bolt hit him. He felt his head snap back. He saw the pain itself inside his brain, an electrical flash behind his eyes. He heard thunderclaps. And then the world went quiet and black.

Forty

THE DEAD WEIGHT OF GUILT

Steve had a sensation of being awakened by being tossed into an icy shower.

But I can't be awake. I can't see anything.

He sensed movement. Side to side and up and down. And a sound. A dull roar.

Okay, the boat is moving, the diesels singing.

He felt the wind rushing by his head, sensed he was in the open cockpit, eyes closed. His face felt raw, like chopped meat, and the salt spray wasn't making it feel any better.

Why can't I move my hands?

A hard, cold rain pelted him, a million freezing needles. A rain so strong, it hissed in the air and *ping*ed as it hit the deck.

He felt the boat ride to the top of a swell, then slide down the trough.

Great. Tied up, semiconscious, and I'm gonna be seasick, too.

A throbbing pain in his skull seemed to beat time with the engines. The boat was moving fast. Open water. Ocean, not the bay. He could tell that from the waves, even though he couldn't see anything.

His mouth felt dry. He licked his lips, tasted blood. He felt the spray hit his neck, the boat splashing down the side of a swell.

So why can't I see anything? Aha, my eyes are closed.

He tried to crank them open. A crowbar would have helped. Eyes swollen shut. He wanted to use a finger to push open an eye, but there was a problem. His hands seemed to be tied behind his back.

He concentrated on his right eye, tried to crank it open. It started to come up slowly, like a Venetian blind pulled by a piece of dental floss. He used his tongue to explore the inside of his mouth. He had bitten though his lip, and he spit out a chunk of tooth.

The rain came even harder, a solid wall of daggers. His teeth chattered. He had never been this cold in his life.

"How you feeling, Solomon?"

Kreeger's voice. The eye opened just enough to see his face, rain soaking his bare chest. The boat on autopilot, Steve figured. With any luck, maybe they'd hit an iceberg. If not, maybe run aground on Bimini.

"Where's Maria?"

"Warm and toasty in the master stateroom. She'll serve her purpose after I dispose of you."

"Bastard."

"That the best you can do, Solomon?"

Steve managed to get both eyes open a crack. "Ugly bastard."

"You don't look so good yourself."

Steve felt like he'd been hit in the face with a baseball bat. Now he saw it was a shovel. Kreeger was leaning on the garden spade Steve had seen in the storage compartment.

"You'd have two black eyes if you'd live long enough for the bruises to show," Kreeger said. "But as you've no doubt ascertained, this is your last boat trip."

Steve's vision cleared a bit, and he saw that Kreeger was wearing surfer's trunks and was shirtless and barefoot. He looked powerful, with wide shoulders and a deep chest. A dive knife was strapped to a sheath on one ankle.

My feet feel funny. I can't wiggle my toes. What's that all about?

Steve looked down. His feet were in one of the aluminum pails he'd seen earlier, his legs sunk up to his calves in cold mud.

No. Not mud. Wet cement.

"You've got to be kidding, Kreeger."

"We wouldn't want your head popping up on the Fifth Street beach, scaring the tourists, would we, Solomon?"

"You've been watching too much *Sopranos*."

Steve wriggled his feet, just enough to lift them off the bottom of the pail, but not enough for cracks to show on the surface. The cement was hardening fast.

"Maybe we can work this out, Kreeger."

"The shyster wants to settle the case. What's your offer, Counselor?"

"I get you help. Not guilty by reason of insanity."

Kreeger barked a laugh. "Got a better deal right here. Not guilty by reason of not being caught."

"The cops know I came after you. You'll be the only suspect."

"Suspect in what? There'll be no body, Solomon. They'll figure you either fled to South America to escape your legal problems or committed suicide." He shook his head, almost sadly. "This isn't the way I planned it. You were supposed to be safe and sound. How else to suffer the torment of watching your nephew go through hell?"

Steve focused on keeping his feet moving. A small crack appeared in the wet cement around each calf. The pouring rain was helping, too. If only he could keep the cement from setting around his feet, he would have a chance.

"I blame myself for your predicament," Kreeger continued. "I've never been so late leaving the dock."

"Because you had to go to the store to buy cement, that it? Run out after you killed that girl from the Redlands?"

"Always start with a new bag." Kreeger dabbed at the pail with the blade of the shovel. "Leave no evidence."

"Let Maria go. Like you said, I won't be around to be tormented. Why torture Bobby?"

"I'm afraid that ship has sailed. The girl can identify me. Or do you think that she'll so enjoy our forthcoming encounter that she'd never testify? Maybe start sneaking over to my house instead of yours?"

"Ugly, sick bastard."

Kreeger laughed again. Took the dive knife from its sheath, crouched, and stuck the blade into the pail, testing the cement. Steve kept his feet still a moment.

"Quick-dry," Kreeger said, sounding pleased, "even in this fucking downpour. Be ready in a couple minutes. Now, don't go anywhere, Counselor."

Kreeger scrambled up the ladder to the fly bridge, picked up his binoculars, and scanned the horizon in every direction. Not wanting a passing freighter to see him toss a man overboard, Steve supposed.

He wriggled harder now. The cement was firming up, the tops of his feet encased in a solid block. But he had kept it from hardening along the sides and underneath. If he was stuck to the pail, there would be nothing he could do. But if he could lift his feet out, he had a chance.

Steve tried working on a plan, but his subconscious interfered. The dead weight of guilt bore down on him, heavier than the cement. He'd let Maria down. But not just her.

I screwed up everything.

Foam spritzed over the gunwales and stung his face.

I let you all down.

Bobby would grow up without him. Victoria would move on to another man. Even his father would take it hard. Steve's throat clenched.

Jeez, am I crying?

He couldn't tell. Tears taste the same as the sea.

* * *

Moments later, the sky darkened even more as they rode through a squall. Gusts pushed the big boat sideways. On the bridge, Kreeger pulled back on the throttles. Steve felt them slowing down. In seconds, they were at idle speed. The boat was at the mercy of the waves now, sliding up one face, rocking down the other.

Kreeger slid down the ladder, facing the cockpit, nimble as a sailor hurrying to his battle station.

"There's a thick patch of sargasso weed just ahead," Kreeger told him. "Bet there are some fine sharks looking for lunch down there."

"Let's just get this over with."

"Whatever you say."

Kreeger bent down, dipped the knife into the drying cement. Steve studied the knife. Ridged handle, easy to grip. Titanium blade, maybe five inches long, serrated on one edge, sharp as a razor on the other. You could saw through bone with it.

Kreeger stood, looked down at Steve. "Time to say good-bye, Solomon." There was a tinge of regret in his voice, as if he were going to miss his old buddy.

Steve focused on his own quadriceps. They were the lifters. He didn't know how much weight the cement added to his feet. It didn't matter. He had strong quads and glutes, and an abundance of quick-twitch muscle fibers.

Kreeger looked down, sliding the dive knife into its sheath. As he did, Steve swung his legs up, high and hard. His feet came out of the bucket with astonishing speed. The bucket stayed on the deck. The jagged clump of cement on Steve's ankles caught Kreeger on the forehead. Steve heard the impact, saw Kreeger spin backwards and bounce off the deck. The knife skittered toward the stern.

Steve pushed himself up and tried hopping toward the knife, but he was like a man in a sack race, and with the boat pitching, he fell, then skidded across the slippery deck.

Kreeger got to one knee and wagged his head, as if trying to stir himself awake. Another second and he was on both feet. Shaky but standing. A flap of skin six inches wide hung loose on Kreeger's forehead, and blood poured into his eyes. Rain slashed down. He used both hands to try to clear his vision. *The bastard should have a concussion,* Steve thought, *but look at him. A wounded bull, fixing to charge.* "Kill you, Solomon," the shrink muttered. "Kill all the lawyers."

He staggered toward the stern. Woozy, knees seeming to buckle with each step. Where was he going?

The knife!

Steve saw it, propped on the edge of a scupper at the stern. He couldn't stand. No way to get there.

Spitting blood, Kreeger leaned over, picked up the knife, and wheeled around. He tried using his forearm to wipe the river of blood from his eyes. First one arm, then the other. It wasn't working.

He can't see and I can't stand.

But Kreeger must have seen enough, because he stumbled in Steve's general direction, flailing away with the knife. Wild swings that started above his head and came straight down, like a man using an ice pick. Blood sprayed everywhere from his forehead.

Steve scooted backward on his butt, great white waves sloshing over the gunwales, soaking and chilling him. Kreeger braced himself against the onslaught, then kept coming, swinging the knife sideways now, like a scythe. "Cut your balls off. Your balls off." His voice droning, devoid of emotion.

Steve spotted a graphite tarpon gaff, maybe six feet long, bracketed to the bulkhead. Pushing off with his hands, moving backward on the deck, he slid that way.

Kreeger changed the knife to his other hand. Came at Steve, slashed left, slashed right, edged between him and the gaff, cutting him off. The boat climbed to the top of a wave, seemed to come to rest, then slid back down again.

Steve had run out of room. Inching backward, he'd come to rest against the bulkhead. Nowhere to run, nowhere to crawl. He brought his knees up to his chest, protecting himself from the deadly blows that would come.

Gasping for breath, spouting blood, Kreeger shambled closer.

Steve made one last desperate effort to grab at the gaff, but it was out of reach.

Kreeger stopped three feet away. Wiped the blood off one hand to get a better grip on the knife. The boat slid sideways up a wave, and Kreeger skidded slightly, widened his stance to keep his balance.

Steve felt the boat crest the wave. Would it go over or come back down? After a second it slid down the trough, and Steve straightened both legs, his cemented feet thrust between Kreeger's braced legs. Steve kicked straight up. At the same moment, the boat pitched wildly at the bottom of the wave, the port rail dipping to the waterline. Steve rocked backward hard, felt both knees pop with a searing pain. Kreeger teetered on Steve's ankles like a kid on a seesaw, then sailed over the gunwale headfirst and into the deep blue sea.

Knees flaring as if on fire, Steve hoisted himself up and grabbed the gaff from its bracket. He spotted Kreeger splashing in the water, dangerously close to the props that churned slowly at idle speed.

"Help! Help me!"

A wave washed over him. He vanished, then bobbed up again, kicking and whaling away at the water, trying to close the distance to the dive platform.

Steve hobbled toward the stern, using the gaff as a cane.

Some things you plan, he thought. Some things you do by instinct, by notions of decency and humanity. A man goes overboard, you rescue him. No matter who he is, no matter what he's done. You haul the man aboard, take him in, let the system deal with him.

Steve leaned over the rail, holding the graphite gaff.

Kreeger reached for it, missed, went under again. He came back up, and Steve dangled the gaff in his direction.

But sometimes, all notions of decency and humanity give way to something else. Call it revenge or justice or maybe just certainty. The certainty that Bill Kreeger would never ever again hurt anyone. Or was that overly complicated? Was the explanation simply hard-wired into our DNA by millions of years of evolution? Maybe all of us carry the fingerprints of the homicidal animals who came before us.

Threaten me or mine, I will kill you. Yes, I will. Even a normally mild-mannered, semi-law-abiding officer of the court like me will kill you dead.

Kreeger would appreciate that explanation, Steve thought. Proving his thesis right after all these years.

A powerful swell lifted Kreeger, nearly catapulting him out of the water. Down he came, his head slipping underwater. Then, another lift, another slide, this one bringing him closer to the boat. Again, Kreeger grabbed for the gaff. Again, he missed. He shouted something drowned out by the wind's roar. Another wave carried him closer to the stern. Steve held the gaff; Kreeger reached for it; and suddenly, Steve pulled it away. He hadn't planned on doing it. The motion was involuntary, his body not willing to follow his brain's instructions, not willing to save the bastard.

Kreeger swam toward the boat, yelling something. Steve could only make out a single word.

"Just . . ."

The rest was lost in the wind.

Kreeger came closer, reached for the dive platform, shouted again.

"Just like . . ."

What was he saying?

Bracing himself on the slippery deck, Steve drew the gaff back with two hands until it was poised over one shoulder. A batter with his Louisville Slugger.

"Just like me!" Kreeger yelled over the wind. "You're just like me!"

Steve swung the gaff as hard as he could, rotating his hips for power. The flat side of the steel hook hit Kreeger squarely across the temple with a shock Steve felt in both arms. A shuddering impact, like driving the ball up the middle.

Kreeger's head snapped to the side and stayed there, his neck at an unnatural angle. A wave hit, swirling him in white foam, spinning him around, and dragging him beneath the cold, gray sea.

SOLOMON'S LAWS

12. When you cut through all the bullshit of
    career, status, and money, at the end of the
    day all that matters is love and family.

Forty-One

THE TEMPLE OF SOLOMON

Steve lay on his back on a rickety raft that rose and fell with the waves. In the distance, lightning illuminated a shroud of fat silvery clouds, and a thunderclap smacked the water. Steve felt the raft pitch and roll, even as he realized he was home in bed. Painkillers will do that.

"God bless codeine."

He had said that to Bobby. Just a few hours ago. Or was it a few years? He didn't know how long he'd been in bed.

"God bless codeine," Bobby had repeated. "BED-SIDE NOSE CLOG."

Steve had laughed, stinging his lip where the stitches pulled at the skin.

"Everyone at school says you're a total mad dawg," Bobby had said.

"If that's a good thing, tell them thanks."

"You're the best, Uncle Steve."

The boy had smiled. They'd pounded knuckles. Bobby doing all the pounding. Steve couldn't lift his arm from the bedsheet. Still, when he saw the boy's grin, he felt he'd won the Nobel Prize for parenting.

A doctor who had once been a client stopped by. Or was he a client who had once been a doctor? Steve's brain was fuzzy. The doc said something about a hairline fracture of the zygomatic bone.

"The zygomatic?" Steve asked. "The machine that chops vegetables?"

"The cheekbone," the doctor explained.

Steve remembered now. He had defended the doctor in a couple of malpractice cases. Lost them both.

There was some sinus damage, too, the sawbones told him. Steve could expect his eyes to tear up unexpectedly. No big deal. That should go away.

"And if it doesn't?" Steve asked.

"Sue me," the doc said.

Crying wasn't so bad, Steve thought. Might be able to use it in closing argument sometime. Then there were the dozen stitches in his fat lip. Plus torn cartilage in both knees. Ice, anti-inflammatories, and rest.

"Don't worry, Steve. You'll be playing eighteen holes in no time."

"Great, Doc, because I've never played one hole my entire life."

Now he was cold. Both knees were wrapped in ice. On the bedside table were a variety of pill bottles, a pitcher of water, and the local section of the *Miami Herald*. A headline blared: "Lawyer Rescues Kidnapped Girl." He would check out the story later. Steve was reasonably certain that it would be more favorable than his last brush with celebrity, an item in Joan Fleischman's column headlined: "Lawyer Jailed Again."

He heard a pounding. Was it in his head? A dull *thud,* then a *crack,* like wood splintering.

Myron Goldberg and Eva Munoz-Goldberg came by. Myron had Steve open his mouth. Complimented his flossing and advised him to get that chipped tooth crowned. Eva gave Steve a deep dish of caramel flan she had baked. He ate it through a straw. Myron said they were dropping the assault-and-battery case, and Steve thanked him as he slurped up the sweet dessert. Eva patted his arm and said he was as brave as Máximo Gómez and Jose Marti.

Apparently, Maria had told her parents how Steve saved her life. How after Dr. Bill went overboard, Steve came to get her, even though he could barely walk and his face was swollen and bleeding. How he climbed the ladder to the bridge, dragging the chunk of concrete on his feet, moaning in pain. How he brought the boat back, banging into the seawall at the Coast Guard station on Miami Beach, then passing out. Steve was glad Maria told her parents all these things, because he couldn't remember any of it.

"Maria says you're a superhero," Eva told him.

"How's she doing?" Steve asked.

"Better than we could have hoped," Myron said.

"*Bien,*" Eva said. "She's with Bobby right now. Studying."

"I'll bet," Steve said.

"He's a fine young man," Myron allowed.

"Of course he is," Eva added. "He's had good training." Then she reached down and stroked Steve's cheek. "*Eres un melocotón en almíbar.*"

Steve wasn't sure, but he thought she'd just called him a peach in syrup. Sweet. Suddenly, he felt a tear tracking down his cheek, then another. Then a torrent.

"You wonderful man," Eva said, her own eyes welling.

Steve decided not to mention his sinus problem.

Cece Santiago came by as the Goldbergs were leaving. The office phones had been ringing all day, she reported, people calling to congratulate him. No new clients yet. There probably wouldn't be. The newspaper story made it sound as if he were on his deathbed. Cece could only stay a minute. She had a meeting with her probation officer. Translation: another wrestling match with Arnold Freskin. And by the way, Arnie already asked Pincher to drop the charges. With both assault-and-battery cases dismissed, Steve wondered if he had any legal work to do.

He dozed for a while and dreamed his raft was sinking. He awoke to find his sister sitting on the edge of his bed, the soft mattress listing to starboard.

"Hey, Stevie. How you feeling?"

"Terrific. I'm starting to understand what you like about narcotics."

"Reminds me, bro. I got a job. Drug counselor over in Tampa."

"Great."

"As for the other stuff, filing for custody of Bobby, my lawyer says I'd be a fool to do it now. You're like a celebrity or something. Plus, I need the job so I can look good in front of the judge when I come back."

"No hurry, Jan."

She studied him a second. "Are you crying, bro?"

"Sinuses," he said.

He dozed off again to the sound of an electrical band saw. Either that, or a million bees were buzzing away in the living room. He awoke and found Irene Lord in the bedroom, running an index finger over the nightstand.

"You need a maid," she said, lifting a fingertip covered with dust.

"How you doing, Irene?"

"Carl left. Just picked up and left."

"I'm sorry. And surprised. I thought he really cared for you."

"I think he does. Yesterday he wired money into my account. From a bank in Moscow."

"Moscow?"

"E-mailed me, too. Said he discovered the lost treasure of the Romanovs. People all over the world are sending him deposits, claiming to be relatives."

"For a con man, he's got a good heart."

"Stephen, have I told you how dear you are to me?"

"Not that I recall, but I've been heavily drugged."

"I think you and Victoria are splendid together. Well, maybe not splendid. But for some reason, you seem to make her happy. And if she's happy, well . . . I'm quite nearly pleased."

She leaned over as if to kiss him, thought better of it, and withdrew. But she did give his shoulder a pat. "Stephen, are you crying?"

"Sinuses," he said.

He fell back into a restless sleep, dreaming of his father. The old goat was building something. Noah's ark, maybe. He felt lips brush his and opened his eyes to find the most beautiful woman in the world kissing him. Victoria was wearing those stretchy workout pants that stop right below the knees and a flimsy sports top with thin straps. The top was cut low and stopped well above her flat tummy.

"You need a shave, slugger," she said. "And your breath smells like a wet donkey."

"What exactly does a wet donkey smell like?"

She kissed him again. "Never mind. I still love you."

"I love you, too, Vic." He licked his swollen lip and said: "I've been thinking about where we should live. If you want a condo, that's fine. You want a town-house or a real house, that's fine, too. What I'm saying, anywhere is fine as long as we're together."

"You mean that?"

"With all my heart. With all my soul. With my last stinky breath."

She gave him an angelic smile and gently ran a finger across his bruised lip.

The pounding started again. Louder.

"Damn. What is that?" Steve said.

"You don't know? I thought Herbert told you last night."

"Last night, I was running a dogsled in the Iditarod. Although it's quite possible I was hallucinating."

"Come on," she said. "I'll show you."

She eased him out of bed. He threw an arm around her shoulder and she helped him down the corridor.

The living room was far too bright.

What the hell?

There was no back wall. Just a couple of vertical studs, the plasterboard blasted to smithereens. Herbert stood in the middle of the rubble, wearing khaki shorts and a yarmulke, holding a sledgehammer. His bare chest was covered with plaster dust. Steve vaguely remembered something about his old man building the Temple of Solomon, but this still didn't compute.

"The hell you doing, Dad?"

"What's it look like?"

"Vandalism."

"Ah'm extending your house into the backyard."

"Why do I think you're better at knocking down walls than building them?"

"Don't complain till you get mah bill. A new master bedroom with walk-in closets, and a family room."

"What for?"

"For you and Victoria, *schmendrick*."

Of course! His brain was still fuzzy, but it made sense. All the room they would need, even though the roof might sag and the walls would be out of plumb.

"Thanks, Dad. I saw this flat-screen TV the other day. Big as a garage door. Great for the family room."

"I was thinking about a piano for the family room," Victoria said.

"Big TV would be better. High-def for the ball games."

"I looked at this Steinway. The Living Room Grand model. It would be perfect."

"Only if you're living with Rachmaninoff."

"I'd like a grand piano."

"And I'd like a big-ass TV."

Herbert pointed the sledgehammer toward the opening in the wall. "Ah s'pose Ah could add a music room, if we encroach on the property line."

"Good compromise," Victoria said.

"I'm in," Steve said.

He wrapped an arm around both of them and gave a good squeeze. Bobby came into the room from the kitchen, nibbling on half an Oreo cookie. "Hey, Uncle Steve. What's going on?"

"I'm counting my blessings, kiddo. You want a group hug?"

"No way. Hugging's for babies."

Steve let his gaze take them all in. His father, his lover, his nephew. His blessings. He felt his eyes tear up.

"You crying?" Bobby asked.

"Sinuses," Steve lied.

SOLOMON'S LAWS

1. Lying to a judge is preferable to lying to the woman you love.

2. Thou shalt not screw thy own client . . . unless thou hast a damn good reason.

3. When you don't know what to do, seek advice from your father . . . even if he's two candles short of a menorah.

4. If you're going to all the trouble to make a fool of yourself, be sure to have plenty of witnesses.

5. When a woman is quiet and reflective, rather than combative and quarrelsome, watch out. She's likely picturing the bathroom without your boxers hanging on the showerhead.

6. A creative lawyer considers a judge's order a mere suggestion.

7. When you run across a naked woman, act as if you've seen one before.

8. Love is chemistry and mystery, not logic and reason.

9. Q: What do you call a judge who is old, cantankerous, and flatulent?

   A: "Your Honor."

10. You won't find it in Darwin, Deuteronomy, or Doonesbury, but it's an essential truth of human nature: we'll all kill to protect those we love.

11. I won't lie to a lawyer's face or stab him in the back, but if I have the chance, I'll look him in the eye and kick him in the *cojones*.

12. When you cut through all the bullshit of career, status, and money, at the end of the day all that matters is love and family.

ABOUT THE AUTHOR

PAUL LEVINE worked as a newspaper reporter and trial lawyer, practicing law for seventeen years, trying cases in state and federal courts and handling appeals at every level, including the Supreme Court, before becoming a full-time novelist and screenwriter. The winner of the John D. MacDonald fiction award, Levine is the author of the Jake Lassiter novels, which have been published in twenty-three countries. *To Speak for the Dead,* the first Lassiter novel, was a national bestseller and honored as one of the best mysteries of the year by the *Los Angeles Times.* He is also the author of *9 Scorpions,* a thriller set in the U.S. Supreme Court. *Kill All the Lawyers* is the third in the series that began with the bestselling *Solomon* vs. *Lord* and *The Deep Blue Alibi.*

He was co-creator and co–executive producer of the CBS television series *First Monday* and has written extensively for *JAG.* He lives in California, where he is at worth on the fourth Solomon *vs.* Lord novel.

THE SUSPENSE WILL KILL YOU....

VICTOR GISCHLER

GUN MONKEYS	$6.99/$10.99
THE PISTOL POETS	$6.99/$10.99
SUICIDE SQUEEZE	$6.99/$9.99
SHOTGUN OPERA	$6.99/$9.99

MORAG JOSS

FUNERAL MUSIC	$6.99/NCR
FEARFUL SYMMETRY	$6.99/NCR
FRUITFUL BODIES	$6.99/NCR
HALF-BROKEN THINGS	$13.00/NCR
PUCCINI'S GHOSTS	$22.00/NCR

ASA LARSSON

SUN STORM
$22.00/$30.00

STEPHEN BOOTH

BLIND TO THE BONES
$7.50/NCR

CODY MCFADYEN

SHADOW MAN
$24.00/$32.00

LISA GARDNER

THE PERFECT HUSBAND	$7.99/$11.99
THE OTHER DAUGHTER	$7.99/$11.99
THE THIRD VICTIM	$7.99/$11.99
THE NEXT ACCIDENT	$7.99/$11.99
THE SURVIVORS CLUB	$7.99/$11.99
THE KILLING HOUR	$7.99/$11.99
ALONE	$7.99/$10.99
GONE	$25.00/$35.00

BD SUS 9/06